AF352001
deception

deception

THE SINNERS OF NEW ORLEANS

NATALIA LOUROSE

For the girls who want to be collared and free.

Nothing ever ends poetically. It ends and we turn it into poetry. All that blood was never once beautiful. It was just always red.

KAIT ROKOWSKI

FAMILY TREE

Carmine Costello (deceased)
Married Elizabetta Costello (deceased)
Children: Caterina, Carlotta, Cosetta, Carmine Jr.

Caterina Costello Ricci
Married Al Ricci (deceased)
Children: Marcus Ricci and *Madalena Ricci*

Carlotta Costello Romano
Married Damien Romano
Children: Lily Romano (deceased) and *Lana Romano*

Cosetta Costello Vitale
Married James Vitale
Child: *Johnathan Vitale*

Carmine Jr. Costello (Junior)
Married Giulia Costello
Child: *Sam Costello*

*Italicized names will have book in the series.

PLAYLIST

Toxic 2WEI
House of the Rising Sun Lauren O'Connell
Pyrokinesis 7Chariot
Control Halsey
You asked for this Halsey
Twisted MISSIO
Sinner DEZI
Until I Com Home Two Feet, Grandson
Serial Killer Moncrieff
Deep Dive Zaryah
Under My Skin Claudia Kane
Terrible Thing AG
Keep Lying Donna Missal
Chanel Perfume Derik Fein
Sick Thoughts Lewis Blisett
Pain King Princess
Met Him Last Night Demi Lovato, Ariana Grande
Baby Came Home The Neighbourhood
Do It For Me Rosenfeld

This is What Makes Us Girls Lana Del Rey
Still Don't Know My Name Labrinth

Full Playlist

CONTENT WARNING

Deception is a mafia romance that contains certain aspects that may be triggering for readers. Some of these aspects include: animal abuse (mice only), sexual assault, foster care/foster care abuse, sex trafficking, abuse towards women/domestic violence, and specific mentions of Hurricane Katrina and the aftermath it caused.

DECEPTION ALSO CONTAINS graphic sexual content including spanking, collar/ownership, and lots of praise.

John

I'm tugging at my tie, trying to loosen the damn thing, when I hear the gunshots. Five distinct bangs that have my head darting toward my uncle's million-dollar home. My feet bounce off the cement, bolting for the front door of the Filmore mansion Junior bought when his wife was still alive. Despite her having died twenty years ago, he still lives in the oversized house filled with her memories next to all the other rich people of New Orleans.

With my gun gripped between my fingers, I push through the wooden door and into my uncle's home. My lips are sealed, and my breathing is quiet as I search for the source of the gunshots. My father taught me to use a gun when I was ten years old, placing the metal contraption in my hands and telling me to watch my back. And I do, as I navigate through the entryway and into the hallway. I check each corner, in every direction, for the shooter. A door slams, and instantly, all the hairs on my body perk. The sound confirms my worst fears. Someone was in here.

"*Zio*," I call out.

"Johnny." His voice is low and muffled. When I spin around the corner, I find him sprawled out on the living room floor in a growing puddle of his own blood. He grips his hand against his abdomen, trying to limit the red liquid that leaks through his clenching fingers, staining his white shirt as it drips down to the carpet.

My eyes scan the entire living room, over the hardwoods and cream-colored walls, the beige couch and walnut furniture. I come up empty, and when I make a move to chase down the attacker, my uncle's gurgling voice stops me.

"No." He reaches out with a blood covered hand. "He's gone, Johnny." He inhales a deep, rattling breath.

Junior's naturally ruddy cheeks are pale and sweaty. He looks almost ghostlike as he struggles to breathe, each inhale producing a crackly gasping noise.

I was supposed to meet him here to pick him up for tribute. We had gotten into the routine of me driving him. He enjoyed having extra time to spend with me. Junior has always been like a second father since I was a kid, and adulthood has limited our time together. Now I have responsibilities, a life. Sam is better at making time to see his father, but I have a relationship with my own parents to maintain.

I spent a lot of my childhood in this very house. Sam and I chasing each other through the halls, jumping in the pool out back to see who could make the biggest splash. For the tough, take no shit attitude Junior displayed to the world, he was a softie inside these walls.

Blood pools at the corner of his mouth while he stares up at me, a frail shell of the man I've known my entire life. His glassy eyes pierce mine and his lips tremble as he tries to speak, desperate to get out his last words.

"Who did this, *zio?*" I ask, wanting to gut the man who dare hurt my uncle.

"Sam," he answers breathily, causing my brows to draw inward with confusion. "Protect him." He exhales the last word as he lets his eyes softly close.

"*Zio.*" I shake his arm gently, but he doesn't inhale another breath. The hand gripping his wound goes limp and more blood seeps between his fingers. "*Zio.*" I try again, this time shaking his body with more force. But nothing changes. He doesn't wake.

My heart thrums, the beating rattling through my body as I furiously try to wake my uncle. I press my ear to his mouth, listening for any sound, hoping for the heat of his breath to touch my skin, but I get nothing. My fingers find the side of his throat, feeling for any semblance of a pulse, even a weak one, something to tell me he's still hanging on.

But there's nothing there.

I lean back, my red-stained palms resting against the cream carpet. Junior would scold me for this. The man loved a clean house, shouting anytime Sam and I walked on this rug with our shoes still on. I can remember being forced to scrub dirt from the thing as a child.

But he's not yelling at me now. He sits silent while the flowing blood seeps into the material.

I don't know how much time passes before police enter the house, guns gripped and at the ready. Fog has taken over my mind, and I slip into a blank state of nothingness. Numbness. "*Clear,*" they call out one by one as they sweep through the house.

"We got a body," I hear next to me, but my own body still won't move, still can't leave my uncle's side.

I should do something, I think. I should move or tell these cops what happened. But my eyes stay glued to Junior's pale face. His dark hair is graying at the roots, all of it slicked back. His *famiglia* ring is still looped around his thumb, and I reach out, trailing my fingers over the metal that matches the ring on my finger.

"Hey, you can't touch him!" one of the uniformed officers scolds me.

I break free from my numb state with a snap, lunging for the officer who spoke. "Don't fucking tell me what to do." Adrenaline courses through my veins, reinvigorating me. Arms wrap around me, pulling me back from the timid cop who scolded me.

"I got a murder weapon," another officer calls out. When I turn my gaze to him, I find a sealed evidence bag dangling from his fingertips with a gun inside.

"Run it for prints." My eyes clash with the owner of the unfamiliar voice. He's not sheathed in a black uniform like the others. He wears black dress pants and a button-down shirt with the sleeves rolled several times. A gold detective's badge hangs from his neck. "And get Vitale outta here."

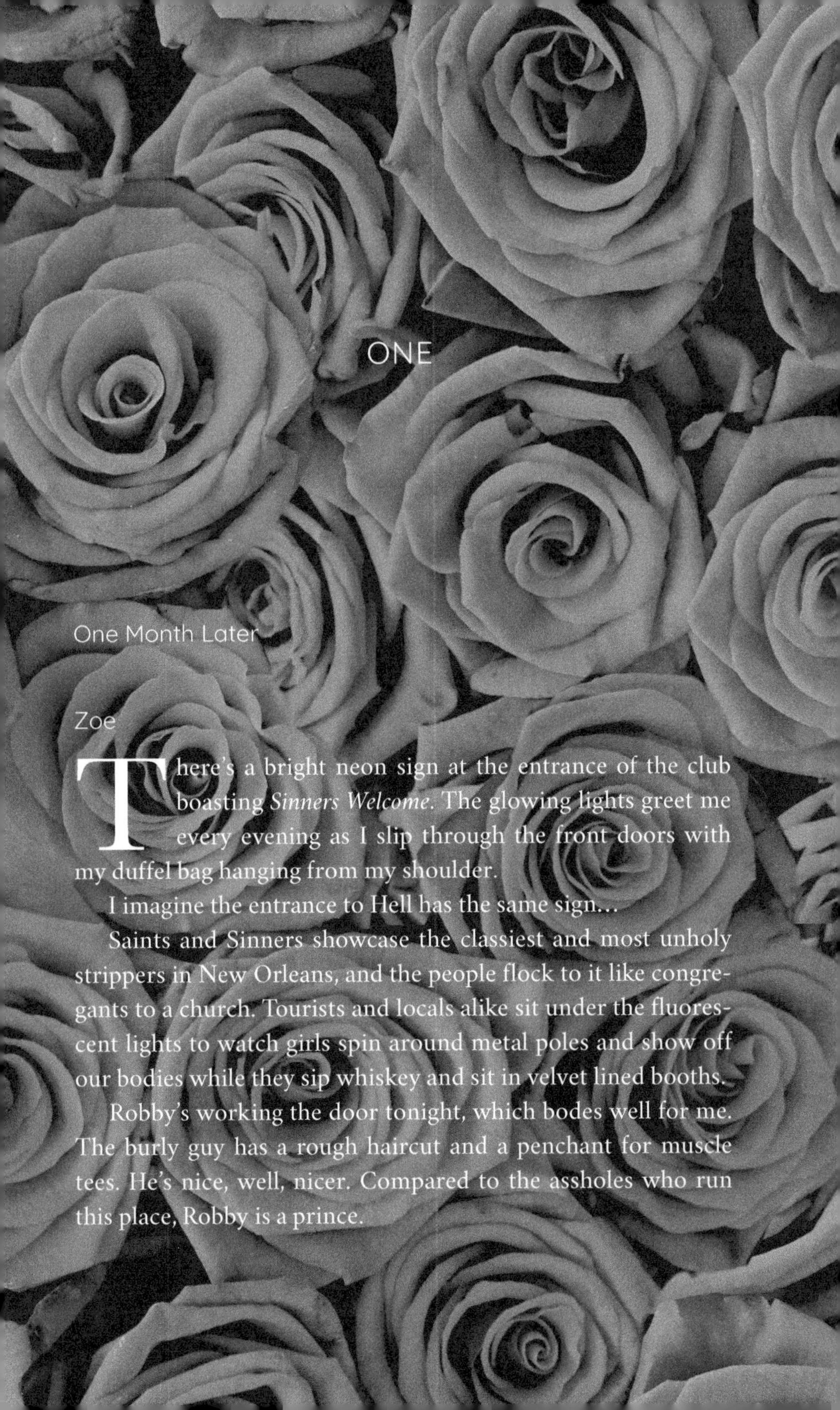

ONE

One Month Later

Zoe

There's a bright neon sign at the entrance of the club boasting *Sinners Welcome*. The glowing lights greet me every evening as I slip through the front doors with my duffel bag hanging from my shoulder.

I imagine the entrance to Hell has the same sign…

Saints and Sinners showcase the classiest and most unholy strippers in New Orleans, and the people flock to it like congregants to a church. Tourists and locals alike sit under the fluorescent lights to watch girls spin around metal poles and show off our bodies while they sip whiskey and sit in velvet lined booths.

Robby's working the door tonight, which bodes well for me. The burly guy has a rough haircut and a penchant for muscle tees. He's nice, well, nicer. Compared to the assholes who run this place, Robby is a prince.

"Meow," he says with a wink, extending his fingers and then curling them inward, mimicking the motion of a cat scratching.

I want to roll my eyes, but that's not how Kat behaves.

Kat, my alter ego, a stripper whose character is the exact opposite of me. She comes out to play when there's a pole on stage and money on the floor. The guys have taken to not using my stage name. They think I'm innocent, too innocent to be a full-grown cat, apparently.

They purr or hiss when they see me, making a show of how it brings a pink color to my cheeks. Well, Kat's cheeks. Because Kat is innocent. Easily embarrassed. They find her blushing amusing.

I'm not like the other girls to them.

I'm *sweeter.*

Not like their nagging wives at home. Or the girlfriend who doesn't pay enough attention.

I'm the fantasy. The sweet little girl who does what she's told, whose body sways and spins for them. Whose mind is empty, the only thoughts swirling through it are about *their* pleasure.

Men are simple creatures, really.

"What's a girl like you want with a job like this?" Donnie, the club manager, had asked during my interview. I had shrugged and told him my sob story, Kat's sob story, and he nodded along like he felt bad for me. Then he forced my head down on his cock to test out the merchandise.

That's what women are here; merchandise.

Afterward, when I had wiped his cum from my lips, he offered me the job.

The club is marketed as some sort of high-end gentlemen's place, but in truth, it's no better than any second-rate strip club. The booths are nicer and there's a cigar room, but it's still filled with women working at the whims of men.

Cassie got a job here first. She forbade me from coming in.

She wanted to keep me far away from this place. Now I understand why. Back then, I thought she was playing the role of an overprotective big sister, and I was determined to prove that I was just as much of an adult as her.

Before Saints and Sinners, my little feminist heart loved the idea of strippers. I was a fan of any woman who took her power back, turned her sexuality into a weapon she could yield, rather than something men controlled. But I think that was all a narrative I spun in my head, one with no roots in reality.

Now, I know there are no feminist powers here.

The faux innocence got me the job, though. Men like to see a girl they can push around, one they can teach. That's fresh and unbroken.

Unbeknownst to them, I'm fucking broken. I'm just good at hiding it.

"Hi, Robby." I give him a quick smile, avoiding eye contact. At the club, I push the nausea down. I can't let the men know how I feel about them. Instead, I have to be sweet and charming, innocent and naïve. It's all part of the act.

The sun is still shining, and no customers are here yet. I need to change, apply my makeup, and warm up my body. I have the worst times today, the disadvantage of being the new girl. The only positive is less people here to see me half naked on stage. But fewer people means less money. Even though this is an act, I need the money. More than I want to admit.

I enter the dressing area; a small room lined with mirrors and makeup tables, crowded with chairs and lockers that we use to change and fix our makeup.

The seasoned girls also do their drugs back here. Coke, ecstasy, whatever they can get their hands on. Not all of them, though. Some just like the thrill and the power that comes with stripping. I wonder if those girls will switch over, eventually. Will the sense of power fade away and leave them with nothing but shame and sadness?

Here you have more to risk.

Rape.

Murder.

Addiction.

This isn't the high point of stripping.

"There's a private party tonight," Maxine, the resident redhead, says as she smiles widely while talking to one of the other girls. "Marcus will be here for it."

I shove my bag into the locker and listen. Private parties are where the real money is. It's also where you're going to do more than stripping.

If you're lucky, you'll find someone to take you in. Keep you in a cozy apartment where you'll be taken care of. *Lucky*, I laugh to myself, there's nothing lucky about being a mafia mistress. A *goomah*.

"How do you get in?" I ask Maxine. I don't want a sugar daddy, not that the money would hurt, but what I do want is information. Information that the men in the VIP room have.

She tosses me an unfriendly look. "Why, rookie? Ya think you're a big girl now?"

I smile lightly, plastering on the innocent look that Kat has adopted. "Just need the money." I shrug my shoulders.

Maxine doesn't answer my question, instead she whispers something in her friend's ear and they both giggle, turning their bodies away from mine.

"Ignore her," Daisy says, slipping her bag into the locker next to mine. I don't know what her real name is, but she goes by Daisy, a fitting alias for the tiny blonde with freckles and a round nose. She looks too cute, too naïve. "Max is just a bitch," she whispers, giving me a small smile. "If you want into the party, you just have to ask Donnie." She shrugs. "But be careful, okay?" Her blue eyes look deadly serious as she warns me. "Those guys aren't like the normal patrons."

She doesn't tell me more, but I don't need her too. The guys who attend private parties with Marcus aren't tourists. They dress like businessmen in fancy suits, but they all have guns strapped to their waists. *Mafioso.*

They run this town. New Orleans thrives on the crime and money that the Costello family brings here, and most of us turn an eye, ignoring all the illegal shit they do. It's easier that way. The men who will join Marcus tonight will be *part of the family,* as they call it.

I need to get into that party, need to see these men up close. But first, I change into a pair of black shiny booty shorts, and a lacy bralette paired with my Converse. I'll wait until the last possible second to slip on my cheetah print heels to give my feet as much of a break as I can.

Donnie is in his office, leaning over a chocolate eclair and a cup of coffee. "Donnie," I say, my voice as smooth as honey when I knock on the door frame.

With a grumble, he looks up to meet my gaze. "What, Kat?" he nearly growls.

I enter his office slowly, swaying my body as I move toward his desk. His eyes are glued to the shiny black material that covers my hips and ass. "Can I work the party tonight?" I clasp my hands behind my back, pushing my tits out and giving him a good view. It's the *sweet girl* pose I've adopted, one that works on every man I've come in contact with. Their eyes find my tits and their lips tell me what I want to hear.

"Why would you want to do that?" It's a moment before his eyes finally travel up to meet my face.

I curve my lips into a timid smile. "Money."

He leans back in his chair now, arms crossed, assessing me. "Ah, Kitty Kat. They're gonna eat you alive in there. No." Donnie has a New York accent from the years he spent up north. It stands out in New Orleans. I usually find it amusing; it makes him sound like a real-life Soprano. But today, I'm annoyed by his words while he pretends to know what's good for me.

I frown. There's a certain bonus that comes from being pretty with a good body. It makes it easy to manipulate men. A chance they can get a taste and they're putty in your hands. "Please, Donnie," I try again. He's no different from the other ones. They all like to be begged.

"No." Donnie stands, stalking over to where I am, and places his hands on my shoulders. "I said no. You're not ready."

Only a strip club manager would think he knows me well enough to know if I'm ready or not.

"Sure," I concede. "Fine."

He pats my shoulders and sends me on my way.

TWO

Zoe

I don't listen to Donnie and go to the private party anyway.

I tell Robby that the boss said it was fine as I press my body against his and look up at him with doe eyes and fluttering lashes. He thinks I mean Marcus Ricci requested me himself and takes my word for it, a dumb move on his part. I may look sweet, but I have a plan, and I'll do whatever I need to achieve it.

My grandmother once told me you should enter every room like you are the solution to everyone's problems.

I don't think she intended for that to include stripping, but it's a fitting saying for my profession. I saunter into the room filled with known made men. Soldiers and capos for the Costello *famiglia*.

The idea of the mafia always felt foreign to me growing up. I would hear things, whispers of the organization that controlled the city. But it never felt real.

Not until now. I've met the men in this room while they

crowd around the bar and throw dollars at my feet on week-nights. The past month has been filled with men, and most of them have been mafiosi.

They're different from the fictional mafia that I'd imagined. They look like high-class businessmen. Something you'd see in the bars on Wall Street at happy hour. Men dressed in thousand-dollar suits with the ties tugged loose and the jackets shrugged off.

The men here talk freely while girls in limited clothing grind on their laps. It's a strange sight to see the mixture of work and pleasure.

In this room, with these men, anything goes. So much money exchanges hands, and the rules are broken, tossed to the wayside. A hand job in the private room? Done. Fuck in the bathroom? Have at it. Want someone to suck your dick in front of your buddies? Sure thing.

Donnie was right when he said I wasn't ready. The idea of sinking to my knees for a few hundred has my stomach churning. But the guy I need to see only comes to this room. He doesn't sit out in the main bar with the tourists and other customers. He's in a private VIP section with waiters and upgraded booths. It's a giant leap from the service in general admission.

Marcus Ricci sits in a velvet lined booth with a girl on either side, Maxine being one of them. She has her hands on his body, eyes focused on him. I wonder if Hugh Hefner got the same kind of attention.

There's a strict no touching policy at Saints and Sinners, but it doesn't apply to Marcus or his friends.

I move to the corner opposite of them, keeping my sights focused on the powerful men that sit on those plush velvet booths. Marcus laughs while his fingers play with a strand of Maxine's hair. Beside him, another man leans back comfortably, watching a blonde dance in front of him.

There's a third man in the booth. His sharp jawline is taunt as he watches Marcus. He has his hands shoved into the pockets of his dress slacks and his ankle crossed over his knee. There's plenty of space between him and the nearest woman. He's not looking at the girls, his gaze intent on the boss.

I try to sway my hips as I walk toward the group of men. Power radiates from them, and I can't tell if it's a projection of my imagination, knowing the things they've done, or if it really fills the room like this.

"Can I get you anything?" I ask in the sexiest voice I can manage. Only one set of eyes rises to find me as I approach. It's the newcomer, the one I've never seen here before. His dark eyes are sparkling with amusement, and I try to shake off his gaze as I lean forward, giving Marcus a show of my cleavage.

Stone-cold eyes rake over my body, looking at me like I have multiple heads. For a moment, I wonder if I read Marcus wrong. I assumed he'd be the type of man who loves a woman that talks sweetly and leans forward, giving him a good look at her tits. But the way he stares at me makes me think he'd rather I leave him to his devices.

"S-sorry-" I stammer, unsure how to backtrack and pull myself out of this one.

"She new?" the mystery man asks, leaning forward in a wide-legged stance and resting his elbows on his knees while his dark eyes continue to watch me.

"Yeah, think so," Marcus answers, his gaze moving from me over to the man. I already feel like I've been dismissed as they talk about me without speaking to me.

"Can I try her out?"

My heart sinks, stomach churns, and I can feel my whole body getting heated. I did this to myself, didn't I? Put myself in a room full of lions and expected none to bite me.

Because I'm desperate.

I'm being too risky, too impatient.

I was supposed to watch first, not get my hands dirty.

And I was definitely not supposed to grab the attention of a man other than my mark. A funny statement, considering my lack of clothing and the room full of men I'm standing in.

But it's been a month, and there's still no sign of where Cassie went. I'm seconds from interrogating every girl who works here, anything to find my best friend.

A deep chuckle comes from Marcus. "You're not too good for my merchandise?" he asks with a bemused smirk. There's something lingering between the two men as they watch each other. "Of course, cousin, what's mine is yours." He gestures toward me without even looking in my direction or waiting for a response to his question.

Cousin.

Said cousin stands and walks to me in two steps. I can smell his cologne, wood and spices, as he presses a hand to the small of my back. There's a door at the edge of the room we're in that takes us into one of the club's private rooms.

With a push from him, I stumble into the private space, and he shuts the door behind us. His dark eyes flash to me as he unbuttons his suit jacket, sliding the smooth material down his shoulders.

My eyes are glued to him as I step back, my thighs hitting the velvet bench. Thick fingers rise to his neck, tangling with the knot on his tie. He tugs at the evergreen material, loosening its grip on him. There's a ring on his pinky, gold, with a flat surface on the top. I can't see it well enough to know what's inscribed there, but my money's on his family crest.

The Costellos, while secretive about how they got their money, aren't hiding that they have it. It's well known that one family owns this city, and the man in front of me is part of that family.

He's not Marcus, my original mark, but he is a cousin. I

could use him. Milk him for information and toss him to the side once I find Cassie.

When his gaze comes back to me, there's something more sinister about it. A few minutes ago, he looked like he had his shit together and wouldn't snap at any moment. Now he looks slightly different, like something in him has shifted.

Darkened orbs rake over my body, taking in every inch of my skin on display.

Already I have the feeling that this isn't going to go as planned.

I try to place a smile on my face, but it feels forced, fake, and I think he can see through me. I'm exposed in my faux leather shorts and the lace bralette that shows most of my tits. Even with my five-inch heels, he still looms over me.

"I'm not going to fuck you." I watch the way his Adam's apple bobs as he swallows. He unbuttons one of his cuffs, rolling the material until it reaches his elbows before he starts on the other sleeve. With the material out of the way, I can see the lines of thick muscles that run up his arms. He looks like a sculpture, like something too perfect. I have to shake my head, snap myself out of the ogling. "What's your name?" he asks.

"Kat." My voice cracks, and it causes one side of his mouth to pick up in a lopsided grin. "What... what are..." I'm not usually nervous when I give a private dance. I'm able to slip into a different head space. But this feels different. The rules disappear when it comes to Marcus, and I have no idea what this man will ask me to do. Or what will happen if I don't comply...

I need to do this, though. I need to get close to him. The anxiety that seeps from me is real, and I let it fill my eyes with a bit of fear as I look up at the Costello man, hoping it will only drive him closer to me.

"Nothing," he answers before I even have the question out of my mouth. His words and his actions are out of alignment. He says he's not going to fuck me, but the way he looks at me tells me he wants to.

And something stirs inside of me with his rejection. The nagging fear that had been gathering in my stomach moments ago as he led me to the private room slowly drifts away as he voices his disinterest.

Then why bring me here?

What kind of game is he playing?

I shouldn't want him to fuck me. Knowing he's a Costello, even with my mission, I should stay far away from that family.

Death hangs over them, killing the innocents they surround themselves with. My heart aches at the thought. God, I hope Cassie wasn't here. In this position, standing opposite of a man she couldn't refuse.

"Why?" I ask, and immediately wish I could suck the word back in.

He smiles, the curve of his lips unsettling, sending a chill down my spine.

"Because this is all a game, kitten, and I plan on winning."

Kitten.

He doesn't think I have claws.

He believes my act, my carefully constructed persona.

"I doubt Kat is your real name," he remarks with a smile, this one seeming more genuine but still just as sinister, flashing his pearly white teeth as he laughs.

"What about you?" I redirect. "What's your name?"

He extends a hand for me to shake, his fingers feeling rough and calloused against my skin. "John," he says.

I mentally recall the Costello family tree. Carmine Costello. Four kids. Six grandkids. Marcus is the oldest grandson and John is… the youngest. I pull the information from my brain. John Vitale is the sixth grandchild, and the third boy. The rich, I've discovered, place all the importance on male heirs, a sort of patriarchal tradition that makes my blood boil.

John stalks toward me, brushing his shoulder against mine before he falls back onto the velvet seat. "So," he starts to say, gesturing his hand to the empty space of the room before us. "Are you going to dance for me, kitten?"

I don't know what I expected when he led us back here, but this doesn't feel like it. I don't like the way my skin burns under the heat of his gaze or how quick my heart is beating. There's music playing, but I can't hear it over the sound of my blood rushing past my ears.

I have to kick-start myself, switch back into my alter ego. Taking a step with my cheetah print heels, I spin to face John. A glimmer flickers across his eyes, and I think it's excitement. He didn't look that interested earlier when I first saw him with Marcus, with girls all around them. He definitely didn't look like this…

The corner of his lip lifts, a sly smirk slowly spreading across his mouth. He looks cute like that; I think.

I sway my hips for him, finding the rhythm of the music and letting it flow through me. Dancing is my favorite part of the job, and with a drink in my system, I can forget the man in front of me. Turning him into a faceless Ken doll while I move my body.

Swinging my leg over his knee, I straddle his thigh and bring my hand to his opposite shoulder. I let myself grind on him, my body impossibly close to his.

I don't block John out, though. I don't let him fade into a faceless blob. My body is still moving with the rhythm, still connected to the flow of the music coming through the speakers, but I'm not lost in my head. I'm not zoned out like normal, instead I'm focused on the moment. I'm *in* my zone, my body moving in time with the beat without my head overthinking the actions.

John's hand finds my shoulder, knocking me off rhythm and snapping me out of it. It's the first time he's touched me, but it doesn't feel sensual.

The look on his face is no longer sparkling with amusement. He looks grim, as if he's shifted back into the man he was outside the private room.

"You should stop." He says the statement clearly, as if my half naked body barely affected him.

I can feel one of my eyebrows lifting. The shock hits me before I can control my features.

"If you don't, I won't be able to control myself, and you're not ready for me, kitten."

THREE

John

My first memory is of a lie.

A hazy recollection of my father buckling me into my car seat when he winks and tells me *this is between us. Ma doesn't need to know.*

Fitting, I think.

After all, the Costello family is built on lies.

I wear a façade, a mask concealing who I really am these days and where my loyalty lies. I had to make a whole ordeal about switching sides, and even with that, I can feel the distrust radiating from the men around me.

Even the men I've known my entire life give me sideways glances, trying to find out if this is all an act.

They're not wrong for distrusting me.

I wouldn't trust myself either.

The Porsche purrs beneath me as I pull into the parking lot outside the Orleans Parish Prison, my favorite cousin's new home. I have to go through security, tossing my phone and keys into a blue basket before they let me go inside. There's an older guard in a blue uniform that slides me the visitor sign-in pad with a sigh. I scribble my name on the list and slide it back over with a smile, using my signature charm. Instead of returning the smile, she taps the button on her control panel. A loud buzzing noise fills the space and the lock to the gate clicks as it's released.

I don't visit the prison frequently. I can't, really. Every stop here is a chance for someone to catch onto me, and if they figure out my true motives, I'm screwed.

As soon as I walk through the chain link gates and into the visiting yard, I see him.

Outside of these walls, Sam Costello is a king. In here? They've reduced him to an animal.

He looks unkept compared to how I'm used to seeing him. His dark hair is shaggy and there are days of stubble on his face. The Sam I know would never have stubble. Even a hint of facial hair had him heading for a razor. He was always put together, dressed in pricey suits and looking like he stepped out of a magazine.

The orange prison jumpsuit clashes with his olive skin, and when his eyes meet mine, I just see two hollow orbs.

I slide onto the plastic bench across from him, leaning my elbows on the table. They have the visitors' room set up outside, letting the ninety-degree Louisiana heat beat down on us. It's unbearable, but prisons aren't created to be fun escapes. They're meant to be torturous for the inhabitants.

"*Cugino.*" The corner of Sam's lips rises just subtly. "Been a while."

He's not wrong. I've only been able to visit him one other time since they locked him up.

Innocent until proven guilty doesn't mean much when they can tie you to the mafia. Law enforcement isn't interested in finding out who actually killed my uncle. They just want to put someone with the Costello name behind bars.

"Can't let Marcus catch on," I mutter.

Sam nods his head. He's in on my plan, so he has no desire to fuck it up, but he's not dumb enough to think that's the only reason I'm not visiting him.

Every time I see him here, see the condition he's living in, guilt fills me. He's here on some bullshit charges claiming he killed his father. And although I was there, and I know he didn't kill his father, he's still sitting here in an orange jumpsuit.

"What's the lawyer say?" I ask. The lawyer is an old friend of gramps, a Harvard graduate who slums around with the mafia. He's good at his job, though. He's defended both our fathers and gramps. If anyone can get Sam out of this mess, it's him.

"They have evidence." Sam runs his fingers through his dark hair. He's stressed, that much I can tell. "Fingerprints on the gun and my cellphone pinged off the tower nearby."

The fucking gun, the one that uniformed officer found while I was staring at Junior, begging him to come back to life. I could slap myself for how stupid I was in the moments after his death. When I should have been acting, trying to figure out what in that home would have incriminated us. Even Junior, in his last moment, told me to protect Sam. But I didn't. Instead, I sat there, numb to my surroundings while the cops got a head start.

"Is that enough to…" I trail off, not wanting to say the words. But Sam knows. Is it enough to put him away forever?

"Maybe." He shrugs. "We don't know yet."

His eyes drift away for a second, his mind going off somewhere before he comes back to me. "How's it from your angle?"

I shrug my shoulder, dropping my gaze from him. "Not great," I mutter. "Marcus is keeping me at arm's length."

Sam nods. "I don't blame him. I wouldn't trust you either."

I also wouldn't trust myself. We may be family, but my loyalty has belonged to my uncle our entire lives. Even getting on my knees and kissing his shoes wouldn't convince Marcus that I'm suddenly on his side. And if for some reason he does believe I'm not spying on him for Sam, he definitely thinks I'm faking it to keep my life. Still not very respectable. He has no incentive to let me in on his plans to take over the family.

"What about Lana?" Sam asks. Junior instilled a core set of values in the two of us, values that didn't seem to rub off on Marcus. Or maybe Junior knew even back then that Marcus was a lost cause.

"She's good. Checked in last week. Ignazio is working with the Luchese *famiglia,* so they're taken care of."

"Good," Sam replies, then his head drops into his hands, and he sucks in a deep breath. He's not as in control as he normally is; he looks stressed and irritable.

"Everything okay here?" I ask. "Need more protection?" Prison has its own inner workings, but they can be manipulated from the outside to an extent. We have men inside those walls, a mini *famiglia* that will protect Sam. I can find him more if he needs it. Some guys are willing to be put away for the right amount of money. Some even like it; the world is a terrifying place, and since prison is smaller, their job is clearer.

"I'm fine," he snaps. It's unusual for Sam to be this pissed off. He's always calm and collected, two steps ahead of everyone else. But prison has made him edgy. I can't blame him. I don't know what it's like to be locked up in a cage.

"If you need something..." I trail off.

"I need out, John. What the fuck else do you think I need?" He slams his palm down on the table, his dark eyes glowering at me. I've seen Sam snap before, but never at me. At Marcus, at other men, but never me.

"Okay." I bob my head, swallowing thickly. "I'm working on it."

Sam scrubs a hand over his stubble, looking exasperated. "Let me know when you have answers for me." He taps his hand on the plastic before standing up. "And, John?" His gaze finds me one last time.

"Yeah?"

"Don't come back here until it's done."

SAINTS AND SINNERS is packed on a Saturday night. There's even a line of people outside the front door, IDs in hand, waiting to be let in. Strippers never interested me. There's nothing alluring about a woman shaking her ass for money. The one from the other night, though, Kat, as she called herself, piqued some curiosity in me.

It was more than her body that caught my attention. Something about her behavior, the way she wrung her fingers together nervously but then jutted out her chest and asked my cousin if he needed anything... she wanted to get close to him, grab his attention. Most girls in her position know who Marcus is, and by proxy know what he... *likes.* It's not a secret my cousin owns the club, and he uses the women who work there freely. Not gently either, and that's saying a lot coming from me. I like rough sex, but Marcus has no regard for human life.

It's always amused me that they dubbed me the family psychopath. As if I'm the one who takes lives aimlessly, like they mean nothing. Sure, I've killed people, gutted them and disposed of their bodies in unmarked graves, to never be found again.

But I've never killed a woman.

It was Junior that had picked me up the second time I got sent to the principal's office for violence. That time, I had gutted the class mouse with my pocketknife. The sight of blood made one of the girls vomit on her desk. Apparently, cutting open animals at school was frowned upon.

Junior didn't yell at me like my dad or scream and cry like

my mom. He took me for hotdogs at my favorite place and we sat at one of the old picnic tables while we ate. Once I finished eating and had moved on to using the back of my hand to wipe the ketchup from my face, Junior started his life lesson. That was one thing my uncle was always good for; wisdom and advice that my parents could never give.

"You can't kill animals." he told me, matter of fact. *"It freaks people out. You understand what I'm saying?"*

I nodded. I could tell by the faces of my classmates that they were not amused by the way the sticky red fluid leaked from the mouse, coating its white fur.

"You can't hit kids either, Johnny." His dark eyes bore into me. I wasn't afraid of my uncle. I wasn't afraid of anyone, really. But with my dad, I expected a fight, fists to fly, and I was okay with that. It was different with Junior. I sat on the edge of my seat when he spoke. I clung to his words, to the wisdom he would impart to me.

I wanted to make Junior proud. Far more than I did anyone else in my life. After a while, it was clear my parents were happy to let Junior do all the parenting, as long as they didn't have to.

"Why, though?" I had asked. *"You hit Uncle Al at the Christmas Party."*

Junior had laughed. *"You're right,"* he said. *"You're gonna have to trust me on this one, Johnny. Sometimes you can hit someone, but you have to know when it's the right time. When it's okay."*

And Junior taught me. He didn't act out of emotion, so I didn't either. I couldn't hit someone, couldn't kill them simply because I wanted to.

I needed a *reason*.

One of Junior's many principles he drilled into my brain was *don't hurt women or children*. It was a red line that I wasn't about to cross. And for Junior, I never did. He gave me explicit permission for when to take a life. It was a serious ordeal removing someone from the world, and it was not to be treated lightly.

The men I kill are liars, cheaters, junkies - worthless men who don't deserve to walk the planet anymore. Marcus kills women once he tires of them.

We are not the same.

"Vitale." Donnie claps his hand on my back. "Nice to see ya." He leans against to the bar and signals for a drink. It doesn't take long for the girl to grab a bottle of whiskey from the top shelf and pour two glasses. She smiles sheepishly as she pushes the tumblers toward us.

I have no interest in her. Not like Kat. She has faint bruises on her forearm and foundation caked on her face and neck, likely covering something up. Between the bruises and the shy actions, I assume she has a man at home, someone who gets their rocks off by hurting her. I feel sorry for the poor blonde bartender. Not enough to do anything, though. That's the other thing Junior taught me. *You don't meddle.* Watch, take mental notes, but don't act on it.

Junior only allowed me to take jobs we discussed thoroughly. There were no passion projects, no side kills for fun. Taking a life was a serious matter, and Junior had the final say.

Mostly, he told me when it was okay, gave me a name and a location, then let me go. Other times, I had to watch them first, report back to my uncle with my findings, and then he would decide. That was always the worst when my fingers were itching for a kill, but I had to wait.

Junior only let me kill a man if he knew for sure that he was a threat to us, our business, our *famiglia*. And if he was, in any shape or form, he was dead.

"Paranoia is a curse, Johnny," he had told me once. *"When men like us get paranoid, bullets start flying."*

It feels ironic, knowing that he died because of a power play, and it left us all a little paranoid. That's the thing about living a lie. You're constantly waiting for someone to catch on to you, and in our line of work, someone finding out your secrets means life in Orleans Parish Prison.

Donnie clinks his glass against mine, and his eyes scan the surrounding club. "You here for ya cousin?"

"Just hanging out." I bring the tumbler to my lips and take a long sip of the amber liquid.

"I don't think I've ever seen you *hang out*." He chuckles skeptically. He's not wrong. I don't make a habit of hanging out at my cousin's club. Or any club. Social activities have never excited me.

I shrug and ignore his statement. I don't owe him an explanation for my newfound interest in Saints and Sinners.

The club is dark, save for the rotating purple and pink lights shining down on the floor. There are comfortable seats everywhere. A sleek couch wraps around the stage, allowing the patrons to have a good view without sacrificing any pleasure.

When I lift my gaze, I find Kat stepping onto the stage, and instantly my eyes are glued to her.

Black boots rise to her knees, clinging to her like a second layer of skin. She reaches out to grab the chrome pole, and I think she's just going to plant one foot and do a simple spin. But she leans forward impossibly slow, letting gravity do its job as one of her legs lift. Right when I think she can't possibly lean forward any farther, her other leg wraps around the pole, and she begins to spin. Her body looks lithe and graceful as she completes a rotation.

Once the heels of her stilettos find the floor again, she leans back, her spine arching with the movement. The little shorts she wears leave nothing to the imagination. From the direct view I have, I can see her tits perfectly as she bends. She slowly lowers her body to the floor, starting with her shoulders until her knees are bent and her back lies on the ground.

A toned arm reaches for the heel of one of her boots, pulling it back while she stretches the other one out until her legs are spread wide and the only thing keeping the leering men from seeing her sweet cunt is a thin strip of fabric.

Heat races to my heart, the organ being flooded with a burning sensation. I want to stalk up there and toss a blanket over her, keep everyone in this audience from seeing her.

Seeing what's *mine*.

But she's not mine.

Something about her makes me want her. In a possessive way, like a jealous fuck who thinks he needs to own someone. It's not that I want to own Kat, per se. I just want to see her be utterly consumed by me, completely at my mercy. Maybe I have control issues.

It doesn't matter, though. I scrub a hand down my face. Whatever I'm feeling for this girl needs to stop. I can't be attracted to her and still get my job done. And my focus right now needs to be on Sam, on figuring out who framed him and how to get him out of this mess.

Kat is just a girl. She's pretty, obviously. With what she does on the stage, I can only imagine what she's like in bed. And her cute little doe eyes make me think she'd look stunning on her knees staring up at me. And sure, maybe she's a liar. Clearly, she's keeping something a secret, but that doesn't make her dangerous, doesn't make her worth investigating. She's just a kid who's in over her head. Not my problem.

When she lifts herself up from the floor, she starts with her ass, leaving it raised in the air as she drags her torso up. Every movement is sensual, lulling me in as she sweeps her hair over her shoulder. From this distance, I can see as she tugs her bottom lip between her teeth and her gray eyes scan the room.

It takes effort to restrain my dick. It wants nothing more than to imagine what it would be like to sink into her, to feel her clench around me.

These feelings, this lust, need to exit the picture. I can't risk fucking this thing with Marcus up, and if I get close to the little liar, I risk her figuring out my secrets before I learn hers. And my secrets could get me killed. Marcus learning that I'm betraying him, that my loyalty has always belonged to Sam, that would be a death sentence.

So it doesn't matter how pretty or how intriguing the girl is.

For now, she gets to keep her secrets.

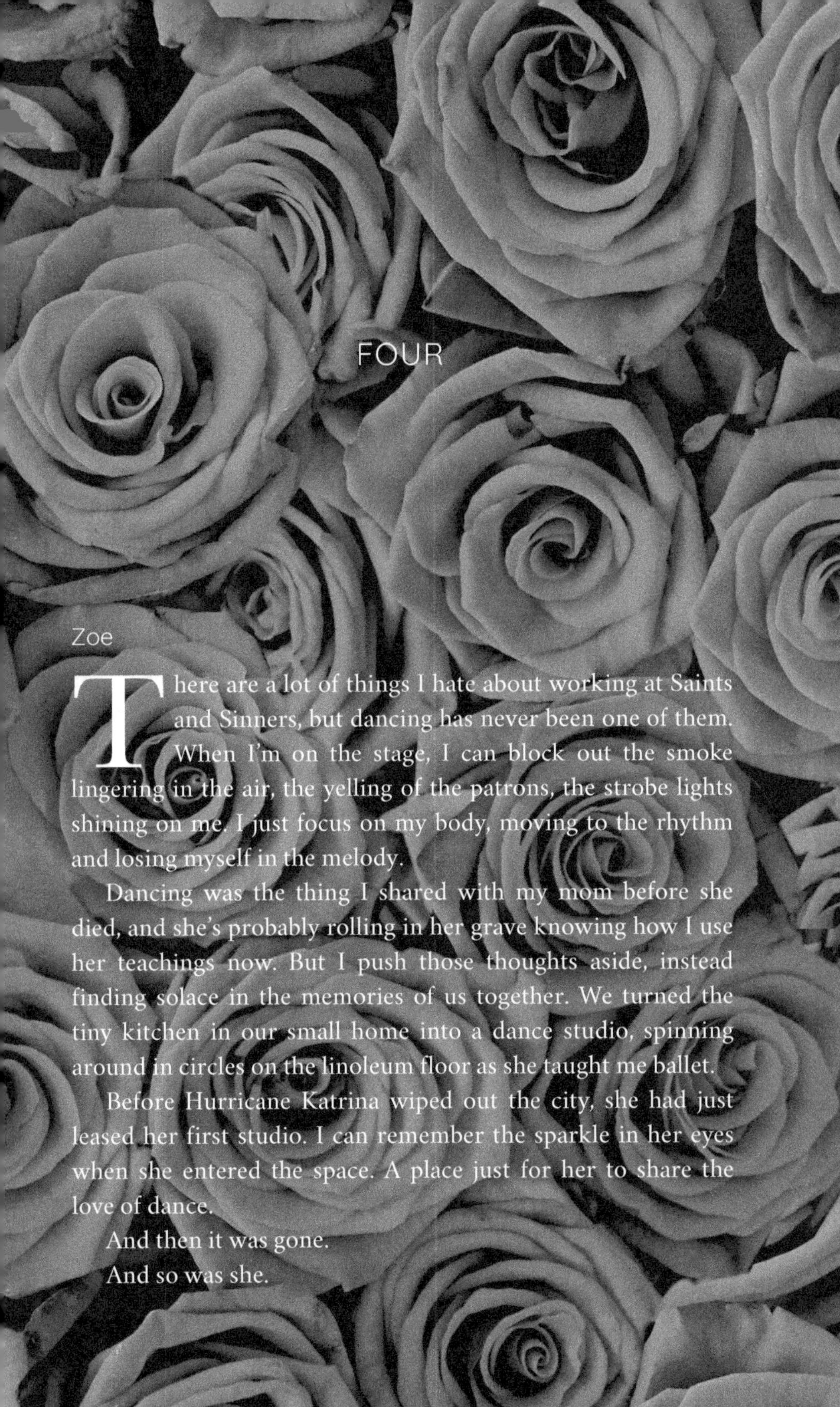

FOUR

Zoe

There are a lot of things I hate about working at Saints and Sinners, but dancing has never been one of them. When I'm on the stage, I can block out the smoke lingering in the air, the yelling of the patrons, the strobe lights shining on me. I just focus on my body, moving to the rhythm and losing myself in the melody.

Dancing was the thing I shared with my mom before she died, and she's probably rolling in her grave knowing how I use her teachings now. But I push those thoughts aside, instead finding solace in the memories of us together. We turned the tiny kitchen in our small home into a dance studio, spinning around in circles on the linoleum floor as she taught me ballet.

Before Hurricane Katrina wiped out the city, she had just leased her first studio. I can remember the sparkle in her eyes when she entered the space. A place just for her to share the love of dance.

And then it was gone.

And so was she.

Stripping isn't the same as ballet; dancing in pink shoes comes with more structure and rules. Dancing on this stage is loose, freeing. People just want to have a good time, and watching me move my body and spin around the pole sparks joy in them.

When the song ends, the fake reality I've created for myself drifts away and the truth comes into focus. I'm not dancing my heart out for my own pleasure, or because it feels good. No, I'm in a darkened club with flashing lights. There are men leering at my body, and crusty one-dollar bills are scattered on the stage.

I pick up my money as gracefully as I can and step off the platform. The part I hate most about this job is mingling with the clientele, and that's what comes next.

I stuff the bills into the waistband of the faux leather booty shorts I'm wearing until I can get to the back to store them in my money bag. In between dances, I'm supposed to hang out with the customers, try to entice them into spending more money to see me alone. Private dances are my least favorite. With a wall separating them from the security guard, their hands start to forget the rules and their mouths start to run.

I'm thinking about heading to the bar when I feel someone grab my wrist, pulling me backwards. I stumble over my feet before landing on the man's lap. He wraps his other arm over my waist, pinning me against him on his chair. "You're fucking beautiful." He slurs the words, and I can smell the vodka on his breath.

"No," I tell him, using my hand to push against his thigh in an attempt to straighten myself. "Let me go!"

I can feel his erection poking against my ass, and for the first time in the month I've worked here, my blood runs cold. I knew what I was getting into. Hell, Donnie introduced me to the life during my interview.

But this feels worse, dirtier, more dangerous.

"Don't be a cock tease." He chuckles, a bit of spittle landing on my face.

"Let. Me. Go," I repeat, pushing against his chest. I don't even care if I land on the filthy club floor, I just want to get away from him.

The man leans his head in, his tongue finding the crook of my neck, and he licks me there. My stomach churns, my entire body stiffening at the action. His hand roams down my bare stomach, over the hem of my shorts. There's barely any material over my ass, and just a thin strip between my legs. He pushes them apart easily and his finger traces the small bit of fabric.

I feel like I'm dying as this man touches me, his fingers burning through my skin and my dignity with every second they're on me. Clearly uncaring about my protests, he continues his assault, his finger slipping under the material between my legs, where nothing is left to protect me from his touch. I punch my fists into his chest, but he's too big, an immovable object.

Until he isn't.

Everything changes in a matter of a mere fifteen seconds.

I'm yanked from the man's lap and right onto my feet, and then he's on the floor, blood pouring from his nose.

John Vitale stands over him and he doesn't let that be the end. He hits the stranger again. And again. Until he's curled into a ball on the floor, his hands covering his face as he whimpers like a child.

"Fucking scum," John snarls. "You like to touch girls without their permission? You don't know what the word *no* means?" The man mumbles an unintelligible response, but that doesn't satisfy John. He leans down so his face is hovering over the man's. "If you ever touch her, or another girl in this place ever again, I will fucking end you. *Capisce?*"

Robby pulls John back, hoisting him up from the armpits while the man who touched me clutches at his bloody face. John shakes the bouncer off, straightening out his suit jacket before he turns, his gaze landing on me. As soon as our eyes connect, something in him shifts.

The hard lines of his face soften, and he brushes his knuckles against his pant leg, wiping off the remnants of blood. He moves to me in two slow steps, his dark eyes glued to mine.

"Are you okay?" he asks, like a completely different person than the one who just defended me seconds ago. That version of him looked happy to punch that man, and now I'm too afraid to even look at the man who was just touching me. There's blood on the floor, splattered on the stage, and on John.

It's too much, more than I would have ever caused from hitting a man. I knew John would be stronger...but that's a lot stronger.

That version of him has drifted away. This one looks calm, nicer even, as he approaches me. "Are you okay?" he asks again.

"I don't know," I mumble. "Is he?"

John knows who I mean, and he glances over his shoulder at the man still on the floor. People are standing around him, with Donnie bent down next to him. There are a few girls with their backs pressed against the wall, too scared to move.

I should be scared, I think.

On some level, I am. But then I look into John's eyes, serene oceans of inky black. He doesn't feel a thing about what he just did.

"He's alive," John answers, uncaring. "Let's get you cleaned up." His eyes drift down my bare legs, and when I follow his gaze, I realize I have blood on me too, splattered over my thighs and knees.

How hard did John punch him?

Strong arms wrap around my waist, and before I know what he's doing, John has me cradled in his arms. I think I should be pushing my way out of his grasp, but I don't. Instead, I let him carry me to the back, through the door marked *staff only*. He brings me into the private bathroom reserved for the staff and sets me on the counter.

Dark eyes assess me, roaming my body and looking for injuries.

I watch him as he wets a paper towel and brings it to my knee. He looks at me first, his hand hovering over my skin, waiting for permission. I nod slowly.

Gently, John begins to wipe the blood from my legs.

"Why did you do that?" My voice betrays me, the words sounding weak as they leave my lips.

Muscles ripple through his fitted dress shirt, and his black pants are taunt around his thighs as he squats in front of me to clean my skin with the damp paper towel. His dark eyes look up to me, framed by thick lashes. "Because, you said no." He continues on as if the explanation was simple enough.

And maybe it should be, but that's not how things work here. My life has been a series of events where no one has ever been there for me. Fighting my own battles has kind of become my thing.

But John was there so quickly, not just helping me but defending my honor.

Protecting me.

I shudder.

My hand reaches out, suddenly wanting to touch his skin, and I rest my palm on his cheek. "Thank you."

"Don't thank me," he says as he wipes the rest of the blood from my skin. He tosses the paper towel into the trash can and washes his hands with soap in the sink. When he's done, he finally returns his attention to me, his eyes roaming every inch of my skin as if he's looking for more. More blood, more bruises, more pain hiding beneath the surface.

I've hidden my pain for so long, and still, John looks at me as if he can see it. Like he can see through my mask. My alter ego.

"Tell me your name," he whispers, and I can see his hand

twitching at his side, like he wants to reach out and touch me. In some sick way, I want him to. I think his hand could erase the feeling of that stranger's on me, could make me forget about the men who think they can touch me, use me, own me.

"Why?" My voice is so low I doubt he hears me.

"I want to know you, kitten. I want to know everything about you."

"I-" My voice stalls. I can't tell him my name. It's rule number one; the most important rule of stripping. Don't give out your name, or any other identifying details, to the men that come here. Some of them become obsessive stalkers who think they can have you simply because you shed your clothes in front of them.

Maybe John isn't a creep who's going to follow me to my car. But I can't risk that...

Even with that thought stopping me, though, my emotions war inside my chest, because something inside me thinks I should. Maybe it will bring me closer to him...and that could bring me closer to Cassie.

Just as I'm about to open my lips and tell him my name, against my better judgement, the door to the bathroom swings open. Donnie stops in his tracks when he sees the two of us, me sitting on the counter and John standing in front of me.

"Johnny." He nods his head at the man. "Whenever you're done." His eyes drift to me as if to say, *whenever you're done with her*.

John nods his head and Donnie backs out, shutting the door behind him. Suddenly, a weight presses down on my chest, a reminder of what I've gotten myself into.

John isn't some kind of knight in shining armor; he's a made man. Mafia.

I jump down of the counter, balancing on the heels and straightening out my top. "Thank you, again," I say, ignoring the look on his face. I spin around to check myself in the mirror before I walk back out there. My reflection glares back at me, and instantly, I can see what's missing. My fingers reach for my throat, searching for the tarnished half heart necklace.

It's gone.

"Are you sure you're okay?" John asks, one of his dark eyebrows ticked up.

"I'm good," I tell him, shaking off the nausea that's rolling through my stomach. I never take the necklace off; I've worn it since the day we bought them. Tears prick at the corners of my eyes, but I know I can't tell this stranger that I'm crying over a cheap necklace, so I swallow the burning sensation and smile through my lie.

I'm not good, though. My body is buzzing, burning with shame and adrenaline and the persistent feeling that I've made a mistake.

FIVE

John

It's not hard for me to find Richie Williams. A low-level dealer who spends his free time and money at Saints and Sinners. He's the kind of douchebag who thinks he can touch any girl he wants.

I think Junior would approve of this kill. At least, that's what I tell myself as I watch the pathetic sack of a man wake up tied to a metal chair.

There's fear coating his features. I can see it in the way he strains his body, testing out the duct tape I used to secure him to the chair. He shakes, the metal hitting off the concrete floor and the duct tape holding strong. I can't help but to laugh at his struggle.

Fucking idiot.

"Not so strong now, huh?" Richie's head whips around as he makes out my figure in the dark warehouse. The fear increases when he sees me, and the blubbering starts, a flow of words I can barely make out escaping his lips. Mostly, *sorry* and *please.* A beautiful soundtrack, music to my ears.

"It doesn't fucking matter," I tell him, standing up from my own metal chair. This warehouse is empty save for the two of us, the plastic tarp under him, and the two metal chairs.

Richie is stark naked in his seat, and as the waves of realization hit him, the crying and begging increase. I could tape his mouth shut, but I don't want to. There's no one here to hear him scream, and I like the sound they make in their final moments, when they realize they're about to die because of their actions.

"Whatever you say," I pause to give Richie a lopsided smirk, "won't save you. You decided your fate the second you laid a hand on that girl at the club."

"Her?" he cries. "That's what this is about? I'm sorry, I didn't know she was yours!"

"Mine." I say the word, liking the way it tastes on the tip of my tongue. She's not mine, though. She can't be mine. But damn, does it feel good to pretend she is.

I let the idea linger in my mind, lying to myself a little bit more by pretending that she could be. That I could lay her out on my bed and kiss every inch of her body, devour her the way I want to.

I could never *keep* her. I'm not cut out for relationships; love is a loser's game, and I'm not interested in playing. Even if she was interested, I can't give her all the things she wants.

But I can give her this. I can take this piece of scum off the street.

My fingers twist the cheap silver chain I found on the floor under Richie's body when I dragged him from the club. It's a silver heart, half of a best friend necklace. I would have tossed it in the trash, but then I remembered the way my kitten touched her neck as she watched her reflection in the mirror. She was missing something.

Is this it?

Did she lose this necklace, and that was what made her look

so sad, so worried. Her façade broke, and for a moment I saw beneath it. This necklace has something to do with it, and I want to know what?

I'm too intrigued by the girl. I need to rid her from my mind, wash her down the drain like I'll do with Richie's blood.

"You're right," I tell the man. I take slow, deliberate steps to the edge of the plastic tarp where I set my knife. I pocket the necklace. "She is mine. And after tonight, you'll never touch her again."

"Wh-what are you going to do?" he whimpers.

I gesture to the three gift bags with bright pink tissue paper that sit at the edge of the plastic tarp. "You get to pick," I tell him. I can't help the grin that rises on my lips. Secretly, I love this part of it.

"You're not supposed to like killing," Uncle Junior had told me. It was funny to think that this family had made their millions by spilling the blood of anyone who wouldn't bow to them. But the idea of me *enjoying* a kill is some type of sin.

But I do like killing. And right now, my finger wraps around the black base of the knife as I stalk toward the man. The stupid fucking man who put his hands on my kitten.

He won't make the mistake again.

"See, one bag has a knife, one bag has a gun, and one bag has nothing. I'm going to use whatever's in the bag you choose. And if you pick the empty one, well…" I shrug my shoulders. "Then I'll let you go."

Richie sobs again, gulping in air through his tears. *Pathetic.*

"Pick one," I demand.

"Middle." He shakes as he nods his head toward the middle bag. I make a show of digging inside, moving the tissue paper like I'm searching for something. I can see the anticipation on his face, and for the briefest moment, he believes he chose the empty bag.

And then I pull out a long, sharpened knife.

The truth that he'll never know is that they all had knives in them. I just like the look on their faces when they think there's a way out, and then the sadness when they find out there's no hope.

"I'm going to start with your hands." He whimpers as I near him. "See, every time I cut you, you're going to tense up. It's a natural response. So I'm going to slice between each and every finger, so even when your entire body tenses, you won't be able to get the slightest bit of release."

"Please!" he shouts as he begs for his life, but I don't pay much attention as I slide the webbing between each of his fingers. Then I get to work, slicing into his skin and relishing in each moment.

When the tarp runs red, and Richie takes his last breath, I finally stop.

Inhaling in the relief.

Bye-bye, Richie.

DETECTIVE MATTHEW ELLISON drives a Mercedes Benz. That's the first sign that something is off to me. Sure, a nice New Orleans detective could drive a Mercedes. Maybe he has family money or a rich wife - but Detective Ellison has neither of those. On his salary alone, that car would eat up his entire paycheck.

It's not surprising to know that the New Orleans police force has dirty cops, as Junior had paid several of them over the years to turn their heads. What does surprise me is that a dirty cop is the detective on my uncle's murder, and my cousin is still behind bars.

Ellison may be working for the Costellos, but it's not Sam who's paying him.

My fingers drum against the steering wheel, itching to wrap

around his throat while I demand answers. But that's not how this works. Junior would want me to follow him more, to be sure that he's on Marcus's payroll. If they're smart, I'll never catch the two of them together. But I don't believe for a second that my cousin is that smart. One of these days, he'll slip up.

Ellison pulls his fancy car into the station, and I park my four-door Ford Escape across the street. I prefer my Porsche, but it's hard to tail someone in a car like that. Plus, the mid-size SUV is good for… other things.

He stands from the car, brushing off his suit jacket. Summers in NOLA are sweltering, but he dons the fancy black suit anyway. Tucking his phone into his pocket, he grabs his brief-case from the backseat before heading for the entrance.

I see her then. Strands of dark brown hair fly behind her as her converse slap against the pavement. She runs to him, her hand reaching out to stop him. I'm shooting up in my seat, grip-ping onto the steering wheel.

I was not expecting this.

Ellison turns to look at Kat, pulling his aviators off his face. He looks annoyed, angry even. She's animated in whatever she's asking him, her hands raising with her words, and when he responds, they drop quickly, slapping against her thighs. She's frustrated with him, I think. But why?

They exchange words I want to hear. Nobody looks happy in this situation. He clearly wants her to go away, and she does, spinning on her heels angrily. He calls something after her, and she stops but doesn't look at him again. Whatever he said pisses her off, and she stomps away from the police station.

Well, that's something new.

Without thinking, I put the car into drive, my brain navi-gating from muscle memory. I don't even realize what I'm doing until I'm in the Filmore neighborhood, driving among the rows of mansions and right to *his*.

Junior was my go-to person.

But he's not here to lean on anymore.

I drive past his house without stopping. I wish he was here; wish I could tell him my suspicions about Ellison. We would bounce ideas back and forth, wondering why a dancer from Marcus's club would be arguing with the detective.

Is he using her? Getting information on *la famiglia?* But if that's the case, why would he be dirty? Is he playing both sides?

It doesn't make sense.

Without Junior, and with Sam in jail, I have nowhere to go.

I pull up Donnie's contact info on my phone, tapping the call button and letting it ring through the speakers.

"Yeah, Johnny?" His thick New York accent punctuates my name. I hate when he calls me Johnny, when anyone calls me Johnny other than my uncle. The stupid childhood nickname grates on me, riling up my anger. And I can't be angry now, can't give anyone a reason to think I'm anything but happy to be working for Marcus.

"Hey, Donnie. I need a favor, got a sec?"

"Sure, what is it?" I don't think Donnie would do me favors if it wasn't for my bloodline. Even though Marcus and I aren't on the best of terms, he can't deny that I'm part of the Costello *famiglia.* And at the end of the day, he wants a job, and you can't bank on who will win this civil war.

"The girl, the one who got roughed up the other day, what's her name?"

Even after I helped her, she still hadn't divulged her real name to me. She was smart to only go by her stage name, and if I hadn't seen her with Ellison today, I probably would have let it go.

But now I need to know more. I need to know everything about her.

She intrigued me from the moment she walked into the VIP room, but now I can't get the little liar out of my mind. Something about seeing that man's hands on her made my vision burn red. I'm not supposed to act on emotions, but I did that day. Before I could stop myself, I was across the room and my fist was burning as I hit his face. And then I did it again.

Who did he think he was to just reach out and grab her, to touch her as if she belonged to him? My blood boiled just thinking about his hands on her body.

"Eh, let me see here." I hear a shuffling of papers in the background and then the clicking of keys. "Uh, looks like Zoe, yeah, Zoe Carson."

"Zoe Carson," I repeat, trying her name out on my tongue. It's much better than Kat, but I still can't help thinking of her as a little kitten. *What are you into, Zoe? Is it more than you can handle?*

"Do you know why she's working there?" I ask Donnie.

"Ah," he grumbles, "something about her father, I think. He's sick or something, cancer, maybe?"

That only gives me more questions. What would her sick father have to do with a homicide detective? "Any other family?"

"I don't know, Johnny. She doesn't talk much."

That I did know. She'd been quiet, shy. Maybe that's why I like her. The women in my family talk nonstop; Lana might be the only exception. Madi, my mother, my aunts - none of them can't shut their mouths. But Zoe was all thoughts and no words, watching me with her piercing steel-gray eyes.

"Thanks, Don," I tell him and tap the end call button on my steering wheel.

I have other things I should be worried about, like getting Sam out of prison, for one. This girl is not my problem. If anything, she's Marcus's problem to deal with.

But there's something off here, something's not right.

She's a little liar, and I want to know her secrets.

SIX

Zoe

My stomach aches when I head into work. I took time away from the club after the incident. I didn't think Donnie would agree to it, but John told him I wasn't coming back in, and Donnie didn't argue.

Instead, I spent my time off trying to avoid all the areas of my apartment tainted with memories of Cassie. Stupid, really, because every spot reminds me of my missing best friend.

Three months, and I still haven't moved on.

There's no one else looking for Cassie. The police have written her off as another sex worker who ran away.

"Move on, Zoe," Ellison, the detective assigned to her case, had told me this morning when I caught him outside of the station, demanding an update.

"Are you even looking for her?"

"We've been over this," he sighed. The man looked overworked, tired. New Orleans had been hit with a string of murders lately, and the news was running stories about the killing of Carmine Costello Jr. daily.

"Is the mafia more important than Cassie? Is that it?" I asked, unable to contain the anger that dripped from my words like venom. It's always about the mafia in this city. All of NOLA revolves around the Costello family, and it's beginning to make me sick.

It's their fault that Cassie's missing. I can feel it in my bones. But my opinion doesn't matter much, especially not against theirs.

"Dammit, Zoe." The detective's voice rose the more I asked. *"We've been over this."*

It didn't matter how many times he told me; I would never be over this. Over her.

"Your friend was a prostitute." The word left his mouth like it tasted bitter, as if her profession made her less than. *"Girls like that tend to run away, move on quickly. You need to do the same. She's not going to be found if she doesn't want to be."*

"She wouldn't do that." I waved my hand through the air viciously. Truthfully, I wanted to slap him, but I've never hit anyone in my life, and I wasn't about to start with a detective. I was angry. How was it that a woman could be missing for three months, and no one gave a fuck?

"Why?" he asked bitterly, *"because you said so?"*

"I know her." There was emotion behind my words, emotion I had worked so hard to press down. I had tried to go the crying route with Ellison before, but he didn't care much for my tears. His sympathy lasted about ten seconds before he handed me a tissue and ushered me out of his office.

"Apparently not," he responded.

"I'm going to find her."

"Stop, Zoe. You're going to get yourself hurt."

I tried to ignore him as I spun around, ready to leave him in the parking lot.

"Zoe," he called after me. *"Stay away from the Costellos. You're going to get yourself killed, little girl."*

I shook off his warning and his demeaning nickname. I didn't care about his opinion. No matter what he said, I wasn't going to give up my search for Cassie. She's been my best friend since childhood. Instinctively, I reached up to finger the tarnished silver broken heart that hung from my neck to be reminded again of its loss. My stomach burned, the sickness swirling inside of it. Should I read into its disappearance as a bad omen? Is this the universe's way of telling me to move on?

But what if Cassie is still out there? The other half of the heart still hanging from her throat?

The necklaces are silly. Trinkets we bought from Claire's in our teenage years, before Brett, the douchebag she ran off with. But I can't let go. Can't give up on her yet.

He was part of the reason the police weren't looking for her. *"She has a history of running away,"* Ellison had told me.

But he didn't understand. Cassie had been in a shitty foster home, her temporary father had been handsy, and we both knew what was going to come next. So she ran. Brett was a few years older than her; he took her in, letting her live in his apartment in Baton Rouge.

It was a mistake. We both realized that later. Brett was no better than her foster father, but in that moment, her options were limited.

That concept was foreign to Ellison. All he understood was that she had a child protective services file that labeled her as a runner, and as such, there was no use wasting resources to look for her. He was seeing things in black and white instead of the various shades of gray.

To him, a sex worker with a history of fleeing was a waste of time.

To everyone except me.

"Boss wants to see ya," Robby tells me as I trudge through the entrance of Saints and Sinners. He doesn't meow or hiss at me this time, and I wonder if he feels bad for what happened the last time I was in this club. He should have been the one to protect me from that customer, but wherever he was, it wasn't where I needed him.

"Thanks, Robby." I try to give him a sweet smile, but Kat isn't coming out to play today. Maybe she's just as tired as me.

I drag my feet as I walked back to Donnie's office, the rubber soles of my Converse scraping against the tiled floor.

"Hey, Donnie, Robby said-" I barely have the door open before I stop dead in my tracks.

Donnie's not in his office. Instead, Marcus Ricci leans comfortably against my boss's desk. His thick arms are crossed over his frame, his dark gazed studied on me. Marcus isn't unattractive, but I can already see his hair thinning, and he's no longer the muscular man I assume he once was. His frame is large, but it isn't built or sculpted.

"I'm sorry, Robby told me Donnie wanted to see me."

"It's fine, I asked for you." He gestures to the seat in front of him.

I swallow the saliva that's building in my mouth as I tentatively step toward him. Robby did say boss... I just assumed he meant *my* boss.

It takes effort not to let my nerves show as I sit down before Marcus. He's the man I'm looking to get close to... but this isn't the way I thought it would happen. He doesn't look like he wants to fuck me. No, he looks like he wants to kill me, hurt me.

Suddenly I wish I would have taken Ellison's warning more seriously.

Marcus doesn't move from his position, doesn't sit down on the other side of the desk. Instead, he continues to stand there, uncomfortably close to me and hovering above. It's a power play, I have to remind myself. He's standing over me in an attempt to make me scared.

Whatever he has to say, he wants me to be fearful of him when I hear the words.

And it's working, because I am.

"You danced for my cousin the other week, hmm?"

I'm not sure if it's a statement or a question, but I nod my head anyway.

"Good, did he like you?"

"Uhm." I lick my lips as images of John flash through my mind. Did he like me? I don't know... I danced for him and there was a sinful look on his face, like he wanted to pin me down and fuck me right then. But then he left.

"Did you fuck him?"

My eyes dart up to meet Marcus's when he asks the question. "Of course not."

A smirk rises on his lips. He crouches down so his face is level with mine, bringing himself so close that I can feel his warm breath hit my cheek. "Would you?"

My nerves are on edge, my anxiety manifesting as sweat drips down my temple. "I-" The truth is, I was already thinking about it. Using sex as a weapon to get closer to John in an attempt to extract any information I could. Before John, I played with the idea of sleeping with the man in front of me. If anyone knew what was happening in his place of business, it would be him, right?

But now, I feel dirty hearing the words out loud.

"Why are you working here?" he asks, cutting off my hesitant response.

How many men are going to ask me that question? I feel transparent, as if they can see through my intentions. Maybe I'm not as good of an actor as I think I am. "I...I..." I can't find the words, my heart racing too fast. Thoughts of John flash through my mind, and the lust I feel for him mixes with the fear I feel for Marcus. "Money," I finally say, and it's not a lie... but it's not the truth either.

"How much?"

I don't know what to say when he asks the question. His

endgame is unclear to me, and honestly, I don't want his money. The only thing I want from Marcus Ricci is the truth about what happened to Cassie.

"I don't understand."

He chuckles, a rough, bitter sound. "I want you to do something for me." His hand reaches forward, a calloused palm rubbing softly against my cheek. It takes everything in me not to flinch at his touch.

This is what you wanted.

I know that. I wanted to lure him in, string him along for information. But it was a dumb plan, I think, because I can't control the anxiety that flutters through my body, threatening to expose me. Expose my carefully crafted strategy.

"I want you to get close to my cousin, and I'll pay you for it."

There's a small smile rising on his lips. The tables have turned. I'm no longer using him, he's using me. Though... I don't think I ever was using him.

"Why?"

His smile grows wider, like he's got me now. His finger hooks under my elastic choker, his eyes dropping to the plastic material.

"I want you to give me information. And if you do a good job, I'll reward you."

I swallow. "Reward me?"

He moves in closer, bringing his lips to my ear, his breath skating across my flesh. "Money, jewelry, sex... tell me what you want, and it's yours."

"But only if I do a good job?"

"She's catching on." He grins.

Stay away from the Costello family... Ellison's warning rings through my mind.

Too late now.

"What kind of information?"

Marcus leans back on his heels before standing, hovering

over me again. "I think he's up to something, and I want to know what."

"How am I supposed to figure that out?"

Marcus shrugs his shoulders. "You're a smart girl. You'll come up with something."

If I do this, I'll have Marcus on my side. I'll be able to get close to him… and then maybe I can figure out what happened. Figure out where Cassie is.

"Okay," I whisper. "I'm in."

SEVEN

John

The old duplex in the Seventh Ward looks rough and worn down. I park my Escape down the street after I drive by the place. Donnie did say she was stripping for the money, but still, I expected... more than this.

I tuck my hands into my pockets as I walk down her street. She's at the club now, so I know she's not home. I had my guy run her name, pulling everything he could find on her. As far as he could tell, she lives alone, since just her name is on the lease.

The place looks old. Some of the buildings down here were never rebuilt right after Hurricane Katrina, forcing the residents to live with what they had, and their shitty landlords got away with making them live in squalor and raising the prices every year.

Normally, I don't care. What people do and put up with are their own problem, but I can smell the mustiness of old water from outside the house and it instantly turns my stomach. Who rents out a place like this?

Pulling the lock kit from my pocket, I check over my

shoulder once before I put it to use. Picking locks is easy, but making sure no one notices me is more difficult. Especially in neighborhoods like this, where community tends to be the only thing holding them together. That means they know each other well enough to know when a strange man is entering someone's apartment when he shouldn't be.

I slip through the door as soon as the lock unlatches, shutting the wooden slab behind me. She lives in the upper unit, so the door opens to a narrow staircase that creaks as I ascend.

The apartment is nicer than I thought it'd be from the outside, surprisingly. Rough around the edges, but it's clean and Zoe has made it look cozy. The hardwood floors are covered with a big area rug and there are plants on every surface, green leaves brightening up the apartment.

Against one of the brick walls is a large bookshelf made of cinderblocks and unfinished wood, an easy DIY that houses rows of books stored in order by color. I click my tongue as I walk up to them. I keep mine in alphabetical order, but I'm impressed just to see books.

They vary in hardcover and paperback, most of them looking extremely well-loved by the condition they're in. I wonder if they're secondhand or if she has read each of these copies several times. I like the thought of her in this apartment, laid back in her oversized green velvet armchair with a classic gripped between her fingers. It's easy to imagine the ambience, with the café lights she has strung up casting a warm glow. I bet it's beautiful.

There are candles everywhere, littering every surface, and I wonder if she burns them to get rid of the musty smell from the building. It's not as bad up here, though; it smells cleaner, faintly of Febreze.

I wander down the narrow hallway, peeking into the small bathroom. It's simple, housing only a shower and tub combo, a pedestal sink, and a toilet. I open the medicine cabinet to see nothing out of the ordinary. Toothpaste, Q-tips, dental floss. The shower just has body wash, shampoo, and conditioner. Nothing fancy, Pantene, but I smell it anyway.

Moving on, I find two bedrooms at the end of the hall. I open the first one to be met with an explosion of clothing and items scattered on the floor. The room is a mess, stuff everywhere, covering every surface of the room. It's jarring in comparison to the rest of the apartment.

I check the other room. How is it possible that her house is so clean, but her room is this messy? It feels off, and when I open the second bedroom to find a neatly made bed, plants on the dresser, and a rack of color-organized clothes, I think this bedroom must be hers. But I go back to the other one. Only one name is on the lease, so who lives in this room?

Watching my step, I walk farther into the room, finding a stack of papers sitting on the dresser. My gloved fingers lift the documents one at a time, scanning for something worthwhile. A medical bill from the local clinic addressed to... Cassandra Stephens.

Interesting.

I abandon the documents in exchange for the other room. Everything in this one is neat and meticulous; it soothes me in a way. Order and structure have always appealed to me. I like knowing things are in the right place, where they belong.

Her white furniture pairs well with the brick walls and the ones that are drywall are painted a warm, taupe-ish color. There's a small desk on the far wall in front of the window, so I head for that next.

Everything on the surface is neatly placed, and I start opening the drawers. They're slightly messier, but not by much. I open each one, looking for anything that would tell me something about her. The first drawer has a journal size notebook, one with the band that wraps around the outside. The second drawer has a small plastic baggie of marijuana next to a grinder and rolling papers. I chuckle to myself. So she likes to smoke.

I slide open the first drawer again, the one with the notebook. My fingers hover above it, wondering if I'm breaching her privacy by opening it. Well, I'm already in her house, so I suppose this isn't that much worse.

Unlooping the band and opening it, I flip through the pages. She writes with colorful pens and markers, doodling on the edges of the paper. It's quite pretty, actually. She uses it for a bit of everything. I find a shopping list, a to-do list, and thoughts on a movie she watched in order. I laugh when I read that she didn't like Pulp Fiction. *Too bloody*, she wrote.

Squeamish, I note to myself.

She has a to-be-read list, compiling every book she wants to read. I pull out my phone and take a picture of that one.

I skim a couple of pages, just browsing until I find a page that stands out. It's written in black ink. With no label, and no colorful doodles, it doesn't fit with the rest of the book.

It's been four weeks. No one is looking for Cassie anymore, and I'm losing my mind, she wrote.

Cassie... Cassandra... the roommate.

The detective on her case says she's probably run away, that because of her "history" it's unlikely anything happened to her. He's closing her case.

Detective... it can't be Ellison. He's a homicide detective, not missing persons. But why else would she be meeting him, yelling at him. I keep reading.

I know she wouldn't have run away. Something must have happened. I'm going to find her.

I snap the book shut. I wanted to know her secret, but it doesn't sit right. And it still doesn't make sense. Who is Cassie and where is she?

I need to leave. I have cash that needs to be picked up for

Marcus, and as much as I want to stay here and read every single personal thought of Zoe's, I know I can't.

Sliding the drawer open, I slip the notebook back in its spot before I leave her room the way I found it.

Not even ten seconds out of the apartment, and my fingers are itching, wanting to touch her, to smell her. It's a weird ache, far from my normal wants. Usually, my mind is focused on my next kill, waiting for the right moment, the right victim. But I have no desire to kill Zoe Carson.

No, I want her. All of her. In every possible way.

IT'S hours later when I finally get to the club. I picked up the cash for Marcus first, bringing it to the office at Saints and Sinners and handing it off to Donnie. I don't like doing runs; it's not something Junior used me for - *ever*. But I don't get to pick and choose with Marcus, so I do as he asks, even if it's a job well below my skill set.

He hasn't asked me to kill at all, and other than the asshole that touched Zoe, my last kill was before Junior died. The only thing keeping the itch away is my fascination with Zoe. She's not out on the floor when I exit the office. My eyes search for her under the glow of the flashing lights. There are multiple stages in Saints and Sinners and three bars. Too much space to cover.

I flag down the bartender, "Gin," I tell her, tapping my fingers against the wooden surface. It's the same girl from the other night, the one with the bruises. *I don't care,* I remind myself, but I set down a twenty for her tip when I take the low ball of Aviation gin she gives me.

The place is busy again, the Friday night crowd has taken over the floor. I finally find my kitten on the second stage. She doesn't seem to notice anything as I lean against the brick wall facing her. Her hips sway as she walks sensually to the pole, letting me know she's into her dance. She makes the act look so effortless as she lifts her legs and swings around.

She somehow has on less clothes than the last time I saw her. The sight is beautiful, but then I remember we're in a club full of men and suddenly I want to pull her from the stage and drag her ass out of here, somewhere private where no one can see her body but me. Her black socks extend over the knees with two white stripes at the top and a pair of black closed-toe high heels. She has on a little plaid skirt with the beginning of her cheeks peeking out, leaving me wondering what's underneath it, if anything at all. And the tiny shirt she wears is knotted between her tits and off the shoulder. Her hair is in two long dark braids. It's innocent, adorable, and inherently sexy. I simultaneously want to wrap her in a blanket and rip the clothes from her body. Protect her and devour her.

My fingers thrum against my side, wanting to touch her smooth, creamy skin. But I won't. Not until she asks me to.

She was going to work after that scumbag touched her the other night, but I hated the idea of her being touched by anyone else. I could tell the experience had shaken her up; it scared her when he was on her, shouting for him to let her go. The bouncer, Robby, an unmade man working for Marcus, was distracted. He was watching one of the other girls when he should have been paying attention to the whole room.

I wanted to cut his fingers off, but I thought better of it. Marcus might not like it if I went around torturing his men.

Zoe finishes her song, her knees hitting the floor with a thud. She whips her head around one last time, and I hear a few hoots as she leaves the stage, her money tucked into the waistband of her skirt.

Steel colored eyes find me, and for a brief moment, I see something in her shift. Whatever fake persona she's created for Kat drops away, and underneath is Zoe, the girl who has a shelf of used books and doodles in her journal. That's who I want to know more about.

Then she begins to move toward me, somewhat surprising me, but I don't let it show. Her high heels are tall, several inches, and I wonder what she's like without them; she must be five inches shorter. I want to know what it's like to tower over her, watching her look up, at me through those thick lashes. Her face is coated with makeup when she's here, eyeliner, fake lashes, bright lipstick. She's gorgeous like this, but I want to wipe it all off to see who she is beneath the perfectly constructed version she's created.

"You again?" She smiles the slightest bit, but it's not her anymore. Kat is back in place.

"I forgot to tip you the other night." I pull my wallet from my back pocket and tug two hundred-dollar bills from their place.

She looks at the money for a few seconds, and I can't tell what she's thinking. If she wants to take it.

"You... helped me. I think that was enough." She pushes my hand back toward me with her slim fingers. When my hand presses to my chest, she finally looks up at me, tugging her bottom lip between her teeth. I have the sudden urge for the teeth biting into that plump lip to be mine.

"I watched you dance, kitten. I think the courteous thing to do is at least tip you."

She laughs, a breathy sound. "You don't take no for an answer, do you?"

"I do." I can feel the corners of my lips lift. "But only in the form of a safe word."

Her eyelashes flutter, the only sign that I've caught her off guard. Her lips move, repeating me, but no sound comes out of her mouth. I've wonder if she's even had the kind of sex I like. My dick throbs at the thought. I would make it good for her; I could do that for her.

"It's too much anyway." Her eyes glance down at the money

and then back up. "I would only take that much for a private dance."

"Then how about one of those?"

"John, you don't need to-"

"I want to." I watch her chest rise and fall for a moment. "Can I have a private dance, kitten?"

It takes a second before she responds to me, thinking it over and pressing her cherry painted lips together. "This way," she says finally, nodding her head in the direction she wants me to follow, and I do. I want to have her alone, even though I know I can't act on my desires. Not tonight.

I can make this work; she's not a distraction. Getting to know her will get me closer to Marcus. Maybe she knows something, even if she doesn't think it's important.

This is work, I tell myself. Strictly a stop in my quest for answers. And if she happens to meet my needs along the way, so be it.

EIGHT

There's a pounding in my chest, beating in time with the alarm in my head that's shouting *bad idea*. And maybe it is, but then why does it feel so right? I'm stupid. I have to be. But it doesn't stop me from leading John Vitale to a private room, and for the third time since knowing him, we're alone. He lets his suit jacket fall from his shoulders, folding it neatly before dropping it over the couch.

"How many private dances do you give a night?" he asks while he begins to roll each of his shirt sleeves tediously. Everything about John seems meticulous, thoughtful and neat. My eyes are glued to his motions.

"I don't know, a few, I guess." His fingers work with precision as they turn over the white fabric.

"You like dancing for strangers?" One eyebrow lifts when he asks the questions, and his dark eyes watch me. I'm wringing my fingers together, avoiding answering.

I don't. Of course, I don't. I like the money, the way it pays my bills easier than any other job I've had. I like to know that I can buy groceries and take care of myself. I feel more financially stable than I have in a while. And I don't mind dancing on the stage; that's easy enough. I just move to the rhythm and pretend I'm somewhere else.

But private dances are harder. If he's quiet and keeps his hands to himself, I can stay steady in my illusion. But a man like that is a rarity. I can always expect talking, questions, and fumbling fingers. All of which breaks me out of my spell and makes me painfully aware of where I am and what I'm doing.

"Of course," I tell him.

"Liar." The word whips from his lips so quickly, so accusingly.

"What?"

He steps toward me, two long strides until he's in my space, just inches away from touching me. His smell is intoxicating, like cedar and tobacco, and it immediately invades my senses, taking over my brain.

"I said," he begins with a smile, one corner of his lips rising ever so slightly. "You're a liar. I can see through"—he circles his finger in front of me—"this. So tell me the truth, kitten, do you like giving private dances?"

"No," I blurt out. Too quick. Too honest. But he was right, he was seeing through me, and I was lying. No, I hate giving private dances, but that's not something I would ever say during one. Something about John makes me want to tell him all my truths, despite how naïve and utterly stupid that would be. But his dark eyes drill into me, and I know he sees through my charade. "No," I repeat. "I hate them."

"Then why do this?" He doesn't look condescending when he asks the question, just simply curious.

I scoff anyway, a rough sound leaving my lips. "Everyone asks that, ya know? As if I must hate myself to work here, like it can't just be because of money."

"People do a lot of things for money, kitten. There's nothing wrong with that."

"Yeah, but they're pretty damn judgmental about this."

"Are they? Or are you judging yourself?"

His words smack against my chest like a ton of bricks. This is supposed to be a private dance, not a therapy session.

"I- I'm not-"

"Don't lie to me, kitten." His fingers reach out to me slowly, gaging if I'll flinch, if I'll turn away. When I don't, he gingerly tucks a stray hair behind my ear, his eyes watching me for a reaction the entire time. "You might do this for the money, but there's another reason, isn't there? What are you doing here?"

My chest seizes with panic. How is even possible for this man to see through me so clearly?

"I'm-" His eyes darken, his eyebrow twitching. He knows I'm lying.

I seal my lips closed, pressing them tightly together. What can I say to him now? He's right. I am a liar. But I'm not about to spill my secret to him.

"I can't," I mutter.

"You can't tell me the truth?"

"No."

He looks disappointed at this. He steps back, putting more space between us. "That's okay, kitten. One day, you'll tell me all your secrets. For now, you can just dance for me."

I swallow thickly as he walks over to the velvet lined bench, taking a seat and leaning back against the stark red material.

All that, and now he just wants me to dance for him. Do my job.

Blood is rushing to my ears, and I can barely hear the music over the sound of it. My stomach is twisting into knots, but I move to him anyway, swaying my hips as I go and ignoring the pain my five-inch heels are inflicting onto my feet.

John's fingers rise to his neck, tugging at his black silk tie to loosen the thing. I've seen men do the same thing countless times, but for some reason, with John, the action is more attractive. My eyes are latched onto his thick forearms, watching the muscles tense as he tugs on the material. I'm imagining those same hands on me, tangling in my hair and tugging my head back.

I blink. I have to lose this line of thought. This silly girlish attraction.

"Are you okay, kitten?"

"Yes." My voice comes out as a squeak, too childish, and John chuckles at me. Fuck. Why am I like this? How is he getting this kind of reaction out of me?

I need to focus, need to do my job. The two hundred dollars John handed me is burning my skin from where I stuck it in my panties, and suddenly, I feel the urge to work for the money. To earn it. The amount of money a man gives me means nothing to me. I don't take it as a reflection of me personally. But something about John has me wanting to be worth it for him, when I know I should be running in the opposite direction.

But I can't. Not if I want to get close to Marcus.

Not if I want to find Cassie.

When I'm directly in front of him, I bring my legs to either side of his, hovering above his knees while I grind my hips. I need to ask him something, need to get something out of him. Something I can tell Marcus.

I don't even know what kind of family drama I've gotten myself sucked into, but it doesn't matter. This is not for them. I'm here for me. For Cassie.

"Are you and Marcus close?" I ask, flipping my hair over my shoulder.

"Not really," John tells me, his eyes still glued to my face, not watching my body as it moves in front of him. Men never look at my face, and with him doing just that, it makes me blush, a red heat crawling up my neck and cheeks.

"You're so pretty when you blush for me, kitten." He grins.

I try to shake off his words, shake off him and get back to the task at hand. I stand, turning around and shaking my ass instead. "But you're cousins?"

"Yes. Is there a reason you want to talk about my cousin?" I feel his hand on my hip, then he's gently spinning me around. His hand is touching me so softly, and still, the warmth burns into my skin while his eyes find mine. He's waiting for an answer, one I don't want to give. Getting information for Marcus is going to be harder than I originally thought.

"I-"

"Just ask what you want to know, kitten. I'll answer. In exchange, you'll tell me your name."

Giving out your name is stripper 101; you just don't do it. There's a sly smile playing on John's lips. I'm torn, my brain and heart reaching in different directions. Playing with John feels the same as playing with fire, but the smile on his face and the praise coming from his lips is addictive. I need to remember why I'm here, though... Cassie.

"Okay," I whisper. I've stopped dancing, my feet planted firmly to the ground. "Why are you here?"

He thinks for a moment. "For you. I don't know why"—he shrugs—"but I'm interested in you."

"You don't even know me..."

"Yeah." He nods in agreement. "You're right, I don't know you. But I want to. Now, your turn."

"What? That was barely an answer!""

"You didn't set any rules about what kind of answer it had to be." He chuckles, "Now pay up, kitten. What's your name?"

I huff, taking a step back and running my hands down hips as if I have more than underwear to smooth out.

"Fair is fair, kitten,"

"Fine," I hiss. "Zoe."

He grins at my admission, and somehow, I know that he

didn't need to hear it from me. Donnie has my application, he knows my real name, so John could have just asked if he wanted to. But he asked me instead.

"I want to get you out of here, Zoe." His eyes are still locked onto my face, still watching me with such focus it sends a chill down my spine. No one has ever watched me like he is, looked at me like I was more than a woman they wanted to possess.

"I don't do that." I take another step back, but John stands as I do. "You can't pay me for sex."

He takes a step forward, starting a weird dance between us. Space, no space. "I'm not offering to pay you," he tells me.

The money sitting against my hip burns. He's already paid me.

"So…" he prods. "Can I get you out of here?"

I huff, running my hands through my loose curls. "And what would you do, John?" I breathe. "If you got me out of here?"

Two more steps, and he's in front of me, backing me into the wall until my shoulder blades press into the painted brick, the rough texture biting at my skin.

His gaze travels down to my throat, lingering on the black ninety's style chocker clinging to my neck. He slips a finger under the elastic material. "Well, for starters, I'd replace this with a collar. Leather, probably, maybe even one with a little charm that says *kitten*." His touch feels sensual against my skin, and a fire lights in my core.

I should be disgusted at the thought of this man, this stranger, wanting to put a collar around my throat. I'm not an object, I don't belong to him, but the idea has me pushing my thighs a little closer together. Hoping for a bit of friction to relieve the tension building inside of me.

He's smiling, watching the heat travel over my throat and face, turning me a shade of crimson. The smug bastard wanted to see me embarrassed, and he succeeded.

"Say yes," he whispers, leaning in close enough for his forehead to touch mine. He sucks all the oxygen from the air, suffocating me with his presence.

And his eyes tell me he knows the effect he has on me, but he can see the fight lingering, the desire to deny him what he really wants.

"I want you to say yes, Zoe," he breathes, his minty breath washing over my skin. "But I won't force you. It has to be your choice."

His words hit differently, bubbling up in my stomach. There's no repulsion here, like what I normally feel when a man at this club asks me to go home with him. Then again, they've never said the words *I won't force you*. Instead, it's me calling over a bouncer that finally gets them to drop their proposal.

"No," I murmur. "I can't."

My mind is too twisted, too fucked up. Because I want John, and I shouldn't. This should just be a job for me, a way to get closer to Marcus, but I know if I leave this club with John, I'll do something stupid. I don't have time to be stupid.

A harsh breath leaves his lips, followed by a low chuckle. "Are you really denying both of us, kitten?"

"Yes." The corner of my lip tugs up into a smile, even though he's right; I am denying *both* of us. "I don't know you, John. Why would I go home with you?"

Dark eyes hold my gaze as his fingers lift, tucking another loose piece of hair behind my ear, his touch lingering on the sensitive skin on my neck. "Because you want this as much as I do." He smiles.

"Maybe, but I'm not going home with you. I'm not that easy. You'll have to buy me dinner first." I use both of my palms to push his chest away from me, freeing me from his overwhelming orbit. "Goodbye, John." I don't look back as I walk away, leaving him firmly behind me.

I have a goal, an endgame, and John Vitale is just a roadblock in the way.

NINE

Zoe

The small house on the outskirts of the Quarter looks the same as it did my entire childhood. Since my mother's death, nothing has changed. The same paint coats the walls, the same ugly tile on the floors, even the same knick knacks line the shelves of the curio cabinet. I'm not sure why my father chooses not to update. Maybe renovating after Katrina was enough for a lifetime. Either way, we choose not to talk about it.

"I brought you groceries," I tell him as I place the overstuffed plastic bags on the counter.

"Ah." From my view in the kitchen, I can see his arm wave me off from his recliner in the living room. "I don't need 'em," he tells me, even though if I didn't bring him groceries, he would starve.

My mother's death and our subsequent displacement left my father broken and bitter. And though my father had a job, and our house was able to be repaired, the loss of my mother still kept us both down. We were told to be thankful, that we still had our own lives, but I think we both would have been happier dead than without her. If he didn't have me to take care of, I'm sure my father would have taken his own life.

Even the cancer diagnosis didn't shake him. In some ways, I think he was happy to have death on the horizon. He was looking forward to seeing his wife again. Despite my constant pleas to try chemo, he was relentless. He wanted to die on his own terms, and as much as I wanted to respect that, it still boiled my blood.

I wanted him to fight, to try to stay alive.

For me.

I, unlike my father, had found a way to live with the grief. Mostly in the form of my best friend. I shifted from one reason for life to another. I met the bony ten-year-old orphan the same night I lost my mother. Cassie was tall with thin legs and arms, dressed in a ripped pair of jeans and a white t-shirt when we found her. She was sitting by herself on a cot in the Superdome, clutching a raggedy teddy bear to her chest.

Dad and I were both cold and shaking when we got there. We had left our home too late to escape Hurricane Katrina, and we ended up being rerouted. We had been waiting for mom, as she had boarded up the windows at the dance studio and was coming home for us all to leave together.

We waited a while, listening to the wind whip against the pale blue shutters of our home before Dad finally loaded me into the car. He didn't have to say it. My eight-year-old brain had figured it out by the look on his face. She wasn't coming home.

So instead of mourning my mother, I befriended the girl with no one.

"You need food, Dad," I mutter, loading the groceries into the fridge and cabinets. My father's diet consists of mostly frozen meals, things he can pop into the microwave when I'm not home.

"Ah." He waves me off again, still facing forward in his recliner. "I'm fine."

I want to scream at him, as the anger bubbles up in my chest. He'll sit in that recliner until the cancer eats him, and he'll be fine with it. I seal my lips tight as I head to the refrigerator, yanking open the door to be greeted with a foul stench.

"Jesus," I mutter, pulling out the containers of moldy food. The pasta I made for him is covered in a thin layer of blue and gray fuzz. The cut strawberries that I prepared in a container are brown and mushy. I plug my nose as I clean everything out, replacing all the old food with fresh.

When I'm done, I grab the fresh turkey and loaf of bread I bought, making a simple sandwich.

"Here," I tell my father as I hand it to him. Luckily, he takes it without much of a fight, biting into it right away.

I don't know how he's living like this. Barely eating, never leaving the house. He's given up on life. My heart fractures. I'm not ready to lose everyone; my mom, Cassie, and now Dad. What will I do after everyone I love is gone?

"How are you feeling?" I ask.

"Fine," he grumbles. "You worry too much, Zo," he tells me, waving his sandwich through the air.

"Maybe you worry too little, huh?" I lean back into the beige sofa we bought after the hurricane. The old one had water damage, since the living room had taken the biggest hit. We bought this one with the insurance money, and it's been here ever since.

Before the hurricane wrecked our city and our lives, we had been happy. One of those families filled with love. My mother was phenomenal at everything. Dancing, cooking, mothering in general. We ate dinner around our small table every night, going around in a circle and sharing what we were thankful for. No one was able to see the magic in life quite like my mother.

"Did you bring the good stuff?" he asks, swallowing a mouthful of bread and deli meat.

"Yep." I reach for my purse, pulling out the clear plastic bag of weed from within. My father could easily have a prescription for the plant. With his diagnosis, it's no wonder he wants something to ease the pain. But he doesn't, so instead, I buy it from the guy downstairs.

He knew Cassie first, sleeping with her twice before I met him. He doesn't bring up my missing best friend when I knock on his door, only gives me a knowing nod as he hands me the bag in exchange for cash.

I don't want him to ask, not sure what I would tell him. He probably thinks she's dead, just like Ellison, just like everyone. At this point, I'm the only one holding on to hope that she's still alive. But I can't give up on her. I won't abandon her like everyone else in her life.

No, she's out there. I have to believe that.

I pull over the wooden TV table that holds my father's rolling station and start by grinding the buds.

"How'd you learn to do that?" he asks as I tap the contents from the grinder onto the paper.

"College," I tell him with a smile and wiggling brows that make him snort, and we both laugh, the weight of our problems lifting from our shoulders. It shouldn't be a funny joke, but for some reason, it is. My community college business degree is more than a joke, two years spent taking classes that I don't use.

Before the club, I was a bartender, and both jobs make more than I would be qualified for with my associate degree. Despite my father's hatred for my newfound profession, he can't disagree with the numbers.

I think if he knew more about the club, he might put up a bigger fight. But all he knows is that I work at a fancy club in the Quarter and make good money. He doesn't need to hear the rest.

When I'm done rolling the joint, I light it, taking an inhale and letting the smoke fill my lungs. I breathe it out slowly, the white clouds trailing from my lips into the living room. I pass it to my dad next, something I never expected when I was smoking behind school years ago.

His eyes close as he pulls in the smoke. In a few minutes, the plant will dull his senses, ease the pain that's building up in him. He'll be able to relax.

"Movie?" I ask as he sinks into the recliner.

"Your turn to pick," he tells me with a smile, pulling from the joint again.

I like the easy ritual I've created with my father. At least if he's going to leave me, we can spend some time together first. Maybe that will take the edge off once the cancer finally wins its battle.

I steal one more glance at my father as I pull up the Netflix menu. I want to remember him like this, happy in his recliner with a haze of smoke over him. Laughing along to whatever stoner comedy I put on the TV.

I close my eyes hard, sealing the memory in place, adding it to my collection with the ones of mom and Cassie, my mental scrapbook of the people I love.

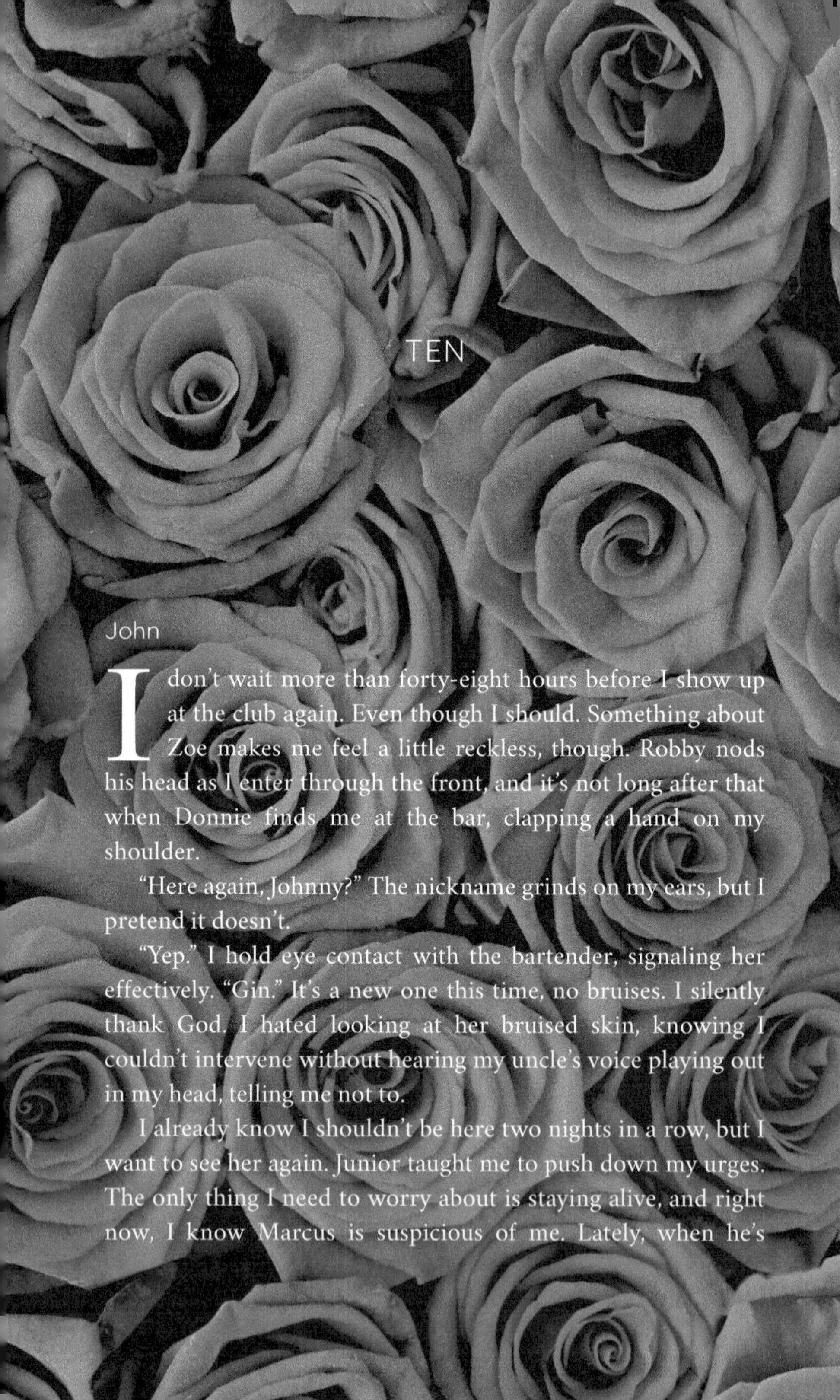

TEN

John

I don't wait more than forty-eight hours before I show up at the club again. Even though I should. Something about Zoe makes me feel a little reckless, though. Robby nods his head as I enter through the front, and it's not long after that when Donnie finds me at the bar, clapping a hand on my shoulder.

"Here again, Johnny?" The nickname grinds on my ears, but I pretend it doesn't.

"Yep." I hold eye contact with the bartender, signaling her effectively. "Gin." It's a new one this time, no bruises. I silently thank God. I hated looking at her bruised skin, knowing I couldn't intervene without hearing my uncle's voice playing out in my head, telling me not to.

I already know I shouldn't be here two nights in a row, but I want to see her again. Junior taught me to push down my urges. The only thing I need to worry about is staying alive, and right now, I know Marcus is suspicious of me. Lately, when he's worried about someone, he doesn't hesitate to take them out of the equation. I suppose he thinks my death will be harder to cover up, and that's why he hasn't killed me yet.

With my uncle, he took out two birds with one stone, or some stupid metaphor like that. He killed Junior and sent his son to prison with one bullet. Like we're part of some monarchy, and he's next in line for the throne. He covered his tracks too, because with Sam charged for the murder, no one else is poking around our businesses.

And without my uncle, he doesn't have to keep me alive. The only person who will scold him if I go missing is my mother, and I suspect her sisters will keep her quiet as long as Marcus is in control.

Money is a powerful drug both of my aunts are addicted too, and as long as Marcus keeps feeding them with it, they'll stay loyal to him.

Donnie is quiet as he looks at me. I'm not that easy to start a conversation with. I don't say much, since I don't really like to talk to people anyway. I think it would be more suspicious if I tried to act like I liked Donnie. It's probably better that I be somewhat real with him, aloof. At this point, most of the men in *la famiglia* know there's something wrong with me, that I'm not completely right. They'd never say it, never insult my grandfather. But behind his back, they whisper, *Johnny Vitale is a nut. Heard he gutted some guy and enjoyed it.*

I'm not sure which I was supposed to be ashamed of anymore, killing people or *enjoying* killing people. Junior would tell me that my brain is an asset, and that we just have to learn to control it. But even with all the controls in place, it never stopped me from being a pariah. And somewhere along the way, I grew to like the isolation.

"Nice talk," I tell Donnie, even though we both know there was no conversation there. I move toward Zoe when I see her, leaving Donnie behind me. It's probably better that they think I'm only here because I'm infatuated with the girl. Makes me seem more relatable, more addicted to pussy like the rest of them.

I've never been one for a steady relationship, but no one trusts a man who doesn't get laid, so being viewed as celibate isn't a good option either. I like women, but they typically want more than I have to offer. I'm not good at being in a relationship. It never feels real to me, more like a game of *don't let them catch on.* I can't produce the feelings women want, the lust and attraction, the *love.*

Women bore me, and I'm only keeping them around for appearances. But I don't find Zoe boring. Not at all.

"Kitten." I smile when I reach her. She just poured a shot down her throat, and she sets the glass back down on the bar. She looks good again, but that's not surprising. Maybe I just like seeing her like this, bared for me, even if I know that she's on display for others too. Some sort of possessive nature inside of me wants to cover her up, hide her body from leering eyes. But I know better. I can't let that part of me act out, not here.

She's wearing all black today, paired with the boots that rise over her knees. There's a crisscrossing of black straps that connect her panties to her bra, and I can't imagine how she even got her body into the contraption. My favorite part of her outfit is the plastic black choker that adorns her throat. My fingers inch to tug at it, and I'm already imagining myself replacing it with something else, something nicer. I can picture a lock hanging from a leather band, the key tucked away nicely in my pocket.

I wonder if my fantasy would get her off the way it does for me...

"Back so soon." She's being coy, and I can see her mask back in place, the version of herself she presents to this world. I think she's the only person who would understand me, who knows what it's like to build your life on a lie.

She's not a stripper.

I'm not normal.

"You said I had to take you to dinner first."

Her eyebrows knit together, probably forgetting the thing she told me the other night. I don't forget much.

"Dinner," she draws out the word, as if needing to say it out loud to understand it.

"You said you wouldn't go home with me because I needed to take you to dinner first. So I'm going to take you to dinner."

There's a shine in her eye, and I can tell she is absolutely interested, but something is holding her back. I can't place it.

"I'm not asking you to fuck me, Zoe. Just give me dinner, hmm?"

There's a war raging inside her head, and I can tell there's a part of her that wants to say no, but there's another part that's urging her to give in. Maybe she feels the spark of electricity. It's a bad idea; I can't shame her for that. She should stay away from me. Nothing good comes from being affiliated with the Costello family, but I hope she tells that part of her brain to fuck off and comes with me anyway.

"So," I prod. "What do you say?"

"Alright." Her eyes flash away, then back to me, and now red is beginning to creep up her neck, coating her cheeks with the prettiest blush. I love how fucking shy she gets around me. "Dinner."

"Good, get your things,"

"Now?" Her eyes widen. "John, I'm working-"

"Not anymore. I'll tell Donnie you're done for the night."

"You can't-"

"I think you're underestimating me, kitten. I'm pretty sure I can do whatever I want." I add, *as long as it's okay with Junior* silently. He's not here to tell me no anymore, so technically, I guess I *can* do whatever I want.

ZOE IS quiet when I take her out of the club. She changed, or put on clothes over her lingerie, I'm not sure. She still looks stunning, and she left the choker on, a fact that makes my dick ache in my pants. The pair of black jeans she pulled on are tight, forming to her thighs and ass with little rips around the knees. She wears a plain white t-shirt on top, so it looks like a casual outfit except for her dramatic makeup and the bold red lips.

I want to know what thoughts are running through her brain, but I don't think she'd tell me the truth even if I asked.

Her fingers twine into her hair, twisting it back into a low bun as we drive. She's fidgeting. I catalog each of her movements as I continue driving.

I could take her anywhere. There are tons of restaurants in the Quarter that are open this late, catering to the drunk crowds. I assume she thinks that's where we're going as I weave my Porsche through the Quarter. When I don't park near any of the restaurants and instead click the buzzer on my sun visor to open a private gate, I see Zoe perk up.

The black gate slides open, and Zoe sits straighter in her seat to watch it. "Where are we?" she asks.

"My house." When it opens the rest of the way, I pull the car through. Houses in the Quarter are tight, pressed together. My father hates it here, claiming there is no privacy to be had when you're practically living on top of your neighbors.

I disagree.

Zoe steps out of the car, her eyes wide as she looks around. There's an archway that leads from the parking spot to the courtyard, and as she steps through, her mouth opens to a wide O shape. "This is…" she trails off, not finishing her sentence as she looks around the space. The courtyard isn't huge, but it's large enough to fit an arrangement of plants, an outdoor dining space, and a seating area. I get her shock, though, because that space alone is about the size of her apartment.

I think she'd pass out if she saw my parent's home, or even Sam's. This is nothing compared to the lavish wealth that my family enjoys. My home is probably the smallest.

"Come on." I press my hand to the small of her back and guide her toward the house. There are two French doors that open out the courtyard, and I take her through those. In the spring, before the heat becomes sweltering, I'll keep them open and let the house fill with the fresh air.

The dining room opens up to the living room, a floating fireplace separating the two; not that I ever light the thing, but it looks good in the space. Creole style loves color, but I opted to keep the design clean and simple. Neutral tones and wood textures that are warm and inviting.

Zoe tugs her bottom lip between her teeth and stares in amazement at my home from the dining room. I could just watch her happily. I don't think I enjoy my home nearly enough for how impressed she looks. I try to see it from her angle; the rich history of this building still peeks through my modern updates. The designer I hired filled the place with French flair and as many original Creole style items as she could find. My dad would have bulldozed the home and replaced it with a more modern one. But I like the original architecture; it's like living in a piece of history, and I did my best to preserve it.

Her silver eyes look around at the slanted ceiling, wooden beams stretching from one side to the other. She finds the custom dining table I had commissioned, large enough to seat twelve, even though it's usually just me. "It's beautiful," Zoe whispers, and I'm not sure if she's talking to herself or me.

"This isn't even the whole first floor,"

"There's more?" Her eyes light up, and in the low lighting, it looks like the silver is glowing.

"It's three thousand square feet." I smile. "Yes, there's more."

I don't know why I decided to bring her here. I could have just taken her to any nice restaurant, but I wanted to see her in my private space. A rarity. I don't share this with anyone other than family and the people I pay to take care of it. I like to keep it to myself, a safe space of sorts.

"Sir." Zoe jumps when Arnold steps out of the kitchen. "My apologies, Miss." He dips his head, but Zoe doesn't say anything, just stares at him in shock.

"Zoe, this Arnold, my head chef."

"You… have a chef?"

Arnold gives her a shy, tentative smile. "I have a few," I tell her, watching the way her eyes widen at the admission.

"So… you're like stupid rich?"

Arnold looks shocked at her statement, but I laugh. It rumbles out of me. I can't remember the last time I laughed without forcing the sound. The feeling startles me, igniting something in me that I've never felt before.

"I was just coming to tell you that your meal will be ready shortly." Arnold tips his head to me before he ducks out of the room.

"We're eating here?"

"Is that okay, kitten?"

Without the heels, she's significantly shorter. I like her this way, with the top of her head barely reaching my shoulder. I want to touch her, feel her soft skin beneath my fingertips, run my hand through her dark waves. But I keep my fingers to myself, not wanting to push her too far yet, despite how much I'm craving her.

"Yeah… I just… didn't expect all… this." Her hand gestures around at my home.

"What did you expect?"

She turns to look at me now, her silver eyes taking me in. "I don't know, John." She shrugs a little. "You're just surprising me."

Her words stir something inside me, and I realize my infatuation is growing for her dangerously fast. I like the way she sees me. I like the way she's surprised by me. She doesn't look at me like some sort of monster, not the way people who know me do. I want to preserve that, even if I know it won't last forever. Eventually, this bubble will pop, and she'll see me for who I am. Who I really am. And then she'll leave. Because no one wants to love a murderer.

"Here." I gesture to the set of glass doors on the far wall. "Let me show you my favorite room." I don't want to ruin this moment by letting my thoughts roam to a dark place, but I also know better than to let myself get attached.

I lead Zoe into my library. This was supposed to be a main-floor master, but I converted it into a study. Every wall of the room is lined with bookcases, each filled top to bottom with hardbacks. I like the old ones, first editions, books that some collectors wouldn't even touch. What's the point of having more money than you'll even need if you don't spend it? I've always preferred books to people, a trait I suspect Zoe shares.

In the center of the room sits a mahogany desk with a leather chair, and off to the side are two armchairs with a smaller end table. One of them is visibly more worn in than the other, a clear indicator of where I sit when I'm reading. For a brief moment, I imagine Zoe in the other one, her feet kicked up onto my knees as we sit in content silence. I shake the thought away; that's not reality.

Zoe looks amazed again, and the sight warms my heart. I don't let people back here, opting to keep this room locked instead. But I wanted to see her face when she saw this room. It has a lot more books than she had on her small bookshelf, and she circles the room twice before she even says a thing.

"This is amazing," she mutters. "Have you read all of these?"

"A lot of them." I shrug. "Collecting books might be a separate hobby."

She grins at that, a full-fledged smile that crinkles the corners of her eyes. She's smiled for me before, but not this smile. Not one that truly shows how happy she is.

I want to make her smile like that again, want to fall asleep to that look every night.

"This is my favorite room." Her eyes find mine, and she looks so sincere as she says the words. I want to capture this moment in my memory, hold on to it.

"Dinner's ready." Arnold's voice cuts through the study, shocking us both out of the moment.

"Do you normally eat dinner at midnight?" Zoe asks with a smile as she follows me back into the dining room.

"No," I hum. "I prefer to eat at six, but you were working, so I waited."

She looks at me, surprised. "You waited all night to eat with me?"

"You said I needed to take you to dinner first," I recite, pulling out a chair for her to sit at. She looks at me thoughtfully, maybe partially amused.

"You didn't-"

"I know," I cut her off. "I know I could have waited until you had a day off, but I didn't want to wait, Zoe. Did you want me to?"

"No," she breathes out the word. "I guess not."

Once we're seated, Arnold uncovers the several dishes he'd placed on the table. I didn't know what to tell him that she liked, so I had him make a bunch of things. There's a bowl of fries coated with a truffle oil that I know are delicious, a seafood ravioli that's Arnold's specialty, a bowl of salad with apples and dried cranberries, mixed vegetables, and grilled chicken. It's more food than we'll possibly eat, but I wanted options. For her.

"This is too much." Zoe's eyes scan the spread of food.

"Yeah, I didn't know what you'd like."

There's an emotion building behind her silver eyes that I can't quite place. She looks teary, as if she might cry.

"What's wrong?"

"Nothing." She smiles, a sadder smile from the one she graced me with just minutes ago. "This is perfect, thank you."

Arnold comes back out with a bottle of red wine and two glasses, pouring us each one and leaving the bottle.

I'm quiet as I watch her fill her plate with food, taking a little bit of everything. She moans when she takes a bite of the ravioli, and I feel a bit of jealousy run through my veins. It should be me making her moan like that, not Arnold's ravioli. But I can't rush her, so I pinch my nails into my palm and slice into my own food.

"So what do you like to do... outside of"—I wave my hand—"dancing."

"Are you asking me what my hobbies are when I'm not stripping?" She purses her lips to hide a smile as she stabs another piece of ravioli with her fork.

"Something like that."

"You first." She takes a sip of her wine, her eyes lighting up as she does. "This is good."

I'm pleased that she likes the wine and the food, and my home. I don't know why, but it warms my heart. I want everything to please her, to keep that look on her face, even though I know I shouldn't. Her happiness shouldn't mean a damn thing to me.

"What do you want to know?"

"What do you like, John? Tell me about your family, your

hobbies, anything." I'm surprised at how fast she shoots off the questions. She's watching me as she waits for my answers.

I don't even know how to answer her question… "I'm an only child," I start. "But my mother comes from a big family."

"I know," Zoe interjects. "She's a Costello."

"So you've done your homework?" I shouldn't be surprised, since it's not like my family isn't well known around here. Plus, I broke into her apartment, so anything she's found out about me is a small change in comparison.

"Maybe." She smiles shyly.

"What else do you know about me, kitten?" I lean forward, resting my elbows on the table. Suddenly the food isn't holding my interest anymore.

Slowly, her smile drifts away, and she tugs her bottom lip between her teeth. "I-" She doesn't want to say it, but I want her to. I'm not sure why, but I like seeing her uncomfortable, twisting her fingers while she tries to come up with an answer.

"What?"

"I know you're into some… shady things."

"Yeah?" I chuckle. "Tell me about these shady things, hmm?"

His discomfort grows as she chews on her lip.

"Stop that," I scold. "Chewing on your lip. Just say it."

"You're in the mafia."

"Does that scare you?"

"Is it true?" she shoots back.

"You first."

She huffs at the back and forth. Apparently, we're not getting anywhere with this conversation. I can see the frustration in her eyes at my lack of answers. "It should," she states. "I'm probably an idiot for not being scared of you, John, but I'm not."

Something inside me warms at her admission. She should be scared of me, but she's not. And I shouldn't be interested in her, but I am. Maybe we're more alike than either of us even realize. Suddenly, my stomach doesn't want the food in front of me.

Instead, I want her, spread out on the table and waiting to be devoured.

Not yet though.

I smooth my palms over my thighs. Not yet. I won't have Zoe until she's ready for me. Until she knows what she's gotten herself into, and still wants to be here.

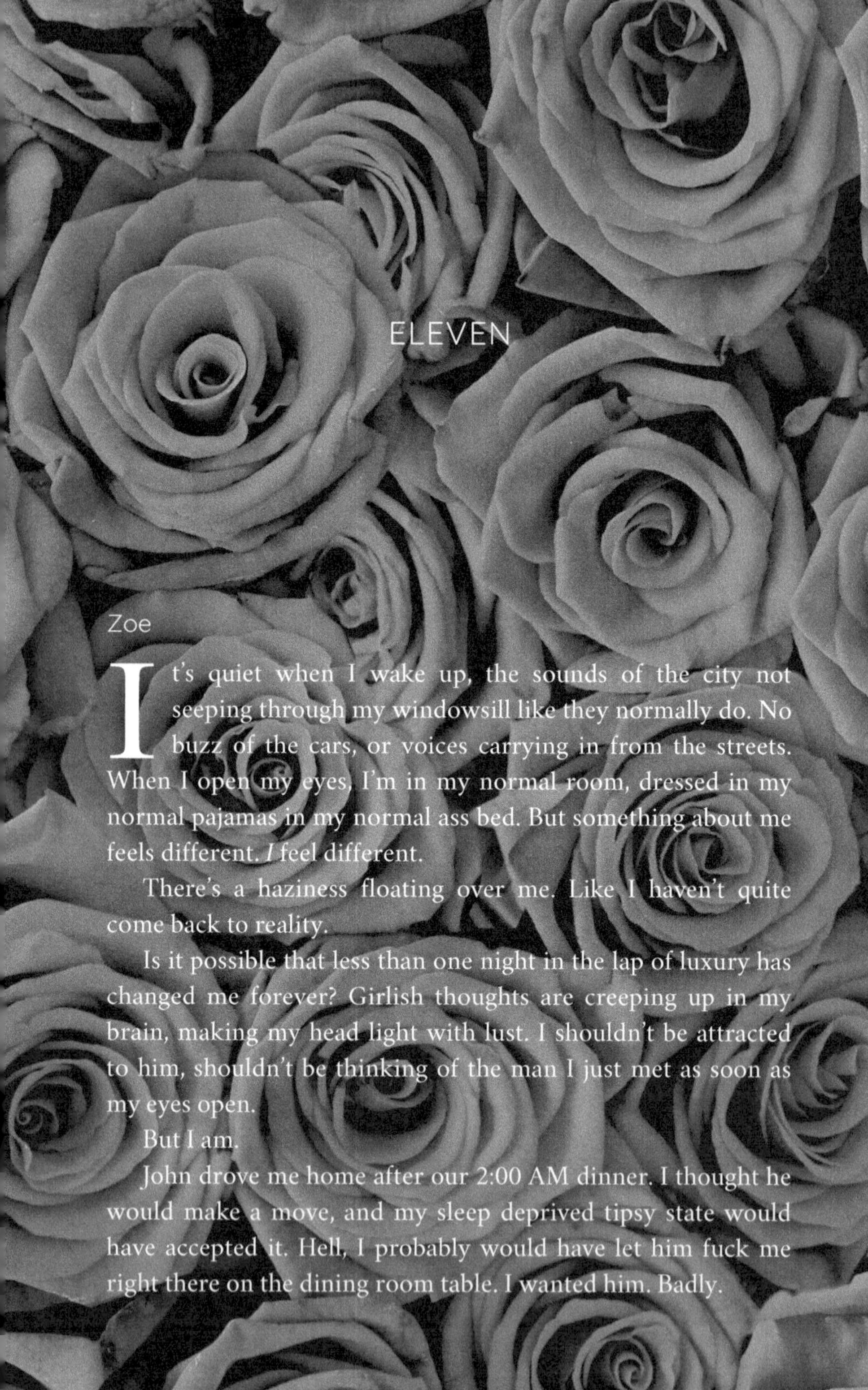

ELEVEN

Zoe

It's quiet when I wake up, the sounds of the city not seeping through my windowsill like they normally do. No buzz of the cars, or voices carrying in from the streets. When I open my eyes, I'm in my normal room, dressed in my normal pajamas in my normal ass bed. But something about me feels different. *I* feel different.

There's a haziness floating over me. Like I haven't quite come back to reality.

Is it possible that less than one night in the lap of luxury has changed me forever? Girlish thoughts are creeping up in my brain, making my head light with lust. I shouldn't be attracted to him, shouldn't be thinking of the man I just met as soon as my eyes open.

But I am.

John drove me home after our 2:00 AM dinner. I thought he would make a move, and my sleep deprived tipsy state would have accepted it. Hell, I probably would have let him fuck me right there on the dining room table. I wanted him. Badly.

But he was polite, telling me that I could stay, but in the guest room. All that to get me to his place and not make a move. Part of me was thankful, but most of me was confused and overwhelmed by my desire for him.

I let him drive me home, too aware that my attraction to him is dangerous. How am I supposed to spy on this man when my stomach rumbles with butterflies every time he comes near me. I don't know what information to give Marcus; I'm not even sure what he wants to know.

The biggest piece of information he *almost* admitted was that he's in the mafia… a fact I'm sure Marcus is well aware of. I need to get myself together. John is a pawn in my plan, so I should be using his interest in me to get information… whatever information I can to Marcus. That's what's going to help me find Cassie. If I want to find her, I need to use John, not fall for him.

I use a hot shower to erase his smell and the lingering feeling of his hands on my body. By the time I get to the club, the dressing room is already packed with girls getting ready for their nights. Daisy has her back to me when I slide onto the bench next to her. She's fidgeting with her makeup bag as I open my locker.

"Hey." When she doesn't respond to me, I turn to look at her, and that's when I see it. Red and purple bruises mark her flesh, a handprint is wrapped around her throat, and the discoloration trails down her arms. She's still fully clothed, but the marks are visible on every uncovered surface. I can see the panic that's rising on her features.

"I don't know what to do," she whispers, and I can feel her pain through the single statement. I don't need to see the rest of her body to know she's covered in more bruises. It's not uncommon for strippers to have some marks, the pole isn't that friendly, but these aren't from being a stripper. She looks like someone beat her up.

"Daisy…" I don't even know what to say, what words would even make this better? "What happened?" I sit down next to her and wrap an arm around her shoulder in an attempt to console her, but I don't know if it will be fine. I don't even know who hurt her… or why. "It's going to be fine,"

"It's not gonna be fine." Daisy hiccups a sob and drops her head in her hands.

"Who did this to you?"

Daisy wipes the back of her hand under eyes, smearing her eyeliner with the action. She doesn't look at me for a long moment, and I wonder if she doesn't want to tell me.

"Daisy." I place my hand on her knee.

"I owe them money," she whispers. "I'm supposed to be working it off." It's on the tip of my tongue to ask who *them* is, but I don't want to interrupt her or make her share more than she's willing. "I just want out." She sobs again, choking on the breath she inhales. "I don't want to do this anymore."

"Kat." Robby's voice makes me jump as he calls into the dressing room. "Boss wants ya."

"It's fine," Daisy tells me through a strangled sob. "I'll be okay, you can go."

I don't like the thought of leaving her, but I do. I'm not dressed yet, still in a pair of leggings and a loose t-shirt as I make my way back to Donnie's office.

I shouldn't be surprised when I find Marcus there instead for the second time, yet I stop in my tracks, staring at John's cousin. He's impeccably dressed, but the Costellos always are.

Marcus isn't much like his cousin, the only resemblance being their dark hair and matching eyes. They carry themselves so differently. John seems more rigid, calculated. Marcus comes off more relaxed, even smiles sometimes - but something feels off about it. His gaze seems more predatory than appreciative.

"You asked for me?" I feel his eyes on me, burning a hole through my clothing as he assesses my body. I'm suddenly thankful I haven't finished getting ready. The t-shirt and jeans I'm wearing provide a barrier between his eyes and my flesh.

"I did." The corners of his lips tilt up into a wicked smile, and it sends a shock wave of fear through my body.

I want to get away from Marcus; nothing good is going to come from this meeting. But I can't let him see my fear, can't let him know that he's getting to me, because that will only let him know how much control he has over me.

Cassie was better at reading people, presenting them the character they wanted to see. It was always a different character, and there were so many versions of her that I lost count. But she needed every single one. That was her survival mechanism. The more people she had on her side, the better taken care of she'd be. If she smiled and pretended, it would be easier. She honed her skills through years of foster families and court dates, and I learned from her.

I pull my hands behind my back, clasping my fingers together in a way that pushes out my tits. I don't want Marcus; the idea of him repulses me, but I want him to think I'm not appalled. I want him to believe I'm a naïve little girl that he's using to get his way, that way he doesn't see me coming.

"Do you have anything for me?" His lips move as he asks the question, but his eyes are wholly focused on my chest.

When I don't move inside the office any farther than the doorway, he stalks forward, shutting the door behind me. I don't know that anyone would help me if I yelled, but having the door closed makes me feel that much more cut off from the world. Trapped within the walls of his office like a caged animal.

"No." My voice is so quiet, a hushed whisper.

Marcus takes two steps until he's directly in front of me, his body too close to mine, sucking all the oxygen out of the room. "Why?"

John doesn't scare me the way Marcus does. There's something intimidating about him, and I know I should be scared, but I'm more... *intrigued.* Every hair on my body stands up on edge with Marcus in front of me. My heart pounds the same way it did when I realized my mother was never coming home.

It's more than intimidation.

The news hasn't been shy about their speculations of what the mafia is capable of. And since Carmine Costello's passing, the death toll in NOLA has been rising.

Would I just be another number? Another statistic for Marcus? Another one dead.

I think of the bruises on Daisy's flesh... did they come from him? Or is Marcus too good, too high up in the rankings to do his own dirty work?

Goosebumps pebble along my arms as the fear settles in my bones.

Marcus reaches out, his fingers intertwining with my hair as he tugs on the locks, not hard, just enough to frighten me. "Why? It's been a week."

"I know." I nod my head, trying to come up with the words to disarm him.

"I gave you a job, girl." He tugs on my hair harder, craning my neck to the side. "I expect results."

"I know." I'm ashamed of how pathetic my voice sounds as it leaves my lips.

"Have you talked to him?" His dark eyes remind me of John's, but the way the bore into me is much more sinister.

"Yes... I-"

"And what did you talk about?"

"I don't know." The pain in my scalp is starting to burn, causing tears to prickle at the corners of my eyes. "I'm still getting to know him; he doesn't trust me yet."

He releases my hair, and for a second, I think he's satisfied, but then his palm cracks against the skin on my cheek. The force from the slap turns my head, my hands clutching at my face. Before I can even grasp what happened, he comes at me again, this time pushing me to the floor.

Marcus hovers above me as he kicks his polished Italian leather shoe into my abdomen repeatedly, the action taking the breath right out of my lungs and sending a ripple of pain through me. He grabs me by the neck when I don't move, his fingers wrapping around my throat in a tight vise as he pulls me up to a kneeling position. I don't think my legs could stand even if I tried. My body burns with rage and shame and pain, tears breaking free from my eyes, completely out of my control.

His free hand reaches for the back of his waistband, tugging free a black metal contraption. I swallow hard when I see the gun he brandishes in front of my face. Somewhere in my head, a voice shouts that he is just trying to scare me, but it doesn't matter because it's working. I am scared.

"I expect more. Do you understand me?"

I nod my head as I choke on the tears now free-falling down my face. I'm blubbering like a baby. The man in front of me has reduced me to nothing. A shell of myself.

I'm not strong, not independent.

I'm nothing.

"Answer me," he shouts.

"I understand."

"You're gonna go home, and you're going to figure out how to wrap my cousin around your finger. I want you to know everything about him. When he eats, when he shits, and what he's fucking plotting. Got it?"

"Yes," I choke out. When he drops his grip on me, I fly backwards, my head hitting off the wall before I collapse into a pile on the floor.

"And, Kat?" he asks, a devilish smile playing on his lips. "If you can't do this, I can't find another job for ya, you know? I

have plenty of boys who would like to sink their teeth into you."
He winks at me before he turns around, as if I'm nothing more
than trash to him. "You can go now."

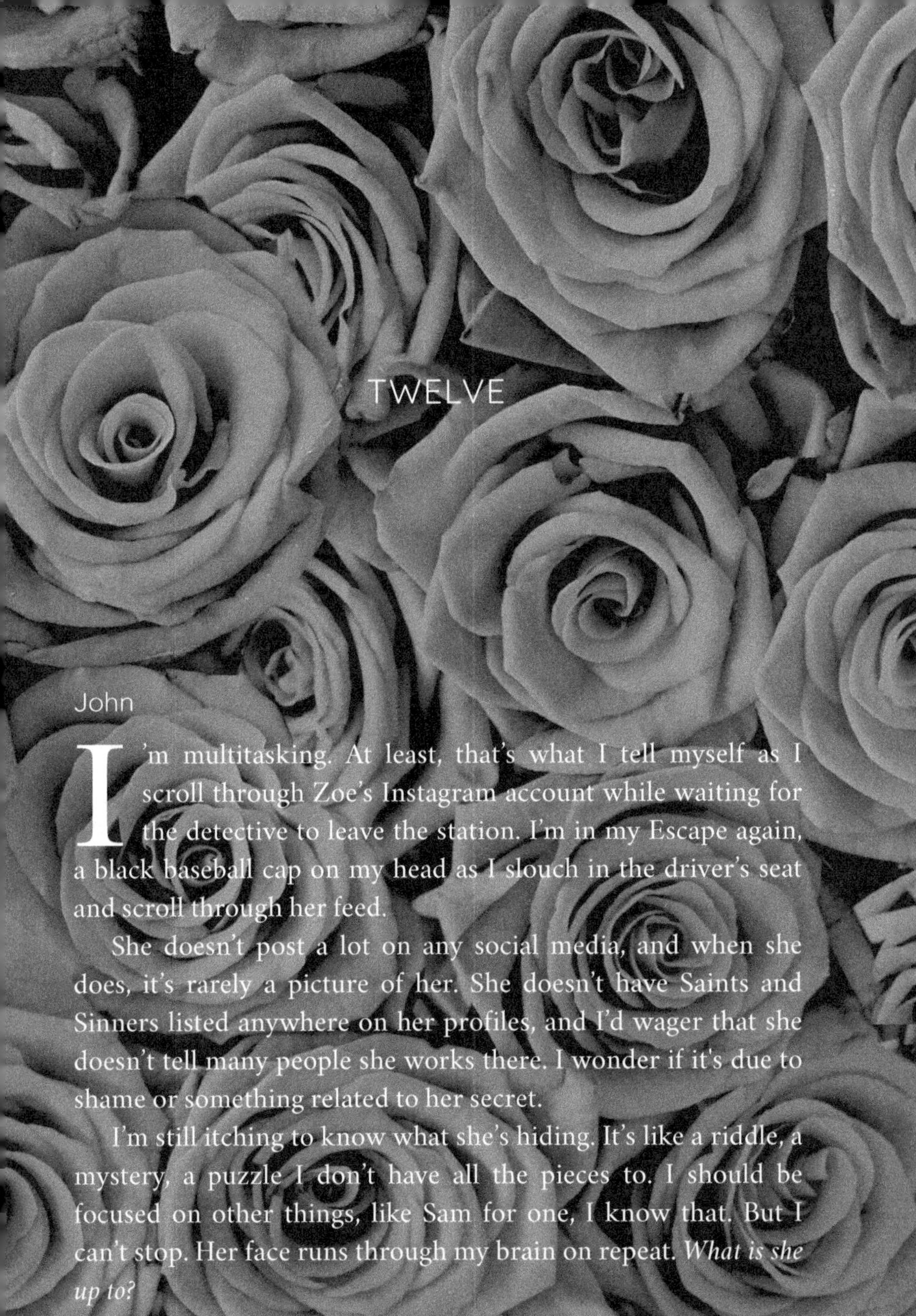

TWELVE

John

I'm multitasking. At least, that's what I tell myself as I scroll through Zoe's Instagram account while waiting for the detective to leave the station. I'm in my Escape again, a black baseball cap on my head as I slouch in the driver's seat and scroll through her feed.

She doesn't post a lot on any social media, and when she does, it's rarely a picture of her. She doesn't have Saints and Sinners listed anywhere on her profiles, and I'd wager that she doesn't tell many people she works there. I wonder if it's due to shame or something related to her secret.

I'm still itching to know what she's hiding. It's like a riddle, a mystery, a puzzle I don't have all the pieces to. I should be focused on other things, like Sam for one, I know that. But I can't stop. Her face runs through my brain on repeat. *What is she up to?*

I scroll through the accounts she's following on Instagram, the platform she's most active on. There are only five hundred of them, but the number seems low to me. She follows a lot of book accounts, and this makes me laugh for some reason. I look through their feeds, cute pictures with string lights, colored fabrics, and books lying on top. Zoe's account doesn't have pictures like this, but I can see which ones she's liked. Social media is such a strange thing.

I take a mental note of the books she tapped the heart icon for and keep digging. She follows some other people, friends, I think. I stop when I come across the account named *itscassiebitch*. The name Cassie rings out to me. *Cassie Stephens*, that's her missing roommate. I meant to look into her more, but I was too distracted with Zoe's room, with her likes and obsessions. I click on Cassie's profile. The circle icon shows me a selfie of a blonde girl sticking her tongue out. Her name in her bio is surrounded by emojis, a high heel, and lipstick. I scroll further.

Cassie Stephens posts a lot of pictures of herself, but what stops me in my tracks isn't her, but the background of her photos. *Saints and Sinners*. She's a stripper too.

I zoom in on one of her selfies, studying her face. I don't recognize her, don't think I've seen her around with Zoe at all. I go to the last picture Cassie posted three months ago. Which makes sense if she is the girl from Zoe's journal entry. *Cassie's been missing for three months.* She had written.

There are a myriad of reasons a girl from the club would go missing. Most likely, she's done working there. But it could get worse, depending on the reasons she is working there, or if Marcus has anything on her. If she's an addict.

My eyes glance out the window in time to see Detective Ellison leaving the building. Just one more second, and then I'll follow him. I just need to know more about Cassie…

I need to check her other social media accounts. But Ellison…

When I look up, his Mercedes is gone. *Dammit.*

THE REST of my afternoon is spent looking for Ellison unsuccessfully. I can't figure out where he went, but around 5:00 PM, I give up and head for my parents' house in Elmwood, silently wishing they lived a little closer to the Quarter. James and Cosetta like their fancy house in their fancy suburb, since everything with them is about appearance. Everything with the Costellos in general is about appearance. We need to maintain the image we've created in this city, no longer the gangsters of the 1900s. Instead, we're businessmen, a self-made family.

My grandfather wasn't interested in continuing to be thugs on street corners. He rose up the ranks of the Black Hand gang shortly after moving here and quickly realized that he didn't want to lead a group of low-level street dealers. No, Carmine Sr. wanted an efficient organization of men who knew how to play the game and break the rules. Make money, but don't get caught.

He turned a group of street rats into businessmen.

It was impressive, really.

My father is in his office when I get to the Elmwood house. I hear the keys clicking and know he's probably plotting out numbers or watching his money laundry software run. He's good at cleaning dirty money, which is part of the reason my grandfather liked him so much. Even before he proposed to my mother, Pap had decided to pay for his accounting degree. He was envisioning the next generation of gangsters who knew how to cook the books. Illegal crimes that *looked* legal.

And the money his school cost was worth it, because my father was good. Still is.

He wanted me to go down the same path, but numbers were never really my thing.

"Johnny," my mother coos when I enter her kitchen. There's a pot of sauce simmering on the stove, and she abandons her wooden spoon to come pinch my cheeks instead. She places a kiss on each of them and pulls back, her fingers gripping onto my shoulders while she looks me over. She's assessing, making sure nothing about me has changed since last Sunday. "You look good." She grins.

My mother can sniff out any change; she reads people like the back of her hand. I learned my skills from her, sitting at her feet while she tapped my shoulders and pointed things out to me in hushed tones. *Do you see the way he keeps looking to the left and covering his mouth? He's lying.*

It always amused me how much my mother was able to pick up about people just by reading their body language. She could spot a lie a mile away, and I was her sidekick. When I got older, she would send me to spy, weaving between the legs of senators and made men, listening to their conversations and reporting back to her.

"I'm good, Ma." I kiss her back, pecking each cheek the same way she did to me. "How 'bout you?"

"Same old here." She dusts her hands down the front of her apron. "Dinner should be ready soon. I made extra sauce for you to take home." She spins around, going back to her cooking.

My mother was trained to be a housewife, just like her mother. She moves through the kitchen effortlessly, and her food is just as good, if not better, than grandma's. But she's smarter than just a housewife, and a flicker of pain passes through my chest whenever I see her here.

She could have worked, could have contributed to *la famiglia.* Her father loved her; she's the youngest girl and as such was treated like a baby, but love didn't equate to power. Her marriage wasn't arranged, but it was heavily implied that James Vitale was a good match for her.

She has an open bottle of red wine on the counter, so I pour myself a glass, taking a healthy sip. My father is always more tolerable to me when I'm intoxicated. He wasn't a horrible father, but I wasn't the son he imagined having. He wanted someone more like Marcus or Sam, someone who would follow in his footsteps.

Instead, he had a son who couldn't feel emotions unless he was cutting someone open. Numbers don't bleed, and therefore, I don't like them.

"Johnny." Dad claps a hand on my back as he comes into the kitchen. His touch burns into my shoulder. I've never lived up to the standards of James Vitale, a fact that's put a strain on our relationship since the moment he knew I was different. Even a simple greeting put me on edge, waiting for the jabs, the mentions of what a failure I am.

Junior didn't think I was a failure. Quite the opposite. My skills were useful to this family, just not for the job my father wanted me to do.

He watches me as we sit down for dinner, his eyes finding me with every few bites. "How's work?" he asks once we're halfway through our pasta. My mother has never dissuaded him from talking about business at the table. She's always stayed quiet and listened, occasionally asking one or two questions. Her mother was the opposite. Sunday dinners were meant for family and not business. But the two have always been so intertwined.

"Fine," I tell him. My mind is already drifting to the club. Zoe works tonight, like most nights. I don't know how busy the strip club is on Sunday, but I'm hoping it's not. I want to watch Zoe, knowing other eyes aren't on her. The thought of other men looking at her makes my blood boil. *She doesn't belong to me.* I need to recite the words in my mind, but even with the mantra, I can't shake it.

"What does Marcus have you doing?" he asks. My father was always loyal to Junior when he thought he was going to take over, but now, after his death, he's stuck just like me. Marcus won't kill us if we don't make a move against him, but he doesn't like us either.

"Pickups." I bring a forkful of pasta to my mouth. "He has me picking up the cash,"

"You're better than that." He stabs at his plate, spearing his noodles as if they're meat instead. I know I am, but that's precisely why Marcus is using me for stupid fucking tasks. He needs to test my patience, see if I'll do any job that he gives me without complaint. And I will. Because the sooner he trusts me, the sooner he'll slip up.

I leave as soon as dinner is over, kissing Ma and slipping out of the house as fast as I can. My grandfather preached that *family is everything*, but I can only handle so much of mine.

It doesn't help that Zoe is weighing on my mind. I want to know more about her friend Cassie. If Junior was alive, I'd reach out to one of the cops on our payroll to run her name through a few databases, but I'm certain that all the dirty cops answer to Marcus now, and if she did work at Saints and Sinners, it will get back to him that I'm asking questions. I need to figure this one out on my own.

I navigate my Porsche back to the French Quarter and park a block up from the club. It's too crowded for a Sunday, but May is still prime time for tourists before the city gets too hot. They fill the Quarter in large crowds that I have to navigate through to get to the club.

It's busy inside, and I can't help but to laugh about the irony of a packed strip club called *Saints and Sinners* on a Sunday. I guess everyone finds their church somewhere, so who am I to judge?

I don't see Zoe on any of the stages or on the floor when I scan the club. I start to study the faces of all the girls I do see, looking for any resemblance to Cassie. Maybe she changed her hair? She could also be going by a different name, so maybe I missed her. But I don't see her either.

Donnie strolls out onto the main floor from his office, tapping his fingers on the bar to grab the attention of his bartender.

"Hey, Don," I slide in next to him. It's the same bruised girl I'm used to, and she doesn't ask for my order before she grabs my preferred bottle of gin from the shelf. She's growing on me, and I have the sudden urge to hunt down her boyfriend and give him a lesson on how to treat women. But I need to focus on Sam first… and then Zoe.

"Back again," Donnie muses. "Looking for your girl?" He chuckles to himself as the bartender slides the two low ball glasses in front of her.

I don't want to confirm my interest in Zoe, but we both know that's why I'm here.

"She's not here," he adds, taking a heavy gulp of his whiskey and saving me from having to ask. "Your girl was sent home. She's not feeling well."

I want to ask more questions, but I refrain. I don't trust Donnie. Instead, I take a long sip of my gin and wait for him to leave on his own accord. People are used to me not responding; they chalk it up to me being crazy, and I allow it.

Now I need to find Zoe.

THIRTEEN

Zoe

The iron railing bites into the flesh of my back as I lean farther into it. I like the sting of pain it gives. A bit of a bite to punish me as my head tilts up to watch the stars flicker in the black sky.

There's a sick part of my mind with ideas I don't dare speak out loud. An aching piece of me that longs to not be here. I should be dead; my life here is meaningless, just a collection of days that amount to nothing.

Because no matter what I do, I won't ever get ahead or pull myself from this pretty little slice of Hell. And Marcus's warning only gave that piece of me more power. Why should I stay alive if all I have to look forward to here is more pain from Marcus, and my father slowly withering away in front of me?

Cassie was the only thing anchoring me to this world, and I can't find her. Without my family or Cassie - there's nothing left for me, especially not in NOLA.

A smart part of me knows I should run, get out of here

before I dig myself a deeper hole to die in. But I want to know, I *need* to know, where she is. And what do I have to lose?

What did my best friend get herself into? And how did I live in the room next to her and not know? I rack my brain for memories of her with bruises. Did Marcus hurt her the way he did me? Did he pound his fists into her flesh? I can't recall anything suspicious, anything that wouldn't have been from the pole. She was happy for a bit before she went missing. She had the bubbly energy she always did when she was fucking somebody.

I can't tell you who, she had told me while shoving a spoonful of chocolate ice cream between her lips. But Cassie was always sleeping with someone, so it didn't surprise me anymore when she kept her partners to herself. Cassie had grown up using her body to get her way, and who was I to stop her.

Is that what she did? Did she sleep with someone she shouldn't have?

I shake the little bit of pot I have left into the grinder. The natural medicine is the only thing that seems to calm the constant chatter in my mind. When I'm done running it through the plastic mechanism, I empty the contents into the funnel that sits in the bong. The smoking device is a work of ark, a colorful blown glass bong with bits of purple and pink that spiral up the long neck. It's Cassie's. I stole it out of her room not long after her disappearance, needing something of hers to cling to.

Lighting the bud, I inhale and the water at the bottom of the contraption bubbles as I breathe in the smoke.

"What are you doing?" The voice startles me, and I puff out the white clouds with a cough, choking on the smoke. My hand clenches against my raspy chest as I look for the source of the voice.

John Vitale stands on the sidewalk below me, his dark eyes pointed toward my balcony. A fitted black suit clings to his body, and the material has a bit of a shine that illuminates him in the darkened night.

"Why are you here?" I ask, peeking over the banister to look at him.

"I asked you first."

Strong hands are tucked into his pockets as he leans back on his heels to look up at me, waiting for an answer.

"Smoking." I lift the bong just slightly to support my answer. The smell still lingers in the air, and for some reason, I feel self-conscious in his presence. John doesn't seem like the type to participate; something about his perfectly tailored clothes and uptight demeanor makes me believe he doesn't have fun. "Your turn."

"Checking up on you." I can see the flash of his white teeth as he answers me. He's charming, that's for sure. Even if something else is off, like he's hiding his own secret beneath that perfectly made exterior. "You weren't at work."

"I'm sick." I think we both know I'm not sick, but between the distance and the lack of lighting, he can't see my face yet.

"Can I come up?" He tilts his head with the question, his sharp jaw angled up toward me. He looks *good,* his strong features extenuated with soft skin and a roguish expression.

"I don't think that's a good idea." It's a horrible idea, really. I can't get any closer to him, to this family. My skin still stings from the hits Marcus landed, and I feel myself slipping deeper into their grasp.

But a sick part of me knows I should say yes. John's here, offering himself on a silver platter for me. I should be thanking him as I pick his brain for details and then report back to Marcus. It's a win-win for me. I can get close to Marcus while still being comforted by John.

My stomach churns at the thought. I don't want to help Marcus, though. I don't know if it's because I'm dumb, or if my persistent client has gained a fraction of my loyalty.

"Please," he says the word softly, but his charm still lingers, and something in me softens for him. He doesn't seem like the big bad *mafioso* I've made him out to be.

"Okay." I find my hand shaking as I slide open the glass door and find the buzzer to open the outside door for John. My pulse ticks as I wait for him to climb the steps before I hear his knock rasp against my apartment door.

A bit of shame lingers in my body as I open the door for John. He steps through the threshold, letting his eyes linger. The apartment is cheap in comparison to other places, but still too rich for my blood. With Cassie here, we split the rent and utilities, making it possible for me to pay my half on a waitress's salary. Without her, it's been tough.

When I shut the door and turn to face him, I can tell the second he sees the cut that slashes across my cheek. The ornate ring Marcus wears broke my skin, slicing me open, in addition to the bruises that mark my cheek and throat.

John's entire body tenses up, his shoulders rigid with the motion.

"Who. Did. That?" He punctuates each word with his deep voice.

"It's nothing." I wrap my arms around myself, pulling my loose sweater closed. "I'm fine."

His jaw ticks when I tell him I'm fine, and I can see the darkness that sits in his gaze, like little black pools of anger he's trying to restrain. "Who did it?" he asks again, the words strained, as if he's holding himself back.

I tug my bottom lip between my teeth, avoiding saying the name out loud. Anger is a new look on John, one I'm not used to. The only time I've seen him with a temper was when he hit the guy who touched me in the club… Every other time I've seen him, he's been flirty, uptight still, but never angry.

The sleeves of his black dress shirt are rolled up to the elbow, and I can see the tight lines of his tense muscles as his fingers clench into his fists. He stares at me silently, waiting for me to answer his question while I fidget underneath his gaze.

Outing my boss, the man who runs the New Orleans mafia doesn't feel like a good idea. I don't know how their organization works, who has more power. Saying his name could have me killed. I tighten my grip around myself, fear bubbling up inside my chest.

"What did he do to you?" John asks, but his gaze is still settled on my cheek, the worst of the abuse I suffered from Marcus's hands.

"Why?" I ask. "Why do you want to know?"

John takes two steps toward me, closing the gap until there's only mere inches separating us. "Because, kitten, whoever touched you is dead. Do you understand?" His dark eyes search mine as he palms my cheek. I'm ashamed of myself for leaning into his touch. Embracing his warmth.

I can feel the haze of my high deepening the moment, intensifying my anxiety, but also the lust that lingers between us. I shouldn't be okay with the words that came out of his mouth.

Dead.

He means he's going to kill a man. Not just any man... Marcus.

"John." My voice is too soft, strangled by his presence.

"Hmm?" His thumb drifts over my unaffected cheek as he waits for me to spit out my sentence.

"It was Marcus," I breathe.

John stills, his eyes lingering on the cut on my cheek before drifting down to the bruises on my throat. His only movement is the slow rise and fall of his chest, even though I can feel the rage radiating from him. He's still, gathering his thoughts before he speaks again.

"Kitten." He blows out a soft breath. "He shouldn't have done that." I don't know what I expected from John; maybe for him to be more like his cousin. Maybe for him to tell me I deserved it, and to listen better next time. But he doesn't say any of that. Instead, his thumb moves to trace my bottom lip, and his dark eyes bore into mine. "I'm sorry."

The apology stuns my heart. I wasn't expecting the softness of his words. His hand tangles in my hair as he smooths it back, his touch gentle even though I know there's strength in his muscular body. I can feel his apology in the way he touches me, the way his eyes find mine. He *feels* sorry.

"It wasn't you," I whisper. Even though a part of me does blame John, because his interest in me is what put Marcus on my path. But then again, I wanted Marcus to see me, talk to me. I wanted to get to know him in the hopes that he would drop me some breadcrumbs, point me in Cassie's direction.

John or not, I put myself in this situation.

"Maybe," he breathes. "But I should have protected you."

"And how would you have done that?"

He opens his mouth, but then closes it quickly. "Let me make it up to you, kitten."

A swarm of butterflies is swirling through my insides, beating against my ribcage as John's heated gaze watches me.

I should tell him to fuck off.

I should make him leave.

I should do anything but lean closer.

But I don't. He meets me in the middle and presses his lips to mine softly, in a gentle, exploring kiss. And then his hand finds the back of my neck and he pushes me forward, fusing my lips to his.

He deepens the kiss, and the butterflies flap their wings harder, my chest aching with my desire. My lips part, and he invades me, taking over all of my senses and filling them with him.

My brain turns to mush, my heart only beating one syllable over and over.

John. John. John.

The weed in my system only intensifies the lust that streams through my veins. My brain is a hazy fog, and the only light at the end of the tunnel is John Vitale.

Suddenly, all the apprehension has vanished, replaced by only need.

He pulls back, his swollen lips hovering above mine, his eyes darkened with his own desire, peering straight into mine. "Kitten," he says. "How high are you?"

I can't help the laugh that escapes me, bubbling up from my chest. I don't want him to use my state as an excuse to stop. "Not that high."

"How much did you smoke?"

"Not that much."

A smirk rises on his lips, his eyes sparkling with amusement.

"I don't want you to stop," I tell him.

"I know." He leans in, leaving one tender kiss on my lips. "Do you have a bed in this place, or do you want me to lay you down on the floor?"

"I have a bed." I barely have the words out of my mouth when John picks me up, cradling me in his arms, and walking us through my apartment.

He doesn't ask which room as he carries me back and right into mine. I shake the thought from my head. It must be obvious; my door was open, hers was closed.

Under the golden hue of the twinkle lights strung along the ceiling, John lays me out on the bed. My heart rate begins to speed up. He's so gentle with me, so protective and soft, and it shocks my system in comparison to the hits Marcus landed.

"Tonight is all about you, pretty girl," John tells me, ghosting his palm over my cheek again. "I want you to tell me exactly what you want. Whatever you need, got it?"

I nod my head feverishly.

John leans forward on the bed, his arms on either side of my head, caging me in. "I need your words, kitten. Understand?"

"Yes," I breathe the word, and a smile rises on John's lips.

"Good girl." His praise sends a spark through my body, electrifying me.

He begins to remove my clothing painfully slow. Helping me sit up so he can pull my cardigan off my shoulders. Next, his fingers come to the hem of my t-shirt, pulling the thin material over my head. Goosebumps rise on my flesh from his light touch and my thighs clench together, waiting for more, for his fingers to find my skin.

He admires my pale pink lace bralette. The tiny scrap of fabric barely lifts my tits, but it's more comfortable than a regular bra. John's hands find the waistband of my leggings, and with unhurried precision, he drags the stretchy material down my legs at an agonizing pace.

By the time I'm naked in front of him, my body is on edge, longing for more of his touch, *demanding* it.

The power dynamic in this room is all off with him in his clothes and me bare. The black dress pants are tight on his thighs, and his matching black shirt clings to his muscular forearms, but he doesn't remove his clothing.

He tucks his hands under my ass and drags me to the edge of my bed before he kneels down. Something about this powerful man on his knees for me only makes my heart beat faster. He parts my legs, spreading them so he can see my pussy.

Humming a sound of approval, he leans forward and presses a kiss against my sex. A moan leaves me immediately, and an ache forms low in my belly.

His tongue sweeps over me. "You're wet," he remarks when he pulls back. "So fucking wet for me, kitten."

His pet name pulls at my heartstrings, and I'm swept into his orbit, intoxicated by him.

I don't know if it's him or the weed, but my body craves him, his touch, his taste, everything about him.

He dives in, licking and sucking until I'm shaking beneath him. Then he adds a finger, sweeping it through my juices before bringing it to my entrance. When he pushes through, my walls contract, clinging to his digit.

"Fuck, oh God," I moan, and I can feel John grin against my sex.

"No, kitten." His voice is deep, a sexy drawl as his breath skates across my wet skin. "Not God. I want to hear you thank who's licking your pussy right now."

My body vibrates with pleasure as he brings his mouth back down on me. "You," I breathe. "John, oh fuck, John." I'm shaking, my fingers tangling in my sheets, gripping the fabric as John's tongue laps over my clit.

The pressure of my orgasm builds in my core, bubbling over the edge until I'm free falling. Everything, all the pressure, all the guilt melting away as I fall and fall with John's tongue and fingers still working on me.

When I finally open my eyes, I'm panting as I come back down to earth. John's dark eyes and white teeth glow under the light of the moon that peaks through my window. He looks devilishly handsome right now.

"Say thank you, kitten."

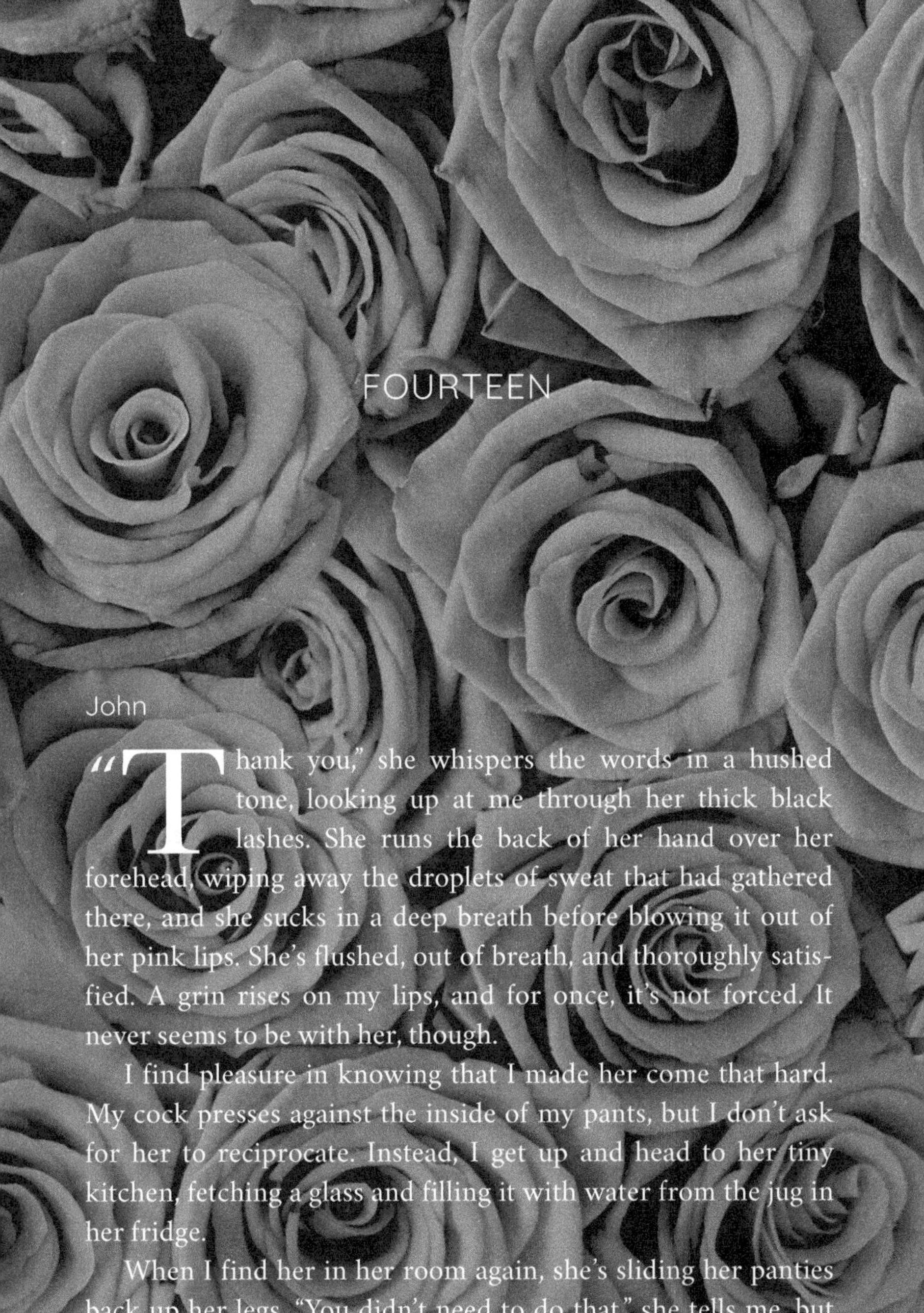

FOURTEEN

John

"Thank you," she whispers the words in a hushed tone, looking up at me through her thick black lashes. She runs the back of her hand over her forehead, wiping away the droplets of sweat that had gathered there, and she sucks in a deep breath before blowing it out of her pink lips. She's flushed, out of breath, and thoroughly satisfied. A grin rises on my lips, and for once, it's not forced. It never seems to be with her, though.

I find pleasure in knowing that I made her come that hard. My cock presses against the inside of my pants, but I don't ask for her to reciprocate. Instead, I get up and head to her tiny kitchen, fetching a glass and filling it with water from the jug in her fridge.

When I find her in her room again, she's sliding her panties back up her legs. "You didn't need to do that," she tells me, but takes the glass of water anyway.

"You're probably thirsty." I shrug. Orgasming is a physical activity that requires rehydration.

Her eyes assess me, almost confused. Has she never been taken care of after sex? What do the men she sleeps with do afterwards? Clean up and leave? The thought nags at me, burning a hole in my chest. I hate the idea of her being mistreated.

I crawl back into her bed, positioning myself between the slate gray sheets. When she sets the water glass down on the nightstand, I reach for her, wrapping my arm around her waist. I tug her to me, and her body melts against mine, relaxing in my grasp.

Who hurt her? It's more than the bruises Marcus planted on her skin. I want to know who wormed their way into her psyche, planting the idea that she shouldn't be taken care of? Or that a man shouldn't stay?

I don't want to exceed her expectations. I want her expectations to be sky-high. I want to have to work for it.

I don't know what it is about the small brunette with steel-grey eyes that makes me want to scoop her into my arms and protect her. She's encrusted in a shell, her attempt to keep the world from hurting her, but it's not enough. I can see right through her act.

"Why would Marcus do this?" I ask the words as my fingers trace the curves of her soft skin. I linger around the line of a bruise on her arm. She's covered in them, her stomach black and blue where I can tell Marcus kicked her. My cousin isn't a good man, but he doesn't beat up women for no reason. Not that any reason would ever be acceptable.

Is she sleeping with him? Did she piss him off? Or is this because of me?

Over her shoulder, I can see her tug her bottom lip between her teeth, biting down on the pink flesh. I reach out, pulling at it with my pointer finger to free it from her abuse. She's not sure what to say. A bit of fear lingers on her features, and I don't blame her. Marcus only gave her a glimpse of what his consequences look like.

The air is so tense, but something grasps at me. My heart is tight in my chest. Being with her makes me feel something. Normally, I need something more gruesome to shock my heart into life. But being in Zoe's presence turns on my emotions better than blood-soaked carpets.

The feeling is heavy now. Worry. Fear. Guilt. They swirl around in the pit of my stomach, warring for first place. Seeing Zoe hurt feels like shit.

And I want to make it better. If only to see what other emotions Zoe could awaken inside me.

"What's your secret, Zoe?" I ask her softly, brushing my knuckles across her cheek. Her eyes drift shut, and she relaxes under my touch. She feels it too; whatever this is, pushing us together, the magnetic pull that has her stuck in my mind.

I've never wanted a woman. Not in the way I want Zoe. The compulsory way. I feel that way about killing people. I have to push the urge down, willing myself to keep it from people who would lock me up for wanting to do the things I imagine.

This feeling is almost like that; strong and unbending.

Even if I did want a woman, the kind of want where you can't be without them, where it feels unbearable to think about not ever knowing her - I know how stupid marrying someone would be. I can't keep a relationship with someone. Not when my schedule includes me stalking and murdering.

I can't kill a man and make it home for dinner on time.

There's no future with me. And I can't force someone into living my life, living with my secrets.

But I want to know hers. Need to know hers. And then, I'll walk away.

"Why do you think I have a secret?" Her voice is light, but she swallows thickly. I can see through her coy attitude.

She's a liar.

Just like me.

Using the arm wrapped around her waist, I roll her to me, flipping her onto her back as I climb above her, letting my body push hers against the mattress. I'm careful not to put too much weight on her, not to crush her already sensitive skin.

She doesn't push me away. Instead, her body moves to mine, closing the space until we're tightly pressed against each other.

"Why did he do this?" I ask again, watching her gray eyes as I do. She closes them quickly, trying to escape my prying. "Kitten," I breathe. "Look at me." Her lids flicker open at my demand, finding my gaze again. "Tell me," I urge, softer this time.

There's a soft light peeking in through Zoe's window, probably a streetlamp, casting its yellow glow across her smooth skin as she stares up at me. I like her like this, tucked beneath me and illuminated in the night.

They call New Orleans *The Big Easy*, because life moves slowly here, the pace calm and peaceful for locals and tourists alike. My life never felt like that, though. Even before Junior's death and Sam's arrest, life wasn't calm. It's always been one thing after another, one more battle, one more problem to solve. There's always something else. And I think, for a moment, I could let everything weighing on me float away. I could wrap my arms around Zoe and pretend nothing exists.

But then the light shifts just enough to show the bruises that mark her skin, from the fingers that wrapped around her throat and squeezed tightly. That burn returns to my chest, firing up the anger that lingers there. That was always the easiest emotion for me to feel, the one that came most naturally. I only cared about things when they pissed me off.

"You can't act on the anger, Johnny." Junior's voice floats through my mind. I will myself to calm down, to snuff out the fire before it heats up my head and takes over. No, I don't act on emotions. I push them down and formulate a plan.

Something in my gaze must change with my thoughts, though, because Zoe exhales a long stream of breath, finally answering me. "He wants me to… spy on you."

Admitting the truth pains my little liar.

"Yeah?" I laugh. "What'd you tell him?"

Her brow creases and mouth gapes as she looks up at me, searching my face. "You're not mad?

I can't be mad at her. Not when part of me blames myself for her pain. Maybe if I wouldn't have shown any interest in her, Marcus would have left her alone. I'm not dumb enough to think Marcus wouldn't try to spy on me. I just didn't plan on him using her to do it. I didn't plan on getting close enough to anyone for him to use, let alone feeling protective over this girl.

I lower my face slowly until I can press a soft kiss on her forehead. "I'm not mad, kitten."

"You don't even know if I told him-"

"Tell me what he asked you."

She swallows. "It wasn't specific. He just wanted me to flirt with you and see if you slipped up… I don't even know what he thinks I'll see."

"You weren't made for this world," I whisper. She wasn't. She's too pure. Sure, maybe there's a darkness lingering behind those eyes, a trauma she's yet to deal with. But there's still innocence there, a naïve belief that the world is good.

She probably doesn't know what monsters lurk in the streets in this city, what villains she's let past her door.

"What does that mean?" she asks, and I can hear the confusion in her words.

"You know, Zoe, you know who Marcus is, who I am." I can't tell her. I took an oath. My blood dripping from the cut on my palm while St. Anthony burned at my fingertips.

Family first.

Family above all.

You don't tell people about us, what we do in the shadows

when no one's watching. But Zoe's not a dumb girl. She knows what's happening here; she knows that the club she works at isn't very clean. And she knows that what Marcus is asking isn't just a harmless game between cousins. He's scoping me out to determine whether he should kill me or not. Assessing if I'm a threat.

The family above all days are ending. My oath doesn't act as a protection anymore. Not with Junior dead and Sam in prison. We're out in the wild now. Soldiers with too much ammunition and no one to stop them.

Zoe needs to know what she's gotten herself into.

"Mafia?"

"Atta girl." I lean down again, this time peppering kisses along her jaw. I want to reward her for her truths, for being honest with me.

"John," she breathes.

"Hmm, kitten?"

"What am I supposed to do?" I can see the fear still hanging on as her eyes stare into mine. She's not wrong to be worried. Marcus thinks he's going to take over *la famiglia*, and that blind obsession makes him dangerous.

I don't know how to protect her without sharing all my secrets, without getting her in twice as deep as she already is.

"You should leave," I tell her, but even as the words leave my lips, I don't mean them. I don't want her to go anywhere. I want to keep her tucked beneath me. I want to protect her.

But I can't force her to stay.

"I can't..." she trails, her eyes moving away from me, avoiding contact.

"Why?"

"My dad... he's sick. I can't leave him alone. He doesn't have anyone else."

"Then you'll stay, and I'll protect you," I tell her, pressing another kiss to her jaw. She's overwhelmed. I can see the tears that want to build in her eyes, but she pushes them down, swallowing hard.

"Protect me from what?" she asks, the fear seeping through her words as her voice shakes.

"Marcus... my family."

FIFTEEN

Zoe

I woke up buzzing with electricity even though my brain was shouting *bad idea* over and over on repeat. I should be terrified. But I feel alive.

This is too much. Too fast. And my head is reeling, trying to catch up with the new information. My body is sore, and my bruises are still visible. And even though they're Marcus's fault, I still had to come into work today. I spent too much time in front of my bathroom mirror trying to cover the dark marks he left on my skin.

"You have a private dance. Room three," Donnie tells me as I exit the dressing room.

I'm more covered today than I normally am, wearing a black pleather bodysuit. It has a collar that covers some of the bruising on my throat, but a zipper goes down my chest, exposing my cleavage. My stomach is covered and so are my arms, but the bottom of the one piece shows off my ass nicely. I paired the bodysuit with my knee-high boots. It's sexy, in a sort of dominatrix way. Not my usual vibe, but I needed the extra coverage. Even with the foundation and concealer, the marks still showed, and I figure the men here want to see naked girls, not abused ones.

"Me?" He rolls his eyes when I ask the question. I'm not sure what I did to piss off my boss.

"Yes, *you*, Kat. That's what I fucking said, isn't it?"

"I haven't even started yet-"

"He personally requested you." Donnie spins on his heel, walking toward the upper level with the row of private rooms. He must be in a pissy mood today.

I'll give Marcus some credit; his club is nice. But having a nice club doesn't make him a good person or mean that the girls are treated fairly. It just means he knows what his customers want.

I let my heels lead the way as I walk toward the higher level. There are private rooms downstairs, but this level is reserved for VIPs.

Donnie swings the door open for me, gesturing for me to enter.

John stands in the room, his eyes affixed to the shiny chrome pole in the center. Since this is a VIP room, one meant for the men who drop thousands of dollars on a girl, it's bigger, cleaner, with a pole for dancing in the more intimate setting.

I've never given a dance in this room.

"I booked your night," he tells me casually, and my stomach flutters in response. He reaches out with his pointer finger and flicks it across the chrome material. The pole spins and John hums to himself. "I didn't realize they did this. Does it make it easier?"

He turns to face me, his dark hair slicked back, and he's wearing another one of his suits, the dark material clinging to his body perfectly. Did he say he booked my night, and now he wants to talk about pole mechanics? He holds a glass of clear liquid, which I'm sure is some alcohol that's been poured from a bottle that costs more than my rent.

"What?" I can't help the way my jaw falls open when I ask the question.

"It spins." He pushes it again, causing the pole to rotate. "Does that make it easier for you to dance?"

"Sure, I guess… why are you asking me about the pole? Did you say you booked my night?" The words rush from my lips too quickly, but John confuses me. Why would he book my time just for small talk? Why drop a grand just to learn about pole dancing?

He chuckles to himself, but the smile doesn't reach his eyes. "Yes. You're mine for the night, Zoe. So shut the door and sit down."

I swallow audibly as I do what he says, shutting the door to the private room and sitting down on the velvet lined bench. "Why would you do that?"

He shrugs. "I don't want anyone else to watch you dance."

"You can't just-"

"Can't what?" He quirks a brow. "What can't I do, Zoe?" He walks to me slowly, his black loafers tapping on the floor as he gets closer. The power dynamic is off once more, but then again, it always is with him. He hovers over me, his eyes glued to mine as he waits for the answer to his question.

"You can't buy my entire night-"

"But I did," he cuts me off again. He's too smug, too self-assured.

I'm flustered now. "I have to work, I have to-"

"It's covered."

"John, I have to work. I need the money." My fingers grip into the end of the bench. I don't like to be weak, don't like to show vulnerabilities.

"What do you make in a night?"

"I don't want-"

"What do you make in a night, Zoe? Tell me."

"It varies…"

"Is two thousand enough?" He tilts back the glass, finishing it off so he can set it down on the end table. He reaches into his back pocket, pulling out a small wad of hundred-dollar bills.

"I can't-"

"You can." He counts out two thousand dollars before folding the stack in half and extending it to me.

That's a lot of money. I can pay my rent, buy groceries. I can pick up my dad's prescriptions and put food in his fridge. It will go a long way…

But I can't take the money from him. Especially knowing what he's a part of.

He squats down, so he's eye level with me. "Take the money, Zoe. You're in this mess because of me, so take my money and let me protect you."

"How is this protecting me?"

"You're safe. In here, with me, you're safe." He looks so serious when he says the words. Like he believes he can protect me. And maybe he can. Maybe money and power allow you to do anything you want.

"I think you have control problems," I mutter.

"Oh, you don't even know yet." He smiles, and it's a wicked sight that I find myself liking way too much for my own good. I think this is John's true smile, wide and devilish with his darkened eyes.

His words from the other day rise in my mind. "You said you wanted to put a collar on me?" I don't know why I bring it up. The thought shamefully excited me, and I can see the same excitement rise on John's features when I mention it.

"Would you wear it?"

I run my tongue over my lips. Would I wear it? It seems dirty, something too possessive. The kind of thing my feminist heart should be appalled by, but it lights a fire in my core. I have to control my breathing to keep him from knowing how much his question turns me on.

"I like when you wear your choker," he muses, his dark eyes skimming over my face and landing on my throat.

"I thought it would make the bruises less obvious…"

John winces at the reminder, staring at my throat like it's giving him a dirty look. "I'm going to kill him," he mutters. He pushes back to his feet, stalking away from me. The reminder of his cousin changes his demeanor; he's fuming now, silently, and it's almost undetectable, but I can tell. His hand comes to his chin as he paces the room, his other hand clenching at his side.

His words make me think of the news, since the stories lately have been filled with shootings and death notices. When there's not a new case to report, they go back to the death of Carmine Costello Jr. He was shot two months ago in his home, and now his son is in prison for his murder…

I'm naïve to just now be putting the pieces together. John's uncle was killed, and his cousin is in prison. For some reason, I slip into a bubble when it comes to John, only seeing what's in front of me and forgetting where he comes from.

"Are you going to?" I choke on the words.

Marcus is a horrible person… he deserves to die. But who I am to make that decision? Can I let John kill a man and do nothing about it? But what could I even do if I wanted to… I can't go to the police. That's a death sentence.

"Do you want to know?"

I swallow my fears, emboldening myself. But I'm not sure that I do want to know.

"This is a line you can't uncross, Zoe." John says softly. "I can keep you in the dark if you want?" He looks at me, wanting an answer.

Do I want to be kept in the dark? What would that even look like? John books all my time, and I pretend I'm his personal whore who knows nothing about him?

Or do I do this with him? Stay informed every step of the way. Where does that land me, though? If this all goes bad, I'll probably be testifying in court. Or worse, in prison. Possibly even dead.

John was right when he said I don't belong in his world.

"My dad…" I whisper, trailing off.

"What about him?"

"If something happens to me, there's no one left to-"

"Hey," John interrupts me, taking quick steps until he's back in front of me. His knees drop to the floor, and his hands find my shoulders, gripping onto me. "Don't say that. I'm not going to let anything happen to you."

"You barely even know me."

"So tell me about yourself. I'll listen to every fucking thing you want to say, and I'll stay, and I'll still protect you. Just let me do that, hmm?"

"What do I tell Marcus?" I can't let John protect me, can't put myself in his hands when I barely know him. A good orgasm can't be enough for me to put my life in his hands. But the alternative is helping Marcus, and that actively hurts John.

"I'll figure it out. I'll give you enough to satisfy him."

"And then what…" My words are hushed whispers, barely audible above the blood rushing through my head. "You'll…" I can barely say the words.

"I'll take care of him," John finishes for me. "You'll be okay, Zoe."

This was silly. Chasing after Cassie might be the death of me.

What the fuck did she get herself into?

John

I convince Zoe to stay at my townhouse. She begrudgingly agrees after I offer to go to her place first. She grabs a duffel bag and fills it with clothes and a small bag of makeup. Then she takes the journal from her drawer, a pack of pens, and a single book, slipping them into a separate bag.

It's funny seeing Zoe with clothes on. Most of the time I've seen her has been at the club with her body on display. She changed before we left, putting on a plain white t-shirt and a pair of tight-fitting leggings. Her hair is loose, dark locks that hang from her head, reaching the middle of her back.

I want to wrap her hair around my fist and tug, but I resist the urge; she's not ready for that yet. It's not that late when we slide back into my Porsche. We left the club before her shift ended, which she didn't seem thrilled about. She has an anxious energy about her now, probably realizing she's in over her head.

I don't know how to comfort her, how to make her feel like

this isn't some sort of death sentence, like she hasn't attached herself to *la famiglia*. But she has. Marcus knows she means something to me now, and he's not going to stop trying to use her. I can spoon-feed her information, control what she tells Marcus enough to keep both of us safe while I come up with a better plan, one that ends with him at the morgue and Sam out of prison.

Marcus needs to die, but I need to get Sam out of prison first. His death will create a power vacuum, one I can't fill on my own. I can't do this at random, reacting out of anger. No, I need to plan this out. It needs to be organized.

Get Sam out.

Kill Marcus.

In that order.

Zoe bites at her cuticles as I drive us out of the Seventh Ward and back to my house.

"Ask me something,"

She startles at my question. I can see her body twitch as we pass under the streetlamps. She doesn't ask anything for a moment, just squeezes her hands together.

"The news…" she mumbles, her voice soft and fearful as she begins her question. "They say your family is fighting or something. Is that true?"

The sound that leaves my mouth is a mix between a scoff and a laugh. The news likes to speculate about *la famiglia*. "They're not completely wrong." And they aren't. We are fighting. A civil war that is threatening to destroy everything my grandfather built.

"That's why your uncle…"

My fingers grip harder onto the steering wheel as Zoe trails off. I still see red when I think about Junior's death. It clouds my vision, and I squeeze the leather, trying to rid it from my head.

Killing Junior was the worst thing Marcus could have done.

He was the patriarch of our family, especially after our grandfather's death. I scrub a hand down my face. Maybe it was a bad idea to have Zoe ask questions. I wanted to make her feel more comfortable, but it's having the opposite effect on me.

"I'm sorry," she mumbles, wrapping her arms around herself.

"It's fine." I inhale a deep breath, letting it fill my lungs and clear my head. Junior was the one who taught me to breathe when I got angry, such a simple solution to a complex problem. *Inhale, exhale,* he'd told me, *push it down until you can control it.*

I gather control of my emotions again, pushing the anger back into its box. "I was close to my uncle," I tell her, hoping that explains my reaction.

"I'm sorry," she whispers. "His death must have been hard,"

"Yeah," I mutter.

"What about your parents, are you close to them?"

I picture James and Cosetta Vitale. "To my mother," I tell her. I don't want to dive into the reason me and my father don't get along, the lengthy stories about my childhood. Visits to the principal's office where he made me feel like a piece of garbage. A broken child who couldn't be fixed. Junior was the one who rebuilt me, who taught me how to use my differences to my advantage.

Zoe doesn't ask another question for a minute. I'm not giving her much; that was another thing Junior always reminded me. My answers are too short, so they don't make for good conversation. Who wants to talk to a person who only answers in a few words?

I swallow. "She's a good woman, stayed home with me, cooked, baked, that kind of stuff. She's nice."

I can see the flicker of Zoe's smile. "She sounds kind."

My mother was never the problem in my house, but she wasn't the solution either. She chose to parent by ignoring anything she didn't like. When I was sent home early, she just pretended that nothing happened. That I wasn't getting into fights and killing rodents. She just batted her eyes and moved on.

Part of me respected her for it, but another part of me wanted her to say something. Anything.

"What about your mom?" I ask. *That's how conversations work, Johnny,* Junior would tell me, *you give, you take.*

I'm better at acting when I don't care. When I can slap on a persona and pretend. But I'm not pretending with Zoe, and that's what throws me off. I don't know how to behave when it's not an act.

But she wears a disguise too. She's not as confident as she pretends to be when she's slipped into her stripper heels. It's funny with Zoe; the more clothes she wears, the more guarded she becomes.

Maybe we're both a little fucked up.

"She died during Katrina." She doesn't look at me when she shares this fact. Her fingers are twisted together again, and her eyes are staring out the window, watching the city pass by.

"I'm sorry," I say. I think that's the right thing to say, and I am sorry. What would it be like growing up without a mother? "How old were you?"

"Seven." She tugs at the skin around her nail bed.

"Stop." I reach across the console to place my hand over hers. "You'll make yourself bleed." She's silent as she squeezes her hands into her thighs to stop her nervous habit. "It's a bad habit," I tell her. "If you do that in front of Marcus, he'll know you're nervous, or worse, that you're lying."

She thinks this over for a moment. "Is that how you knew?" she asks. "That I was lying?"

I smile at the thought. There were a few things that tipped me off. She was too interested in my cousin, and her eyes were too clear, with no drugs in sight. Most of Marcus's girls are doped up with track marks on their arms. Not Zoe. "I could see through your act," I tell her. "But it's not that bad."

She hisses out a breath. "What do you mean? Does-"

"No, I think Marcus and Donnie think you're there for real. You're young, you need money, and he probably thinks you haven't considered your other options. But you're not there for real. You're looking for something… are you going to tell me what?" I ask the question right as we pull up to my house. The black gate slides open, and I pull through. When I turn to look at Zoe, she's wringing her fingers together.

"You're wrong," she says. "I'm just there for the money."

Her statement stabs my heart. I thought we were being more trusting with each other, opening up.

"Don't lie to me, kitten. You forget, I can see right through you."

Her head spins to face me, those gray eyes shooting daggers at me. "You don't know me, John." Her arms cross over her chest and she presses her lips into a thin line. She's closing herself off from me, trying to create distance. She's scared, acting out like a child because I know she's up to something.

"I told you before you could have your secrets for now." I lean forward over the center console and close the gap between us. "But one of these days, you're going to tell me, kitten."

Dark brown locks flip over her shoulder as she turns away from me. She pushes open her door and hops out of my car, marching to the back door of my house.

The corners of my lips lift as I watch her hips swing. She can pout now, but eventually, I'm going to pull all her secrets from her.

IT'S ALMOST midnight by the time Zoe comes back downstairs. I left her alone in my bedroom to unpack her things and get settled. It's probably best that I don't push her too hard tonight. But a sick side of me wants to. I want to break her, watch come undone, but only for me. And then I want to build her back up, turning her into a queen.

I gave Arnold the night off, so I have to dig through the fridge to find something for Zoe to eat. Luckily, Arnold left cheeses already cut up, so I slice an apple and grab some nuts from the pantry, pulling together a tray for her. I leave it on the table and fill the teakettle with water, then grab two mugs from the cabinet.

My evenings are normally spent at home, in my office, with a glass of gin and a book. I don't want Zoe drunk, though. I want her to be fully aware for all the things I want to do to her.

I need her to be able to say no, to keep me from going too far.

She's showered and changed when she comes back down-stairs. Her face is clear of makeup, and she wears an oversized pink sweatshirt and a pair of navy-blue pajama shorts. Her wet hair falls heavy down her back. She looks small and innocent like this.

"I made some food. Or plated it, I guess." She smiles when she sees the plate of cheese and snacks. "I have some water boiling for tea."

"How do you know I'm not a coffee person?"

"I don't," I tell her, even though I do know because she posted a picture on Instagram of her drinking tea and reading a book. The caption read *Coffee or Tea? I like tea...* But I don't tell Zoe that part. "You seem like the type to drink tea, though."

Her lips press together, but they curl up at the corners as she tries to suppress her smile. "Am I right?" I lift an eyebrow as I question her. I know I'm right, but I want to hear her say it. I take two steps toward her, until I'm in her space again. "You can tell me, kitten," I breathe out.

Her beautiful gray eyes peer up at me through thick lashes. "You're right."

Right as the words leave her mouth, the tea kettle begins to hiss. I want to kiss her, to lean in and press my lips to hers. I haven't kissed her since I came to her house and found her bruised and broken. She's still bruised, and her ego is sore, but she's better now.

I spin around instead, heading for the kettle and making our tea.

"I never answered your question earlier..." Zoe's voice sounds from behind me.

"Yeah?" I pour the water into the two mugs, soaking the bags. Grabbing the mugs, I head back into the dining room. My eyebrow lifts, and my cock immediately begins to harden.

"You asked if I would wear a collar..." Her cheeks flush a pretty shade of pink as she trails off, too embarrassed to finish the question.

I set the mugs on the table, moving back over to her and placing each of my hands on her shoulders to anchor her. "Only if you want to, kitten." She tugs her bottom lip back between her teeth. With as much as she chews on it, I'm surprised it's not bright red and bleeding.

"Is that what you like-"

I lean forward, licking along the seam of her lips until she releases the bottom one, and then I kiss her. Gentle at first, and she responds, opening herself up for me as her hands rise to grip onto my shirt. My arms wrap around her body, pulling her closer to me while my mouth devours hers.

When I pull back, she's flushed with the pink color, her eyes are hazy, and her lips swollen. "I'd love to see you in a collar, Zoe, but I'll take whatever you're willing to give and nothing more."

She smiles slowly, looking timid, but I see arousal in the way she stares up at me. "I think I'd like it," she says.

"Fuck," I growl. "Tomorrow, then. Tomorrow, I'll go out and get you one."

"And tonight?" she asks, her eyes looking sinfully sweet.

"Tonight," I grin. "Tonight, we'll make do without one." My cock is already hard, straining against the zipper of my pants. I want nothing more than to bend her over the dining room table and fuck her until her throat is dry from screaming my name, but I don't want this to be quick. I want to take my time with her. "I want you to tell me what you like, kitten, and what you don't like. Do you understand?"

I can feel her body shudder. She likes when I tell her what to do, when I'm in charge. "Sit on the table."

She smiles shyly as she does what I say, sliding her ass onto my dining room table. "Take these off," I order, grabbing at the hem of her sleep shorts.

"Panties too?" she asks. When I nod my head, she wiggles the material out from under her butt, and I slide them down her legs.

"Good girl," I tell her. She glows under my praise, her eyes glued to me as I place a hand on each of her hips, wiggling them under her ass so I can tug her forward to me. "I'm going to have my dinner now, kitten, so I want you to be very good girl while I eat. Can you do that?"

I can feel her pulse race beneath my touch, and the seam of her lips pops open just slightly. "Yes," she breathes, and I love the sound, so soft and filled with need. I drop to my knees before her and part her thighs with the palms of my hands.

I like seeing her like this, spread bare and glistening in front of me. Zoe gasps as soon as my mouth touches her. I'm not even to her sex yet, just laying soft kisses along her thighs, but she's already heated up for me. She responds to my every touch, and when I finally lick her from bottom to top, she moans as she presses her pussy against my face.

My arms wrap around her bottom, gripping into her as I lick

her again. My tongue finds her clit, rubbing wet circles around the swollen nerve. She's grinding her hips now, arching her back.

"Fuck," she moans, and it has me smiling against her sex. I love hearing her sounds, the breathy whimpers that escape her lips as I continue to eat her out. I bring my finger to her pussy, swirling the digit through her wetness before pushing inside of her. She grinds against it, searching for friction. I add a second finger, pumping the two in and out while I suck on her clit. When I curl them just slightly against the walls of her pussy, she screams out for me.

I don't stop. I continue to move my fingers at a vicious pace while I make quick circles with my tongue on her clit. Her fingers grip into my hair, tugging on the dark locks while she screams out for God.

I want to tell her that he doesn't exist here. That she won't find salvation or Heaven. She'll just find me on my knees, worshipping her.

She falls back onto the table when I pull away, her breath coming out in quick pants. "That was… incredible."

"I'm not done yet," I tell her, watching her eyes as I bring her fingers to my lips, sucking them clean of her juices. She props up on her elbows, eyes darkening as she watches me stand up, licking the taste of her from my lips.

I undo my belt buckle slowly, drawing it out for her while she catches her breath. I strip myself for her, palming my cock as I line it up with her pussy.

"You were such a good girl for me," I tell her, watching her eyes light up. "Now, what do you say after someone makes you come?"

Her tongue darts across her lip, and her eyes lower to where my cock is, watching me as I slide the tip over her slit, wetting it with her and eliciting a whimper to escape from her lips. "Thank you," she breathes.

"Good girl." I reach out, rubbing my thumb over her cheek while I hold her face. She closes her eyes for a quick moment, embracing the show of affection. "I'm going to fuck you now, baby girl."

"Yes, please."

We gasp simultaneously as my cock slides into her soaking wet cunt. She contracts around me, and I pause for a moment, letting both of us get accustomed.

"Fuck me, daddy," she moans, and it's all I need to hear to continue. I pump into her, relishing in the feeling of her wet heat.

"You're fucking amazing, kitten, do you know that?" She smiles beneath me, her hand wrapped around me, pulling me farther into her. "Such a good girl," I praise her, and she rocks her hips faster, her pussy clenching on my cock. She's so fucking close, and I want to see her come as I spill myself inside of her.

I bring my thumb down to where we're connected, dragging it through her juices and up to her clit. She whimpers when I touch it; she's over sensitized and her legs are trembling as I draw quick circles over the tender nerve.

"You've been so good for me, kitten," I tell her. "I want you to come one more time with me. Can you do that, baby?" I flick my thumb over her clit, and she moans out for me.

"Yes, please, daddy." The words are breathy whimpers, and then she coming, her pussy contracting on my dick, and that's all I need to come undone, shooting my release into her.

My hands find either side of her, and I lean down, peppering her with kisses as we both catch our breath.

She mewls a response, her body weak beneath me. I pull out of her and lift her into my arms before I bring her back upstairs. Then I clean her up, slide her pajama shorts back onto her, and tuck her into bed with me.

"You're amazing, baby girl," I tell her.

I sleep through the night without waking up once. The best night's sleep I've had in years, and when I wake up in the morning to find her warm body tucked against my chest, her hair sprawled out on the pillow, I can't imagine ever waking up alone again.

I am thoroughly fucking addicted to this woman.

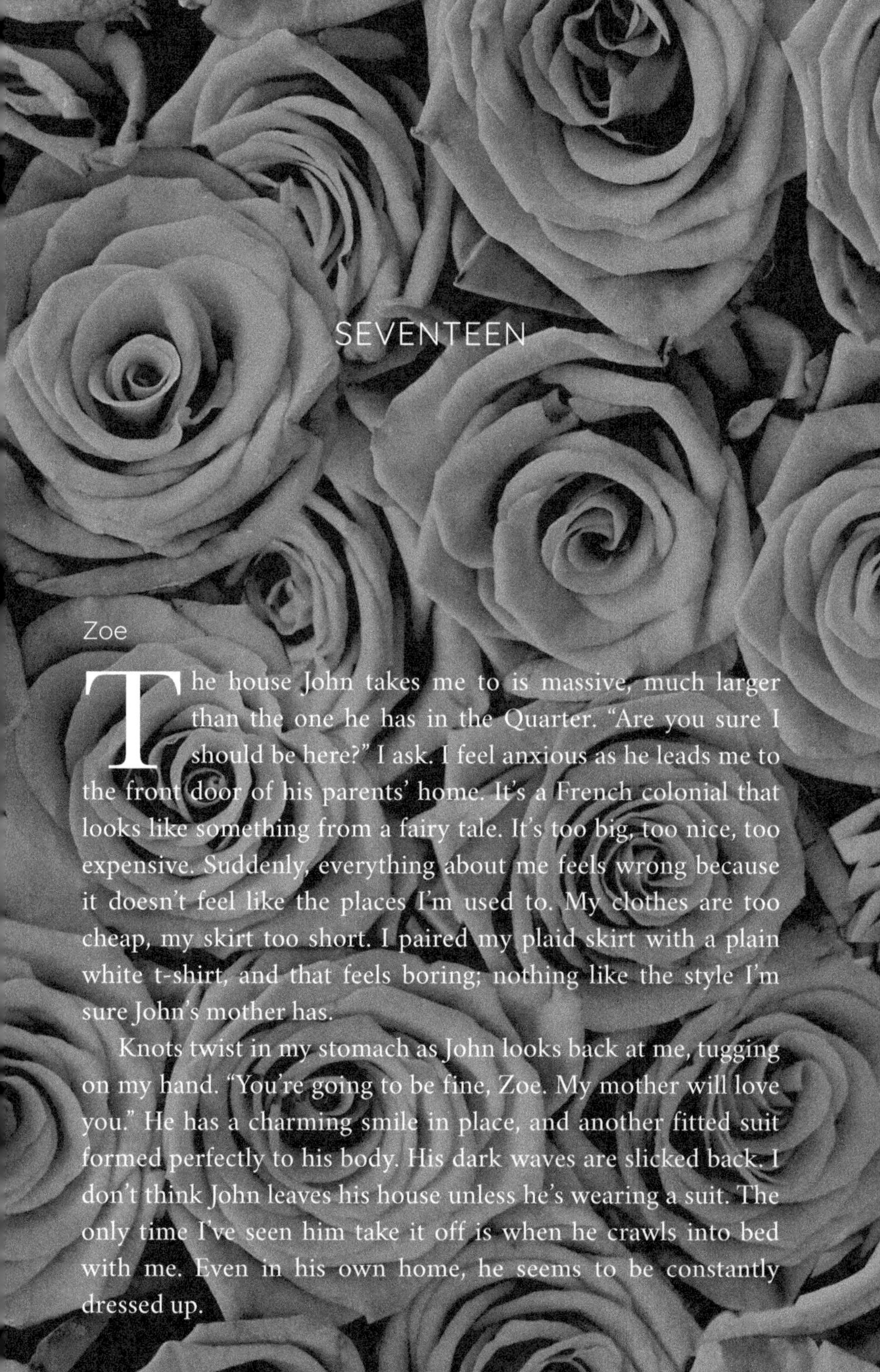

SEVENTEEN

Zoe

The house John takes me to is massive, much larger than the one he has in the Quarter. "Are you sure I should be here?" I ask. I feel anxious as he leads me to the front door of his parents' home. It's a French colonial that looks like something from a fairy tale. It's too big, too nice, too expensive. Suddenly, everything about me feels wrong because it doesn't feel like the places I'm used to. My clothes are too cheap, my skirt too short. I paired my plaid skirt with a plain white t-shirt, and that feels boring; nothing like the style I'm sure John's mother has.

Knots twist in my stomach as John looks back at me, tugging on my hand. "You're going to be fine, Zoe. My mother will love you." He has a charming smile in place, and another fitted suit formed perfectly to his body. His dark waves are slicked back. I don't think John leaves his house unless he's wearing a suit. The only time I've seen him take it off is when he crawls into bed with me. Even in his own home, he seems to be constantly dressed up.

I don't even know why John is taking me to his parents. He gave me bits and pieces of his plan. He wants to sell this as a relationship, something more significant than a stripper he's fucking. If his parents are involved, that should keep Marcus from hurting me and give me more credit to make Marcus believe what I tell him.

That doesn't ease my fears much. What if my closer connection to John makes Marcus more interested in me? But when I expressed my fears to John, he covered me in kisses and made me promise to trust him as he licked my pussy. He was manipulating me with sex, but it was too good. He was too good, more giving than any man has ever been with me. Not that I have a long list to compare him to.

"Johnny," a woman, I'm assuming his mother, coos as she lets us into her home. John told me Sunday dinners are a tradition, and that they used to be held at his grandfather's house, but since his death, they haven't had a larger family gathering.

It's sad, I think, that one death could tear apart a family like this. How do you go from seeing each other weekly to not at all? I didn't press, though. Every time John gives me a bit of information, he expects something in return. He knows I'm keeping a secret from him, but I'm not ready to tell him about Cassie.

Maybe that's stupid of me, maybe he could help me. Or maybe he'll know I'm there to spy on his family, and he'll save Marcus the pain of killing me and do it himself.

A shudder runs down my spine. I don't know if I can trust John.

"Who's this?" the woman asks. She has a charming smile and dark hair that's twisted into a knot at the back of her head. She wears a deep plum lipstick that looks elegant paired with her black dress slacks and silk top. Heels tap against the marble tile, and I think she looks overdressed in her own home, but I wonder if that's where John gets his sense of style from.

"Zoe." I try to smile, curving my features upward, but I'm too anxious today. Too worried that she'll see through me the same way her son does.

"Cosetta." She ignores the hand I extend and goes in for a hug. "Thank you for joining us. I wish I could say my son has told me all about you but..." she trails off as she pulls back, giving John a disapproving look.

"Sorry, Ma." The corner of his lips quirks up into a sheepish smile. It's enough to make her smile before she turns back to me.

"Come on in, Zoe. John's father is just finishing up some work before we sit down for dinner."

The Vitale home is stunning, with dark hardwoods covering the floors, and the walls are painted a creamy beige. There are French accents everywhere, and the furniture feels old but looks new. There's an antique chaise lounge in the living room that I can see myself curled up in, reading a book and drinking tea.

"Your home is beautiful." I can't help how childlike I sound as I compliment the house.

Cosetta smiles graciously. "You're too kind, Zoe. John, why don't you go get your father and Zoe can help me set the table."

John gives me a reassuring look and a squeeze on my shoulder before he leaves me alone with his mother. She leads me into the kitchen, grabbing a set of potholders and opening the oven. The room smells delicious, and she pulls out a bubbling tray of baked pasta that has my mouth watering.

"Ziti," she tells me. "Johnny's favorite."

Cosetta sets the glass dish on the stovetop and moves to the fridge, grabbing a block of parmesan cheese and a bottle of wine.

"So, Zoe, how did you meet my son?" she asks the question innocently, but it feels like her eyes are shooting daggers at me.

My heart thrums rapidly in my chest, and I chew on my bottom lip, avoiding answering her question. "At a club," I finally tell her, leaving out the part that it was a strip club and that her son took me to a private room.

Cosetta laughs. "John? At a club?"

John always seemed out of place at Saints and Sinners, but not enough for me to laugh the way his mother is. "Yeah." I smile. "I'm a… waitress, and he showed up in my section."

"Hmm," she muses, her laughter dying away. "He charmed you, I assume?"

"Something like that." I smooth my hands over my skirt in an attempt to keep myself from picking at my fingers, my bad habit.

Cosetta sets down the things she grabbed from the fridge and walks back over to me, leaning her hip against the kitchen counter. "You seem like a nice girl, Zoe." Her voice changes when she talks to me this time; it's deeper, more stern. "But here's the thing, I know my son well, and he doesn't do relationships. I'm sure you think you're different, or that this is real, but if you're smart, you'll walk away."

Her dark eyes stare at me, waiting for confirmation that I heard her, but I'm still shocked. Is she telling me not to be with John? Is she warning me away from her own son?

"Wh-why?" I stutter over the word, and Cosetta gives me a pitiful look.

"He'll only hurt you. He can't help it. It's in his DNA." She spins away from me, moving on as if she didn't just tell me to break up with her son. "Grab the parmesan, won't you?" She ends the conversation, lifting up the tray of baked ziti and taking it to the dining room.

I'm still reeling from her warning when John and his father enter the formal dining room. "Zoe, this is my dad, James."

James Vitale is an older version of John, with salt and pepper hair and a strong jawline. He's not in a suit, instead wearing a pair of black slacks and button-down shirt with the sleeves rolled up. He extends a hand for me to shake. "Nice to meet you, Zoe." He smiles, but it doesn't reach his eyes.

I wonder if he's genuinely excited to meet me or if he feels the same way as his wife. If he's just entertaining me, knowing I'm nothing but a passerby in this life they've built.

Maybe it's better that way. I'm not meant for the life John comes from. He's purebred, rich and powerful. I'm NOLA garbage, meant to stay in the Seventh Ward.

John wraps an arm around the back of my chair when we sit down, and I see his mother's eyes linger where our skin connects. I feel hot under her eyes, like every inch of me is being scrutinized.

"So, Zoe." James nods in my direction as he piles a serving of ziti onto his plate. "I hear Johnny took you out on our boat, hmm? How'd you like it?"

My body freezes, my mind reeling. What on earth is he talking about? John and I barely know each other. I've only been in his house for seven days. He's never taken me on a boat. I didn't even know they had a family boat.

James sees the confusion on my face and starts to say something, but then an angry look grows on his face, and his eyes dart over to John at my side. Cosetta purses her lips and folds her napkin onto her lap. For a moment, her eyes clash with mine. It feels like she's secretly saying *I told you so*. She wants me to break up my fake relationship with her son.

He's a liar too.

But I knew that. On some level, part of me knew that he was a liar. How else do you live with a family like his? But he lies to them too.

I imagine John lived in two different worlds, one where he was a law-abiding citizen and one where he was mafia royalty. But for him, it's more than that. He presents a different face to every person he interacts with.

He lies, manipulates the truth.

"John." His father slumps back into his seat with a scowl. "What a stupid thing to lie about."

It's an overreaction to a silly lie. But the looks on their faces tell me this is an ongoing problem.

"We didn't go on the boat, dad. That's not what I told you." Slowly, John unravels his silverware and spreads his napkin across his lap. He gives his father a coy expression. "I said I was going to, next weekend. Should you get checked for Alzheimer's, hmm?" John lifts his eyebrow in question, bringing a bite of food to his lips, all while maintaining eye contact with his father.

James seethes from across the table, clearly unamused by John's response. "I'm sure you will, son," he says tightly. "Make sure he takes you, Zoe," he adds. "Don't let him make a liar out of himself."

I try to pull my lips up into a smile as I nod at James, agreeably. I don't really care if John takes me on this boat or not. I'm more interested in why he told his parents he did, or would. Why lie to them? And if he is a liar, what other secrets is he keeping from me?

EIGHTEEN

Zoe

I go back to work on a Tuesday, thankful to be away from John for a moment. Ever since dinner with his family, I've felt suffocated by his presence. Even when he gives me space, he's still there. His scent lingers on every piece of fabric in the house. Everything feels like him. Even my favorite spot, his library, is overtaken by him. I imagine John holding each and every book, wondering what he thought when he read each line. I can't even escape into my own head; he's even taken over that.

He's a liar. He proved that at his parents' house. But he's helping me… or trying to. I can't tell if I'm living in a killer's house, or if I'm being a brat to the man who's just trying to be nice.

And he is nice. He's spent too much time pressed between my thighs while I tell him what I like and what I don't. Before him, the last time I had sex, I was too drunk to enjoy it, even if it was good. But I feel everything with John, every touch, every kiss. Everything he does is sensual.

Which is what's making me crazy in his house. I need to take a breath, get sober for a minute. I can't get wrapped up in… whatever John is.

His mother's warning rings through my head. *I know my son well, and he doesn't do relationships. I'm sure you think you're different, or that this is real, but if you're smart, you'll walk away.*

I should walk away. I should wrap it up and get out of this whole thing before it gets any worse.

But there's still that alarm ringing at the back of my head. The one shouting that Cassie is still out there, and no one is looking for her.

I've been taking it too slow, trying to get my feel of the landscape before I start searching for information, but it's been long enough. I need to find my best friend.

Based on the operations of the Costello family, my guess is this club isn't run that clean. So the financial records are probably all garbage, but there has to be something for employees. Maybe Donnie is a better manager than I give him credit for. If he has a file on Cassie, he might have notes on her, might have some record of what happened the last day she worked, the last day she was seen.

I slip into my outfit for the night first. Daisy's healed, and her bruises have lightened to the faintest yellow she covers with makeup. I still look for them, my mind replacing her with Cassie. Is this an ongoing thing? Marcus using the girls and then beating them up when they don't bring him what he wants?

Am I not the only one he's hurt?

Once I'm dressed, I make my way down the hall, trying not to draw attention to myself. I knock on Donnie's office door first, and when he doesn't answer, I crack the door open. It's empty.

I don't know how much time I have, or how long Donnie will be out for. I go for his file cabinets first, flipping through the tabs of the manilla envelopes. Then I find one cabinet with the names of girls. Each one has the paper application we filled out, sparse with any notes save a red yes or no. I go through the drawer twice, but I don't see one for Cassie. I find my own, and even Daisy's, but no Cassie Stephens.

I go through the rest of the cabinets quickly, looking for anything that stands out. Invoices, receipts, nothing else on the dancers, though.

"Hey." I hear a rough voice behind me right as I slide one of the drawers closed. Robby is looking at me from the doorway, arms crossed over his chest. "What the fuck are you doing in here?"

"Nothing," I squeak, mentally scolding myself for the ass backward plan. "I was waiting for Donnie."

"Why?"

"Just needed to talk to him." I smile and pull my arms behind my back, pushing my tits forward. Robby doesn't look convinced, his eyes narrowing while he assesses me.

"I can come back later," I say, making my way toward him. I place a hand on his shoulder as I go past him in the doorway. "It can wait." I make sure to smile, to brush my body against his.

"You have a job," he growls at me. "Private dance."

I direct my gaze to him, surprised someone specifically asked for me.

"John Vitale called," he adds as I look at him, confused. "Says he wants you in room A for the night. Spent a lot of money on your ass. I don't know what you did to hook him, Kitty Kat, but I hope you know what you got yourself into. Vitale's a psychopath," he sneers. "Better watch your back before he bleeds you out."

NINETEEN

John

I'm not surprised when I get a call from Detective Ellison asking me to meet him at the station. It's been almost three months since my uncle died, and he hasn't interviewed me since that day.

I was the first one to see him, watched as he sucked in his final gasp of air. And the lead detective on his murder investigation has barely spoken to me.

Honestly, I wouldn't have told him more than I did the day I met him. Ellison had one of his uniforms drag me outside where he met me later, tugging the blue booties from his shoes and stripping the gloves from his hands. He spent ten minutes talking to me.

Why are you here? When did you get here? Did you see who killed your uncle?

He didn't ask much more after that. When he offered me his business card, I declined; you don't talk to cops. Even the ones we have on our payroll, we ignore. But even if the cops know they're going to get nothing out of us, they still waste our time with questions and interviews, even trips to the station. Not Ellison, though. He moved right along. He doesn't care what my answers are because he has no intentions of solving my uncle's case.

Not that I would help him if he did.

I just want Ellison to investigate my uncle's case so I can be sure he's a clean cop. So far, he's my best lead on who framed Sam. Ellison was there when the cops found the gun. A Smith and Wesson with Sam's fingerprints. It doesn't belong to Sam, but it's hard to prove who owns an unregistered weapon, let alone convince a judge that someone stole your fingerprints. Add in the fact that you're a known mafioso, no one's going to believe you.

All the trouble someone went through to kill one man and frame the other had to be worth it, and the person to gain the most from the situation is Marcus.

"John." My phone rings as soon as I step out of the station. Something about the place makes me feel irritable, even though the interaction was actually very insightful. Ellison hasn't found anything on who actually killed Junior, which would be fine with me if someone hadn't framed Sam.

Before I can kill him, I need to know that Marcus hired someone to kill Junior. Even in his death, Junior's rules plague me. *You need proof*, he'd told me, *be sure they're a threat before you take them out.*

I don't know why Junior put a leash on me. God knows he had his own list of lives he took. He was the only one in my family that never uttered the word psychopath, but even without saying it, I could tell he knew. Sam didn't need Junior's permission to kill someone, and neither did Marcus.

"She left, John." Robby sounds nervous when he updates me. It's not my fault that stories have been passed around. It amuses me when soldiers are scared of me. I wonder which stories they've heard.

I had asked the bouncer to put Zoe in a private room for me. She wanted to go to work, and I didn't want anyone to see her, so a private room seemed like a fair compromise. I'm not surprised she left, though, once she realized I wasn't there. She's a spitfire; no chance in hell she'll wait around for me.

I don't say anything else to him, just hang up and call Roman. There aren't many men I trust since Sam was imprisoned. I can't be sure who worked with Marcus to incriminate my cousin or who might be reporting back to him, so I don't give anyone anything that could be used against me. Roman, however, was someone Sam explicitly told me to trust, so before Zoe left for work, I asked him to watch her.

"She's home, boss," he says as soon as he answers the phone.

"Her home?"

"Yours." He chuckles. "Arnold let her in."

I can hear her giggle in the background. "Are you inside with her?"

"You told me to watch her?" His voice irritates me, or maybe it's his answer. Either way, I can't stand the idea of him inside my house with her. I told him to watch her, not hang out with her.

Fuck.

I'm thankful I drove the Porsche to the station; it will take me less time to get home with this car. I'm cloudy with rage by the time I pull through the gate and get to the back door.

I see her through the glass before I even reach the door. She doesn't have pants on, just another oversized t-shirt, and I can't even see shorts peeking from beneath the thing. My blood boils. She's in my house with another man, not wearing pants?

My fingers itch at my sides. I want to strangle Roman for being inside with her. But I can't. Not yet. Not unless I know he encouraged this charade.

"You should leave," I tell Roman as soon as I swing open the French doors. He looks surprised to see the anger on my face, probably not understanding why I was asking him to babysit a stripper.

"Boss." He nods his head at me as he moves from the wall he was leaning against. He wasn't even near her; he was leaning on the far wall by the door.

I scrub a hand over my face. She's making me stupid. "What are you doing?" My voice comes out low and harsh, as she has me frustrated with myself. I need to stay in control, but all I want to do is bend her over the table and spank her ass.

"Settling into my new home since you demanded I stay here." She gives me a teasing smile, holding a bright red popsicle, something I didn't even know Arnold stocked in the freezer. The t-shirt is one of mine, another thing that makes my dick stir in my pants. She brings the popsicle to her lips, running her tongue over the surface.

She's teasing me, testing out the waters to see how I'll react.

So, my kitten's a little bit bratty, hmm?

"Kitten," I purr, slowly tugging my arms free of my suit jacket. I lay it over the back of one of the dining room chairs. "Are you trying to be punished?"

"No." Her eyes lift, and she sucks on the tip of her popsicle. "What did I even do wrong?" She flutters her lashes, looking innocent, but she knows damn well what she did.

"You weren't supposed to leave the club," I tell her. My jaw ticks as I take my time loosening my cufflinks and dropping them onto the table. Zoe is looking up at me through hooded lids.

"You weren't even there." She's on the other side of the table from me, sucking the popsicle between her lips. She's doing it too sensually, trying to make me imagine what it will feel like when it's my cock between her lips instead.

"It's too bad." I make a tsking sound as I finish rolling up the sleeves of my shirt, her eyes glued to my forearms. "I bought you a present,"

Her eyes widen, surprise coating her features. "You did?"

"Do you think you deserve it?" I ask as I tug the leather collar from my pocket. I picked it up today, black with rose gold fastenings. It's sleek and pretty, like her.

Zoe nods her head, a small smile rising on her features. I walk around the table agonizingly slow, her silver eyes following my every move. I yank the popsicle from her fingertips as soon as I reach her, swinging my arm out and sending it flying across the room until it shatters against the wall in a flurry of red ice.

She jumps, but then her eyes land back on me.

"That wasn't nice," she remarks.

"You know what isn't nice, kitten?" I lift an eyebrow, but don't wait for her response. "Not listening to me. I booked a room for you at the club, but you came back here. Why's that?"

Her gaze floats between me and the collar that I'm holding. She darts her tongue across her lips.

"You want your present?"

She smiles. "Yes, daddy."

"Then answer my question."

"You weren't there, and I didn't want to wait…" She looks up at me through her thick lashes, looking cute and naïve like this. But she's not; beneath her charm, she's hardened from two decades of wounds.

I hold up the collar for her to see. There's a rose gold lock in the shape of a heart, and I flip it over to show the engraving on the back.

Kitten.

"You're mine, you know that?" I ask her as I bring the leather around her throat. She doesn't respond, but I watch as her lips curve upward, still coated with red lipstick. Her makeup is perfectly intact, probably because she didn't dance at all tonight.

She doesn't stop me as I bring the leather to her throat,

fastening the lock and snapping it shut. I make a show of dangling the keys in front of her eyes before I pocket them.

"What's your safe word, kitten?"

She thinks for a long moment before she answers me. "Roses." She laughs like she told a funny joke.

"Why roses?" I ask, leaning in as I ghost my breath over her cheek.

"Because," she pauses to lick her lips, "that's the stage we skipped. You're supposed to buy a girl flowers before you spank her, don't you know?"

"Bend over," I tell her. She's still grinning, fully aware that she's pushing me. "Do you want to be punished, kitten?" I ask her. My fingers are begging to touch her, but I won't, not until she tells me to.

"Yes," she breathes, looking happy that her bratty plan worked.

She turns away from me, going to the table and bending over the wooden surface. Her fingers grip onto the edge as she puts her ass on display for me. She has on panties, a pair of cotton briefs. I'm thrilled to see them in comparison to the lacy things she wears at the club. Roman might be one of the few guys who hasn't seen much of her.

I wish I could burn her image from all of their minds. They don't deserve to see her. Not like I do.

I feel overly possessive of her. I don't want anyone to have her in the ways I have. From the second she walked into the VIP room, she belonged to me. My fingers slip under the band of her panties, dragging the black fabric down her legs. Her pussy is bare to me, bent over and glistening on my table. I want to feast on her, but not until she's punished.

"I'm going to spank you, and I want you to count for me, kitten," I tell her, and my hand reaches out, my fingertips dragging along her cheek. "Can you do that?" She was looking for a punishment the second she left the private room I booked at Saints and Sinners. She chose not to listen to me.

The way she looks back at me over her shoulder, a grin spread wide on her lips, tells me that she wanted this. She wants to know what will happen if she pushes me. It's a play fight, really, because she's the winner at the end of this. She'll get her punishment, and I'll still make her come repeatedly.

"Yes, daddy." She tugs her bottom lip between her teeth, purposefully driving me insane.

I would have never asked her to call me that, but something about the word, the way she says it, sparks a fire in my chest. She knows it does something to me, that I'll praise her for it. Worship her body while I tell her what a good girl she is.

She wants this as much as I do,

The first smack lands, and she jumps a bit.

"One," she squeaks.

I smooth my hand over her reddened flesh. I want to see my handprint on her ass cheek, want to see her skin bloom red for me... I won't push her that far tonight, though.

I land the next smack on the opposite cheek. "Two." Her voice is already breathy.

"Three!" she yelps when I bring the next two down in the same spot. "Four!"

"Last one," I tell her. She's clenching her thighs together, and I can't wait to dip my finger between them and see how wet she is from me spanking her. The smack lands on the first cheek, and she gasps before hissing out, "Five".

"Good girl," I praise her, smoothing my hand over her ass to soothe the sting. "I'm so proud of you." I lean my body over hers, pressing a kiss to the crook of her neck and up her to her cheek. She curls into my touch. "You did such a good job." I help her spin onto her back and nudge my legs between hers, spreading her open.

Eyes filled with desire are glued to me as I drop to my knees between her thighs. She sucks in a breath when my tongue meets her pussy lips. She soaked for me, drenched from getting her bratty ass spanked.

"You liked that, didn't you?" I ask, pulling my mouth back from her pussy. "Were you bad just because you wanted daddy to punish you?" I laugh, my breath blowing over her bare sex. "All you had to do was ask, kitten."

Dragging my tongue back through her slit, I swirl it over her swollen clit. She moans as I bring my fingers to her entrance, dragging them through her juices before pushing into her.

I pump my finger faster as I suck the bundle of nerves. I wait until she's panting, grinding her pussy against my face, seconds away from coming, and then I pull away from her. The sound that leaves her lips is carnal, desperate. I stand slowly as she pants out curse words, her eyes glaring up at me.

I bring my hands to either side of her, leaning over her body and bringing my lips to her ear. "You act like a brat, you get punished like one."

I pull back again to look at her, the scowl on her face making me grin madly. "Say you're sorry, baby."

She sits up, having to tilt her head to see me. "Sorry, daddy," she whispers, fisting her hands against my dress shirt and tugging me toward her. "I won't do it again."

"I know you won't." I kiss the top of her head. "Now go upstairs and get on the bed so I can fuck you."

TWENTY

Zoe

There's a mix of emotions rushing through my head. My body is betraying me, as it aches for John's touch. I find myself rushing up the stairs, the hem of my t-shirt rising up my bare ass. John is following behind me. I pull the sweatshirt over my head when I get to the top of the stairs. Something about seeing him fully dressed while I'm naked in front of him sends a shock wave to my core.

The power here is off balance. It doesn't matter that I'm the one who's mad, that I'm the one who wants to fight.

John is in control.

John is always in control.

I watch the corner of his mouth rise in a lop-sided smirk as he moves toward me. He stops at his dresser first, then he thumbs a lighter, letting fire flicker to life while he lights the few candles around the room. The metal taps against the wood as he drops it and spins to meet my gaze.

"I said on the bed." His voice is deep, commanding, and I'm forgetting why I was ever mad at him in the first place.

Maybe he is a psychopath. Everything the man does is methodical, perfectly executed. He doesn't even fuck me with unchecked passion. He spanked me with such precision, giving only as much as he knew I could take.

And he's good, I can't deny that.

He reaches into a part of me I didn't know was there. I want to please him. Want to hear him call me a good girl. My brain forgets to work when he's near, turning me stupid for the man.

Maybe this is why people are afraid of the Costello family. They're more than just gangsters; they're manipulative.

The lopsided smirk is still there when he reaches me.

"You're not very good at listening tonight, hmm?" Excitement swirls in his gaze.

If he is a psychopath, like Robby implied, I shouldn't push him. I should just let him fuck me gently while he whispers sweet praises.

But for some reason, I do want to push him. I want to know what he'll do when I tease him. And then I want to know what he'll do when I say *roses*.

"I haven't been, no," I agree, lacing my fingers together behind my back.

"My pretty little slut," he praises, his hand coming to my throat as he traces the line where the collar touches my skin.

He's moving too slow. It's an agonizing pace. I want him to move faster, want to feel his mouth on me again. I need to feel him inside of me. I'm too wound up, too turned on to think straight. He's toying with me, a game of tug-of-war playing out between us.

Slowly, he brings his lips to my ear. "If you wanted me to fuck you, kitten, all you had to do was ask," he whispers. The words send a rush of heat to my pussy.

"Fuck me, John." He looks happy at that statement.

"I will, but you're going to suck my cock first. Can you do that, baby?"

I drop to my knees too eagerly, or maybe I'm just eager for him to finish what he started and make me come again. I start with his balls, swirling my tongue over them while his fingers fist into my hair.

The goal is to make him as needy as I am, as desperate and unhinged.

My tongue trails up the length of his cock, traveling over his head before I go back to the base and start my teasing over. Swirling my tongue over his balls and up to his tip.

"You've made your point," he growls, tugging on my hair to lift my head back to the top of his dick. He doesn't push me down, but the implication is enough. I swallow him into my mouth, listening to him groan above me.

"Fuck," growls.

I keep moving up and down on his cock, my tongue running over the underside. He's vocal about his appreciation, telling me repeatedly what a good job I'm doing. The praise makes me work harder, wanting more like an addict, except I'm addicted to his praise. I take him in the back of my throat, letting it rest there for a moment before I try to swallow.

"Jesus," he moans, his fingers tugging on my hair. The moans that come from his lips tell me I'm doing a good job, and I smile around his cock, proud of myself for making him as needy as he's made me.

"Stop," he tells me, "I don't want to come in your mouth."

He's close, I can feel it, just a few more pumps, and he'll come. I keep going, even as he tugs on my hair to try to pull me off him. I grip my hands around the back of his thighs and keep moving.

I'm not wrong. In a few pumps, he explodes, spilling his cum down the back of my throat. It drips out of the corner of my mouth, and I lick my lips, getting every last drop. Lust fills his eyes as he watches me, panting as I lick the cum from his cock and flash him my winner's smile.

"You think that's gonna stop me from fucking you, babe?"

I hoped it wouldn't. He fits his hands under my armpits, yanking me up and pushing me face down onto the bed. He slaps a hand down on my ass again, making me yelp as he hits the still tender flesh.

He slips his hand between my legs, finding me soaking wet for him. Dragging a finger through my slit before he brings it to my clit and draws slow circles. "You're a brat," he tells me. "But I can tame that out of you." He presses a soft kiss on my shoulder blade. "If you let me."

Abandoning my clit, he slides his finger back to my entrance, thrusting inside me. A whimper leaves me immediately. He adds another finger, fucking me harder until my I'm gripping onto the linen sheets of his bed.

"Do you want to come, kitten?"

"Yes," I pant.

"What do you say?"

"Please, daddy, please, can I come?" I feel unhinged in my need, desperate for his touch, as he swipes his thumb over my clit, and I come undone. Melting around his fingers as my eyesight goes cloudy, and I sink to the mattress.

He leans in close to me, soothing me as he rubs a hand over my back. "Good job, kitten," he coos. "Now I'm going to fuck you."

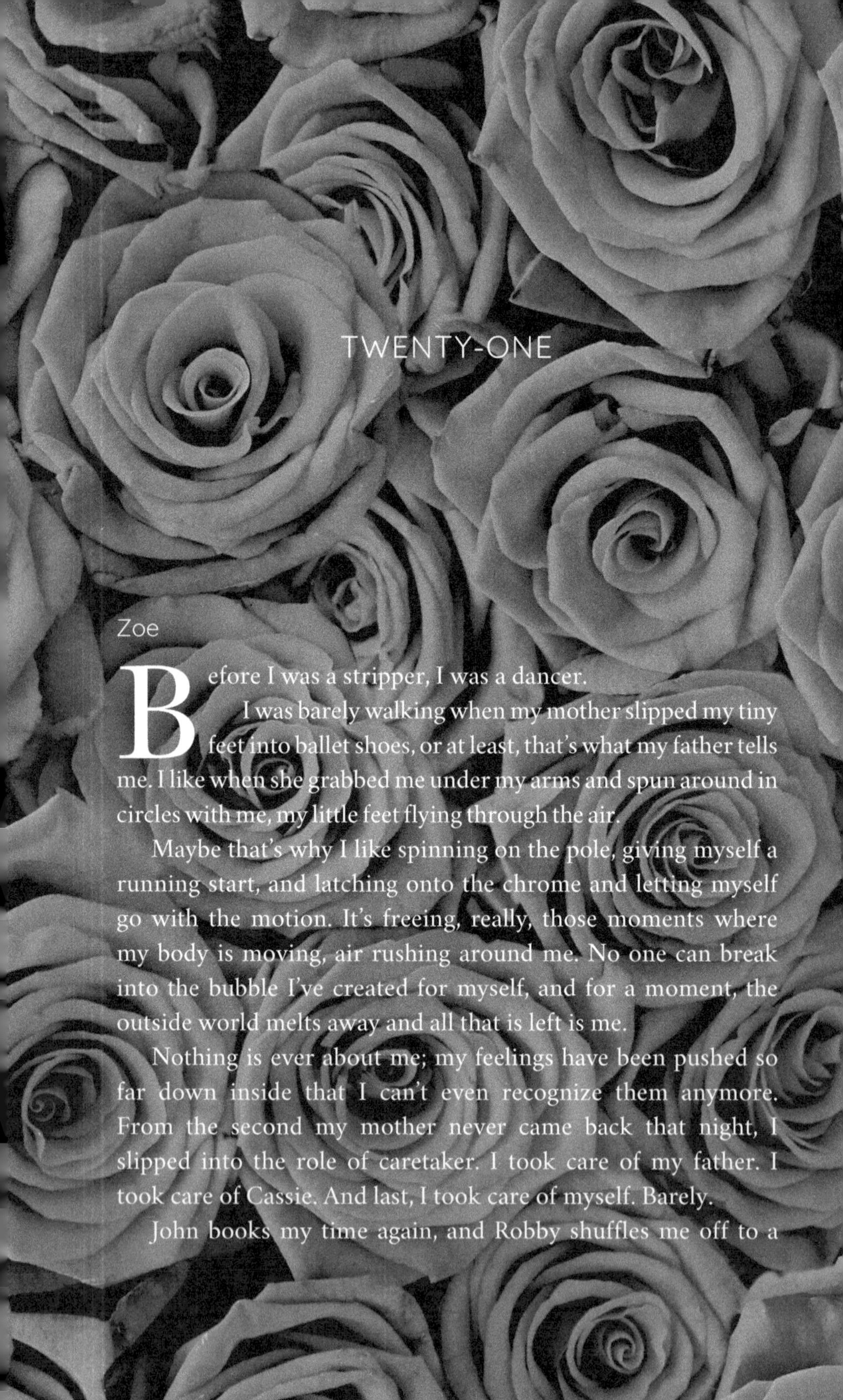

TWENTY-ONE

Zoe

Before I was a stripper, I was a dancer.

I was barely walking when my mother slipped my tiny feet into ballet shoes, or at least, that's what my father tells me. I like when she grabbed me under my arms and spun around in circles with me, my little feet flying through the air.

Maybe that's why I like spinning on the pole, giving myself a running start, and latching onto the chrome and letting myself go with the motion. It's freeing, really, those moments where my body is moving, air rushing around me. No one can break into the bubble I've created for myself, and for a moment, the outside world melts away and all that is left is me.

Nothing is ever about me; my feelings have been pushed so far down inside that I can't even recognize them anymore. From the second my mother never came back that night, I slipped into the role of caretaker. I took care of my father. I took care of Cassie. And last, I took care of myself. Barely.

John books my time again, and Robby shuffles me off to a

private room, one of the nicer ones. I'm not surprised when John isn't there. I'm not mad either, not like the other week when I sat in here waiting for him to show up.

I decide to appreciate the alone time, making a show of dancing for nobody. I do tricks on the pole that I wouldn't do for another. At one point, I link my ankles around the top and let myself hang upside. The only downside is the lack of snacks in here.

I'm hungry. I text John. I see the message flip to *marked as read*, but he doesn't send a response.

"What the fuck did you do to my cousin?" It's Marcus's voice that interrupts my solace. I drop from the pole when he enters, catching me off guard. My ass lands against the tiled floor as he stalks closer, looking down at me.

Robby follows him in, a paper takeout bag in his hand. I can smell it immediately, Chinese food, my favorite. I don't even remember when I told John that.

Marcus is looking at me, expecting an answer. I'm not sure what to tell him. John gave me a list of things to share, the strategic facts he was allowing me to tell his cousin. Part of me was scared to insert myself between these two men. But another part of me was happy I was on John's side.

But without him here, the fear has crept back in. Marcus is large, a tall and muscular man with a bit of a round middle. He has a scowl spread across his face, and his eyes are dark, near black as he looks at me.

"I don't know what you're-" His hand lashes out before the words even leave my lips. His fingers grip around my throat, and I remember what a horrible idea this all was. Why am I even working here? Why did I think this is how I would find Cassie?

My stomach drops, and the only thought running through my head is I need to get out of here. I want to kick and scream, but my body is frozen in place, staring into the dark vortex of Marcus's eyes.

"You better fucking have something for me, girl," he growls.

"I do!" I try to shout the words, but they're muffled between his grip on my throat and the fear coursing through me.

Marcus lets me go, flexing his fingers. "What is it, then?"

"He said something about the charity ball," I sputter. "He has something going on there, I think, some kind of deal?" I rub the skin around my throat, trying to soothe the ache.

My information seems to calm Marcus as he ponders it for a moment. "That better pan out, *slut*," he spits the word at me. It feels dirty when Marcus says it. When John calls me a slut, it's prefaced with praise.

My pretty little slut.

Marcus just makes me feel less than, worthless.

"Why is he paying for five hours' worth of private dances if he's not here?" he asks, his eyebrow ticking up, too much like John's. It's hard to reconcile that the two men share blood.

"He doesn't want anyone else to see me," I mutter. I'd even stopped getting completely ready for the night, knowing that I wasn't performing. My makeup is lighter, I have on booty shorts with a t-shirt over my bra, and my heels are kicked off to the side of the room.

Marcus looks disgusted with me.

"You better hope to God"—he wags a thick finger at me— "that this information pans out. Because if it doesn't, you can kiss this cushy lifestyle goodbye."

Robby gives me a dirty look as he tosses the bag of food onto the bench.

Suddenly, I'm not hungry anymore.

I'm thankful when I find Roman outside after my shift; he has become a new fixture in my life. I find him sitting on the hood of his five-year-old black Audi. "That car is shit." I jab as I slide into the passenger seat.

"You're shit," he spits back with a laugh as he gets in to drive me back to John's house.

"Uh oh," I tease. "Someone's going to get in trouble with their boss now."

Roman shakes his head. "Zoe, you got me in trouble the first night I met you."

I can't help but to smile. My memories of that night are pleasant, even with the spanking included. Unfortunately, Roman was just a prop in my game that night. I think he's used to playing the role of pawn, though, being shuffled around the board at John's demand. Unfortunately, for us, we can't see the board the way he does.

"Did you get your dinner?" he asks as he turns onto the next street. I could walk to John's house from here, as it's only two blocks over from where the club is. But John scowled when I presented the idea. He's become overly protective of me, and I can't tell if it's because of Marcus or if this is just how John is.

"Yeah."

Roman looks disappointed when I don't say much more.

"Was it good at least? He made me sprint over there to fucking fetch it for you." He laughs loudly, turning onto John's street.

"I didn't eat it. I wasn't hungry anymore." I tear at the loose skin on my thumb nail, hoping Roman doesn't ask any more questions.

"Zoe? Did he do something?"

I tug my bottom lip between my teeth. "I'm fine."

Roman's fun-loving attitude dissipates as he walks me inside the French Quarter townhouse. John's there, I can hear him rifling through papers in the library.

"Let me tell him." Roman gives me a sad glance.

"No, I can do it." I haven't even told Roman about Marcus's threats, but I didn't need to for him to know exactly what was going on in my head.

John is sitting at his desk in the library, a tumbler of gin placed neatly on the cork coaster and a stack of papers sitting perfectly straight beside him. He looks up when he sees me, the black framed reading glasses he wears sitting at the bridge of his nose and his dark eyes questioning me immediately.

He has a sixth sense for knowing when something is off.

"What happened?"

"Marcus came to me today."

John stands up before I even have the full story out of my mouth. "Are you alright? Are you hurt?" He moves over to me swiftly, his hands running over my body as if he's checking for injuries.

"No, no." I snatch his hands into mine, pausing their movements. "Nothing like that. I'm fine, I swear."

"Then what's wrong?"

I chew on my bottom lip again, not caring that it's my tell, or that it drives John mad.

"Zoe," he pleads softly. "Tell me what the fuck happened before I start making up scenarios in my head."

"He just threatened me," I mutter. "He said if the information about the charity gala doesn't pan out, then he'll…" I trail off.

"What?" John growls, his anger bubbling over. "Then he'll what?"

"It wasn't anything specific, it was all just vague threats."

"Nothing is vague, Zoe. What the fuck did he say to you?" he's shouting now, and it's making my heart race, my anxiety hammering in my chest.

"That I can *kiss this cushy lifestyle goodbye.*"

John's eyes narrow while he thinks the statement over, then he drops my hands and runs them through his wild dark locks. He mutters to himself, like he's trying to figure out some sort of puzzle.

"What are you even doing at this charity thing?" I ask.

"Nothing." John shrugs. "I just want to see what he'll do with the information."

My stomach twists, knots forming there. There's nothing for Marcus to find, no information for him to gain from this.

What will he do to me when he figures out that John is playing him?

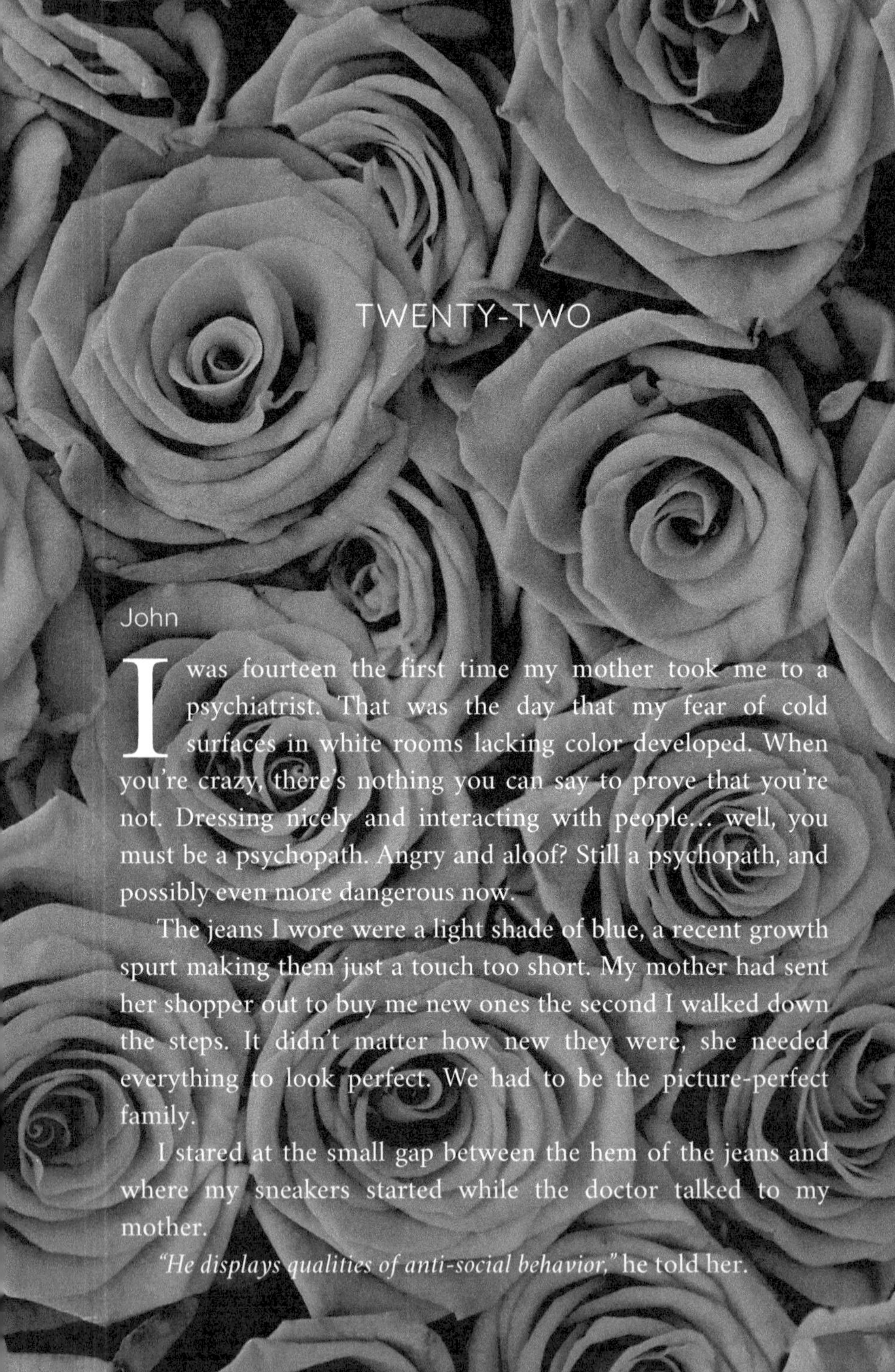

TWENTY-TWO

John

I was fourteen the first time my mother took me to a psychiatrist. That was the day that my fear of cold surfaces in white rooms lacking color developed. When you're crazy, there's nothing you can say to prove that you're not. Dressing nicely and interacting with people... well, you must be a psychopath. Angry and aloof? Still a psychopath, and possibly even more dangerous now.

The jeans I wore were a light shade of blue, a recent growth spurt making them just a touch too short. My mother had sent her shopper out to buy me new ones the second I walked down the steps. It didn't matter how new they were, she needed everything to look perfect. We had to be the picture-perfect family.

I stared at the small gap between the hem of the jeans and where my sneakers started while the doctor talked to my mother.

"He displays qualities of anti-social behavior," he told her.

The features of my mother's face twisted, her lips turning into a frown. *"And,"* she prodded angrily. *"What does that mean?"*

"It means he lacks empathy. He has a grandiose sense of self-worth; he has these ideas..." The doctor looked frustrated. *"That he has unlimited success."*

"So does everyone in this family," I muttered.

"Hush, Johnny," my mother slapped my knee, too hard. It pissed me off, and I clenched my fists at my sides. When I looked up, the doctor was watching me, his eyes focused on the way my fingers curled into fists.

"How do you fix *him?"* my mother asked, because she needed someone to fix me, to change me. I'd become too much for her to bear. Even her nightly wine didn't ease the ache I'd created.

She raised me in a den of lions and was angry that I'd become one.

"What's this?" Zoe breaks me out of my thoughts. She steps into my bedroom, wrapped in a fluffy white towel. The sight of her immediately has my dick hard. Her face is clean and bare, and her dark hair hangs in wet strands. She holds the towel closed, and her eyes are looking at the garment bag laying on the king-sized bed.

"A dress." I rub my hand over my chin. "You're coming with me tonight."

Zoe's steel-gray eyes dance between me and the bag. "To the gala? No." She looks at me like I'm insane. "Your family is going to be there. Marcus is going to be there!"

"So?"

"I- no, John, I'm not going. I don't-"

"You don't what?" I interrupt, taking two long strides over to her. She looks up at me, and her resolve softens when I touch her. She melts against me. "Tell me, Zoe. What do you think you're not?"

"John-"

"No, tell me. You're not pretty enough? Bullshit? Not rich

enough? I don't give a shit. Whatever you're going to say, whatever little lie you believe about yourself, I'll disprove. You're enough, Zoe. You're more than enough. You're stunning and elegant and perfect. *Fucking perfect.*"

Her eyes drop away from me, a feeble attempt to hide the water that's filling them. "You can't just say stuff like that," she whispers.

"Why? 'Cause it's true?"

"You're just… not who I thought you'd be," she whispers the words as her eyes drift up to me slowly.

I'm not who she'd thought I'd be. Not the psychopath that the stories make me out as. But that's just the charm talking, because deep down I am the person people paint me as. I'm just good at hiding it.

"Look at the dress," I tell her, changing the subject from me.

A small smile ticks at the corner of her lips as she goes for the dress bag, unzipping it and exposing the baby blue satin gown. It dips low at the neckline to show a classy amount of cleavage, fitted with an empire waist and a high slit.

"Here." I grab the large black velvet box and hand it to her. She takes it with tentative fingers, holding her towel closed with her armpit while she pulls the case open. Inside is a choker, a simple band of diamonds with a matching pair of earrings. I want to see her wearing it. Even now, as her fingers delicately touch the diamonds, my cock aches to see her with them wrapped around her throat.

"John… this is too much,"

"Don't say that." I wave my hand dismissively. "Nothing is too much for you."

"Please tell me it's fake at least."

I scoff. Does she really think I would buy her fake jewelry? "No, they're not fake."

She drops the necklace, closing the case. "I can't. This is

all..." She waves her hand at the dress, the jewelry, the house. "This is all too much."

It feels like a punch to the gut. I don't want her to feel uncomfortable with the wealth; I want her to own it. I don't think I realized until this moment how badly I wanted to see Zoe in the dress and the diamonds, looking like a queen on my arm.

Money has always mattered to me. I've always wanted more of it, wanted the nicest and most expensive things. Call it psychopathy or a side effect of being a Costello, but either way, I want Zoe covered in the same wealth. I want heads to turn when she walks into the room.

And I want my diamonds wrapped around her throat.

I reach for her, dragging her over until I can press her body into mine. "It's like the collar," I whisper. "You're mine, aren't you, kitten?" I use the tip of my finger to tilt her head up to me, forcing her eyes to look into mine.

"Yes," she whispers, a breathy sound.

"Then be a good girl and wear my collar, hmm?"

***

ZOE LOOKS stunning in the dress I picked, even if she can't see it. She stood in front of the mirror for a while, tugging at the satin and staring at her body. She doesn't see herself the way I do.

"I've seen you dance in front of others with less clothing on and look far less nervous," I whisper as we enter the gala.

"It's not the same." She clings to my arm, her nude heels clicking against the marble tile as we make our way to our table. She's gotten progressively more nervous.

"How?" I ask.

"Those people are strangers, and the club is dark. I barely

even see their faces. This is different…" She scans the room, and I feel her shrink as she does. "These people are judging me."

"So, fuck 'em." I pause before we reach our table, turning to face her. "Who gives a shit what anyone else thinks, kitten. You're here with me. Fuck anyone else."

A small smile tugs at the corner of her lips. "Can't I just fuck you?" she asks coyly.

"Jesus, if you say shit like that, I'll have to bend you over the counter in the bathroom."

She grins. "Don't make promises you can't keep, Vitale."

There are already a few people seated at the table, and my father and Uncle Damien are standing next to each other, speaking in hushed tones. Aunt Caterina and Aunt Carlotta are the polar opposites, sitting next to each other and speaking animatedly. I spot my mother, holding her clutch at her side and schmoozing the mayor's wife. Marcus is the only one missing.

I pull out the seat next to Madi, who's staring at her phone, scrolling through Instagram, for Zoe. "Zoe, this is my cousin, Madi."

Madi's blue hair is tied back elegantly, save the few curls that frame her face. She wears a navy-blue dress a few shades darker than her near turquoise locks. Her gaze flashes up to Zoe and then to me. "Is this your girlfriend?" She looks surprised.

I've never brought a girl home to meet my family. I've never liked one enough to. This thing with Zoe won't last, it can't last. I know this is all just a façade, but there's something that tugs at my chest when my family looks at her. When they see me with her. They don't believe I can love someone. That I can have a family. I lack the empathy they all seem to have.

"He won't be able to control his urges." That's what the doctor had said to my mother that day. I won't be able to have a normal life because I'm not normal. All because some test said so.

"Yes," I mutter roughly. Zoe gives me a look as she takes her seat.

"Nice to meet you, Madi," she says, and the fear she had moments ago slips away and her charm slides into place. She moves in and out of the characters she plays so easily, it makes me wonder if she ever sat in a blank white room. Maybe we're all a bit crazy?

"Mad, can you hang out with Zoe for a sec? I have something I need to do." She gives me a confused look but nods her head anyway.

I leave Zoe there with her and go in search of my cousin. I need to give him something tonight, so he won't come after Zoe. She's supposed to be disposable to me, but the thought of Marcus hurting her makes my chest ache and my fists curl. Somewhere along the line, she crossed over from disposable to indispensable.

I find my cousin with Congressman LaFontaine. That asshole gets on my nerves. I wanted to kill him months ago, before he even laid his hands on my other cousin, Lana. But Junior didn't want to get our hands dirty with the blood of a senator.

Junior didn't want things to be bloody anymore, not like they once were. His anti-violence stance itched at me. He wanted to handle things like men, in fancy offices, over expensive drinks, not like the gangsters of the past.

I wanted to sneak into LaFontaine's mansion and shoot him between the eyes.

Now that Junior's gone, I wish I had. LaFontaine has his eyes set on Madi as I approach. "She'd need to dye her hair," I hear him hiss at Marcus. "And even if I agree, what's to say she wouldn't jump out the window or run away like the other two." His voice is sinister, and the glass in his hand shakes as I approach.

That's the plan, then? Sell off Madi to LaFontaine... anything to make that deal stick?

Marcus wants to start shipping in underage girls through

warehouses, cheap labor to stick in his clubs and sell off like cattle. But he wants LaFontaine's name behind him. They think they're going to be some sort of power couple. And apparently, the Congressman is too stupid to find his own wife, so he needs to arrange an alliance.

"Congressman." I put on my face, dialing up the charm to interact with them. "Good to see you again." I extend my hand, reaching to shake his. "I hear you had a good month, huh? Got your bill passed, is that right?"

His recent bill is for additional Hurricane funds, a deal that seems good on the outside but will put a nice chunk of change in his pocket. He flashes me his signature smile.

They say psychopaths have a superficial charm. I think they should say the same for politicians.

"Johnny," he says, his voice cheerful, as if he doesn't hate my side of the family. There's a line that separates the Costello family right down the middle between the older siblings and the younger ones. My mother has always been loyal to Junior, and therefore, I have, not to mention that the man was more of a father to me than my own. Despite Junior's death, they both know where my loyalty stands; to his son in prison.

This whole encounter is fake. Another charade.

"Business is good as ever." LaFontaine smiles as he tips his glass of amber liquid back, taking a healthy sip.

"John." Marcus doesn't look amused with me. He's wearing a fitted tux, all black with the white shirt peeking out. He casts his glance over at the table where Zoe is sitting next to Madi. "I see you brought your whore with you." He tips his glass in her direction.

My blood shouldn't boil at his comment, but it does. Anger rises inside of me, and my fingers tighten around my fists. Marcus sees my reaction, a smile rising on his lips because of it.

Just like when we were kids.

Marcus always knew how to press my buttons until I

exploded, punching and kicking whoever was closest to me. It always resulted in black eyes, normally on Sam, since he was the one trying to calm me down. And the girls would run. Lana would be the first to break into a fit of tears, pulling at her mother's skirt.

The yelling never helped. My father would scream, but all it did was fuel my anger.

Junior was the one to talk me down, bring me back to earth. Even when we were children, Junior always knew that Marcus was the asshole of the bunch.

"I'll see you later." Marcus taps LaFontaine on the shoulder and gives me one last *I won* smile before he saunters off.

My blood is still boiling, and LaFontaine is looking at me with a smug expression…

"How do you feel about cigars?" I ask, and his expression lightens up.

"Love 'em."

"Smoke with me, then?"

We exit through a side door into an alley since there's no smoking inside. LaFontaine looks around and scoffs. "I'm sure there's a patio out back-" He doesn't get a chance to finish his sentence. I catch him when he turns to look at me, grabbing his neck and wrapping both hands around it. Leather gloves coat my hands as I squeeze.

He's pulling at my wrists, trying to loosen my grip on him while he gurgles out some sort of nonsense.

Pleasure rushes through my body.

It's euphoric.

"You disgust me," I growl at LaFontaine, squeezing his neck a little harder. It's tiring, choking a man to death. My arms begin to burn as he fights back, pushing against me as his face begins to turn purple.

Oh, but the satisfaction. It's even better this way, watching the life drain from him as I hold him in my grasp.

The sensation that comes with inflicting pain is immediate, a rush of endorphins that coats my body, dulling each of my nerve endings. I can breathe. It's blissful, almost as good as sex.

Everything is better after a kill.

And then the euphoria starts to drift away, melting from my skin. Reality starts to come back into focus, and I realize what I've just done. I drop LaFontaine's body, and it hits the cement with a smack.

"Shit."

Junior is gonna be pissed that I killed like this. Nothing was planned or organized. I'm not supposed to act out of anger.

"We have people for that," my father would say. James doesn't like to get his hands dirty. Not that either of my uncles is better. They don't do their own dirty work. Not now. Not when we're trying to look legal. *"We're not thugs anymore."*

The only reason Junior let me kill was to organize my chaos. He knew when I was ten that I wouldn't be able to stop myself. After I killed the class mouse, he could see it in my eyes. He couldn't fix me. But he could manage me.

I tug my phone from my pocket, pulling up his contact and pressing the button to call him. It doesn't ring, going straight to voicemail, and that's when I remember.

My uncle is dead.

If only he would have had a backup plan for when he wasn't here to manage me. I slam my fist into the brick wall. "Damnit," I hiss.

I call Roman instead, and he picks up on the first ring.

"Boss?"

"I need you to clean something up for me," I tell him, scrubbing a hand over my face.

TWENTY-THREE

Zoe

"Do you want to get a drink?" Madi doesn't wait for me to answer the question before she's out of her chair, her hand grasping mine as she drags me away to the bar. "You're not ready for them," she says.

Perfectly manicured nails flag down the bartender. "Shots, tequila. Do you like tequila, Zoe? You look like a tequila girl." The words leave her lips in a fast-paced flurry, and the bartender is already grabbing a bottle from the top shelf before I have a chance to say yes.

I imagine this is how all conversations with Madi go.

"Tequila's fine."

The man behind the bar gives Madi a sly smile as he sets the shot glasses down. His eyes roam her body, from the turquoise color of her hair to her bare shoulders that lead down to the low neckline of her dress. She doesn't even notice or pay him a second of her attention. "Costello," she says, sliding me one of the glasses. "And two hurricanes please."

At least she said please.

"You got it." He winks before going to make the other drinks.

Madi holds her shot, clinking the glass against mine before we both drink them. The liquor burns my throat as it slides its way down. Madi winces and slams the glass down on the bar. "So," she says. "You're dating, John."

I feel simultaneously overwhelmed and at ease by her personality.

"Something like that."

"Have you met his mother?" Her eyes are wide.

"Cosetta? Yep. At Sunday night dinner."

"Oof, how'd that go?" The bartender slides the two drinks in front of us, his eyes still fixed on Madi, who's completely unaware. Or maybe she's just used to the attention that comes with being that beautiful, and a Costello. I can't deny the good genes that run in John's family. The whole table looks like a cast from a James Bond film - beautiful, timeless, extremely fucking wealthy.

What have I gotten myself into?

"Not great," I tell her.

"Well, well, well, what do we have here? Madalena Ricci." The man that interrupts us also looks like something out of a magazine. Easily ten years older than Madi and dressed in a fitted midnight blue suit with a shiny white tie and matching pocket square.

"Adrian Russo." He grins, showing off a set of sparkly white teeth as he extends his hand to me. "I didn't know Madi had any friends." He laughs at his own joke, but Madi doesn't. She crosses her arms over her chest, her eyes shooting daggers at the man.

"Zoe." I shake his hand politely.

"Zoe," he repeats, still grinning. His dark hair is slicked back, and he has neatly trimmed facial hair. "Nice to meet you."

"Adrian here is a fancy ass lawyer." Madi gives a mocking

smile and takes a heavy sip of her drink. "Aren't you? Criminal attorney, keeping bad guys on the streets. Isn't that your slogan?"

I wince at her insult, but Adrian just chuckles, taking a sip of the amber liquid he holds in a crystal tumbler. "I'll have to share that one with the marketing department." He winks at her and Madi hisses out a breath. "Do you have a moment?"

"I'm busy, Adrian."

"Too busy for me?"

"Always too busy for you." Madi loops her arms through mine, clasping her drink firmly between her fingers. She spins us away from him, walking quickly toward the door. "I need air."

"What was that?" I can't help but to laugh.

"He's an asshole," she huffs, leading me toward an abandoned bench. The back patio of the venue is huge. Lights are strung over the gardens, connecting to the gazebo. There are flowers in full bloom and intricate pathways made with brick pavers.

"A good-looking asshole." I laugh.

"Don't let his looks fool you," Madi says sternly. "Adrian Russo is a shark."

"Bad blood there, then?"

She shakes her head, looking away for a long moment. "How much has John told you about our *famiglia*?" Her voice is low, serious.

"Enough," I answer, matching her tone.

"Adrian wants to marry me."

"And I assume you don't want that?"

"It's him or Congressman LaFontaine," she mocks, gagging. I've seen Congressman LaFontaine on billboards and ads. I even think my dad might have voted for him. He's handsome, but Madi's reaction tells me she has no interest in marrying him.

"Why do you have to choose between two men if you don't like either of them?"

Madi laughs, a full-bodied sound that has tears brimming her eyes. "Oh, you precious naïve thing." She looks over at me wistfully. "I don't get much of a choice."

"Who's forcing you?" My question comes out more demanding than I mean for it to.

Madi has dark brown eyes that resemble John's, and when she looks at me, I can see they're glassy. She rubs her pink painted lips together and sighs heavily before she answers. "My brother. What you have to understand is that marriage in this world is an alliance, so he's using my life to strengthen his business ties." She takes another gulp of her drink that's almost empty. I can't blame her, though. I smoke to push away my feelings. If I was being forced to marry someone I didn't want to, I'd be drinking too.

"I'm sorry."

"Fuck, I shouldn't have told you that."

"I won't say anything." I rest my back against the bench, my shoulder pressing against Madi's. We sit in silence for a long moment.

And then we hear it. A loud thud, following the hiss of a curse word.

"What was that?"

THREE BODIES.

Two alive. One dead.

That's what we see when Madi and I follow the noise to the alley next to the building. John's eyes are dark, watching me as I slowly move toward him.

"Zoe-" Madi and Roman both speak at the same time, trying to stop me from going any farther.

I ignore them both. Stepping forward until I'm in front of John and the body. He doesn't say anything to me, not even as I kneel down to see his victim.

Is this what John's mother was trying to tell me before?

He's not like us.

He doesn't feel.

The face in front of me is contorted; it looks like he was screaming before he died.

"How'd you do it?" I ask, swallowing all the salvia that's built in my mouth.

John's face doesn't change much. "Strangulation."

He says it so seriously, so precisely. Not *I choked him, I wrung my fingers around his throat and drained the life from him.* No, *strangulation.* Matter of fact. To the point.

I tilt my head, trying to make out the face of the dead man in the dark alleyway.

"Is that…"

"Yeah," John says, void of any emotion.

"LaFontaine," I mutter. One of Madi's prospective husbands. My gut churns a bit. It's shameful that my first thought upon seeing the dead man at my feet is *at least Madi won't have to marry him.* "You killed a congressman?"

"Keep your voice down," Roman hushes me.

John is staring at me, his dark eyes glowing under the moonlight. "You're not scared?" he asks. His question freezes the alleyway, all four of us standing in silence. I wonder if I should be doing something. Calling the police, checking his pulse. Aren't those the things you do when you see someone dead? I think there's a checklist taught in CPR classes, *clear the scene, check for a pulse…* But we don't do any of those things.

My gaze flashes to Roman; he didn't come to the gala with us, so did he show up here just to help John clean up the body? Is this the event John had me tell Marcus about?

"Terrified," I say clearly, watching him frown as I do so. "What do you do now?"

He looks surprised by my question. "Roman's going to take the body-"

"John," it's Madi that interrupts this time, "are you sure..." she trails off, but the way her eyes dance between John and I tells me all I need to know. I'm an outsider.

He ignores his cousin, stepping over the congressman's body to be in front of me. When I don't protest, he takes another step, and another, until he is practically pressed against my body. "Are you going to run, kitten?" His voice is hushed, barely above a whisper. I'm not sure if Roman or Madi can even hear us.

"Should I?" I ask. I know I should. I know my feet should be pounding against the pavement. But I don't.

"Yes." He smiles wickedly. "But God, I hope you don't."

"I'm not going anywhere."

"Madi." John doesn't look away from me as he speaks to his cousin. "Go back to the gala."

"John-" she starts to protest, but he doesn't let her finish.

"Go." She huffs loudly, but I hear her heels click against the pavers, slowly sounding farther away. "Roman, you got this?"

"Yeah, skip." As soon as Roman answers, John's hands are on my waist, spinning me around. He faces me in the direction I came from, his hand on the small of my back as he pushes me forward.

My breath lodges itself in my throat, a mixture of fear and excitement swirling through me. He leads me inside, and then immediately veers to the side, down the hall and into a private bathroom. "On the counter," he demands, his fingers pressing the silver button to lock us in. I do as he says, pushing myself up onto the marble surface.

Every nerve ending on my body burns with anticipation as he undoes his cufflinks, slowly and with precision. There's a small entryway table beside the door, and he sets the metal pieces down with a soft clink.

"You surprise me," he says as he strips the suit jacket from his limbs, hanging it on the hook on the back of the door. "I'm very proud of you, kitten."

The comment shoots a stream of pleasure through me. My mind gets hazy with his praise, wanting more of it like an addict.

"What's your safe word?" he asks, his tongue darting across his lips.

"Roses," I whisper.

"Will you use it if you need to?" he asks, his fingers coming to the sleeves of his white dress shirt, rolling one side and then moving to the other. Dark eyes flash to look at me, his eyebrow raising as he waits for an answer.

"Yes."

It's then that he begins coming toward me. His hands come to frame either side of my waist, and he uses his knee to push my thighs apart. Soft lips meet the column of my throat, leaving a trail of kisses until he reaches my lips.

"Lipstick," I whisper, but he only smiles.

"I'm not afraid of a little lipstick." His lips meet mine, soft and gentle, so different from the way he fucks me.

He pushes up the fabric of my skirt, using the slit to expose my bare legs. Trailing his fingers over my skin, goosebumps rise in his wake. When he reaches my center, his fingers drift over the pair of nude lace panties, a sly smile forming on his mouth. Deft fingers slip beneath the fabric, and his smile widens into a full grin when he finds me wet.

"Full of surprises," he whispers.

He starts with my clit, drawing small circles around it before he moves to push a finger into me, then a second. His thumb is working on my clit while his fingers fuck me, his mouth finding my ear, whispering his praises to me while I moan from his touch.

"Such a pretty slut," he breathes and my body bursts into flames. "That's it, baby."

I come undone at his words, the sparks exploding in my stomach and firing off all my nerve endings. The feeling radiates through me, burning every inch of my skin until I don't know where I end, and he begins.

When I suck in my next breath, oxygen bringing me back down to earth, he's grinning at me as he shoves his cock inside me, making me see stars again.

One hand finds the back of my head, holding me so I don't smack it off the mirror as he pounds into me. His cock reaches all the sensitive parts of me that set me alight once more, making me hold in a scream.

When I come undone the second time, he joins me, jumping off the cliff and free falling. It shouldn't be this good; he has no right to make me feel like the world has melted away and all that's left is here and now.

Right and wrong have ceased to exist and nothing outside of the four bathroom walls even matters. It should feel dirty and wrong to be in this bathroom with him, but it doesn't. Maybe it's the niceness of the features, the expensive amenities. Or maybe I've become too wrapped up in John.

Either way, the fireworks take over my mind, making it all feel *perfect*. And when I come back down from the high, John is there whispering sweet nothings in my ear while he kisses me softly.

TWENTY-FOUR

Zoe

John cleans me up using a towel from the bathroom. "This will never get old," he murmurs as he smooths the skirt of my dress down my legs. "Seeing you spread out for me, my cum dripping from your pussy. This is possibly the hottest thing I've ever seen."

Pink heats my cheeks. I turn into a child under his praise, addicted to him, hanging on every word. Maybe it's stupid, trusting this man so much, and maybe it will come back to bite me in the ass. But I can't seem to detach myself from him. I'm sucked into his aura, overtaken by his scent of cedar and tobacco.

John presses a chaste kiss to my lips before he opens the bathroom door. I can almost see the mask he slips back on as we reenter the ballroom. Not a killer, not the man who just fucked me on the bathroom counter - now he's back to being the doting son and Costello grandchild.

My body thrums with adrenaline as I sit down for dinner, cutting chicken and steak, pretending John didn't kill a man in the alleyway and then make me cum in the bathroom. It takes effort to keep me from blushing as John's family asks me questions.

How did you meet? How's John treating you?

James asks me how the boat trip was, and my face heats under his scrutiny.

"Change of plans," John answers for me. "I went to meet her father instead."

James huffs but doesn't ask anything else. I catch him and Cosetta sharing a look, though, and I wonder what they're thinking.

Marcus stares at me for too long, his eyes shooting daggers into my chest and filling me with anxiety. The only thing that soothes me is John's hand resting on my thigh.

All the remaining Costellos are here. I meet Madi and Marcus's mother, Caterina; the oldest of the Costello children. She's dressed in a sleek black gown with wide gaping sleeves. She doesn't pay me much attention though, and I'm not sure if I should be offended or not. I notice she has no husband or partner here, and I don't ask why.

Next is, Carlotta and Damien. I learn from Madi during a bathroom break that they have two daughters, one in New York and one who passed away. I say I'm sorry and don't ask any more questions once I see her face fall while thinking about it.

"Lana was my best friend," she offered up anyway. *"But she needed to get out of here."*

It's on the tip of my tongue to ask why, but I bite it back, instead following her back out to the table.

Then it's John's parents, James and Cosetta. The youngest of the four Costello children is John's uncle, the one who passed away months ago. No one brings him up.

Despite the casual conversation and the shared drinks, something lurks at the Costello table, a nagging sense that all is not what it seems.

"You did good, kitten," his smoky voice whispers into my ear. "I know this was a lot. I'm proud of you."

Maybe he is a psychopath. Charming, manipulative… he checks off the boxes.

"Your family is… interesting."

He laughs at that, his head tipping back. His dark eyes stare at me for a moment. "Ask me, ask me the questions that are swimming through that pretty little head of yours."

"Your cousin Lana… Madi said she moved to New York?"

"Yep." John nods his head as his arms wrap around me. He leads, guiding me through a slow song. "She was supposed to marry Congressman LaFontaine." His voice is low as he shares this with me.

"Is that why you-"

"No. I helped Lana get out of the city a few months ago. No one knows that, though."

I go to open my mouth, ready to ask another question. "Uh - uh," John cuts me off. "My turn." He extends his hand, spinning me in a circle before dragging me back into him. "What aren't you telling me?"

I swallow thickly. I don't want to spill my guts to John, there's still something inside me nagging that I shouldn't trust him. But he's shown me so much of his life. Taken me in and protect me. Not to mention the way my body reacts every time I see him. My heart beats faster and butterflies swarm my stomach. He brings me back to life in ways I haven't felt since I was a kid. But then at night, when my body calms down, I feel at peace tucked into his chest.

He both excites me and makes me feel at home.

The feeling soothes some sort of ache in my chest, a burning sensation I had dulled over the years with a mixture of pot and fantasy novels. But John has ripped off the band aid and fixed the real problem.

"My best friend is missing," I tell him, the honesty coming with a rush of relief.

"And you think Marcus has something to do with it?"

"Something like that..." I draw out.

"Why does it matter so much to you?" He doesn't ask the question with any malicious intents. He looks nothing but curious as he waits for my answer.

"She's all I have," I whisper. "I met her when I was seven. She was in foster care most of her life. I just... I don't want to abandon her like everyone else has."

John gives me a pitiful look, and I feel shame creep up on me. "That's kind of you," he says. "But she's not your responsibility."

"I'm not *your* responsibility, yet you're taking care of me." He pauses at that statement, his eyes darkening as he looks down at me.

"Well then, I guess sometimes you take care of the ones you love."

"Do you love me?" I ask.

"Is that your next question?"

There are so many things I want to know, so many things I want to ask. I debate if I should be wasting my question on something so trivial. But I nod anyway.

"I don't know what love feels like, Zoe," he answers, his voice raw, and I think it's lined with honesty. "But if I had to guess, I think this is it."

My heart swells, the organ growing too big for my ribcage, making my chest ache. This wasn't the plan; I shouldn't be falling for this man. He's in the mafia, he's a killer. I've seen him with a corpse at his feet, yet I can't help the way my body heats at his words, or the way butterflies swarm in my stomach.

"I love you too," I whisper. He grins at my admission.

"Can I cut in?" Neither of us are happy to see John's father. His hand extends, reaching for mine.

John glances at me, checking that it's okay, before handing me over to his father, leaving me with a kiss on my forehead.

The dance speeds up into a waltz as James takes my hands. John's father is an attractive man, an older version of his son. He's dressed in a black tux with a shiny silk bow tie. "So Zoe," he starts, "How's my son treating you?'

"Very good." I try to smile, slipping my charm into place. I can woo John's parents. I can make them love me. *I think.*

"Good, good." He pauses, pursing his lips together before he continues again. "You should know my wife wanted me to come talk to you."

My stomach sinks at his words. "Yeah?"

"Yeah, I have to say, I agree with her on this one. You seem very nice, and John... John just doesn't do well with *nice* girls."

I swallow the lump that's building in my throat. "With all due respect, Mr. Vitale, you and your wife don't know me."

James chuckles. "True, but we know our son."

"I think our relationship is between me and him, don't you?"

"Sure, sweetie." He smiles. "But here's the thing you need to understand: my son isn't going to have a *relationship* with you. He'll chew you up and spit you out, and when he's done with you, it's not him who's going to be left in a ditch crying."

A chin runs through my body. "Are you warning me or threatening me?"

He grins, a sinister smile that makes my stomach churn. "It was very nice seeing you again, Zoe." He passes me back to John, and I watch him walk away back to Cosetta, who sits at the table watching us.

"Are you okay?" John asks as he takes me back into his arms.

"Why does your family think you shouldn't date me?"

"Well," he begins, "it's nothing about you. You could be the Queen of England and they would still have those looks on their faces." I glance over to see his mother still watching us, and she looks concerned.

"Why?"

John shrugs.

"Robby told me you're crazy."

He laughs again. I didn't realize I was so funny tonight. "I'm serious, John. Tell me the truth."

There are other couples on the dance floor, and none of them close enough to hear our whispered conversation. His eyebrow ticks up as he looks down at me, deep in thought. I told him my secret and now I think it's time he does the same.

"Okay," he muses. "I scored high on a checklist. They think I won't be able to have a normal life. Therefore, they don't want me to get close to someone they believe I would eventually hurt."

"What does that mean? What checklist?"

The corners of his lips lift just a bit, a small smile. "They think I'm a psychopath, kitten."

I swallow. "And are you?"

John shrugs his shoulders and extends his arm to spin me in a circle before he brings me back into him. His lips come to my ear. "Aren't we all?" he whispers.

My only knowledge of psychopaths comes from watching bootlegged versions of Dexter, and that only convinced me that his psychopathy was created. He was placed into a box and repeatedly told how dangerous he was.

John doesn't look crazy. He's too well dressed in his fancy suit and expensive shoes. He looks perfectly tailored, perfectly made. Not like a killer who might lose it at any second.

But I saw him an hour ago with a body at his feet.

How much more proof do I need than that?

"What are you thinking?" His voice slices through my thoughts, interrupting my spiraling internal dialogue.

"It's overwhelming," I say.

The song begins to change, and the next one is too fast for a slow dance. "Let's go outside." John presses his palm to my lower back and leads me to the door. He checks over his shoulder to see if anyone is following us, and I wonder if he's always been paranoid or if I'm just starting to notice it.

The back patio is large, overlooking the water. There are tables scattered around, lounge chairs too, but we walk to the railing. My eyes watch the inky dark water ripple as John continues.

"Tell me what happened to your friend."

"She didn't come home one night." It feels surreal to say the words. I wouldn't shut up about it when she first went missing. Trying to grab the attention of anyone who might care. "I got nervous. She'd never been gone that long, and then to ignore my phone calls... It was unlike her. I waited a while and then I went to the police."

"They didn't do anything?" John asks. He's listening intently to me, hanging on my every word.

"They said she was an adult. I waited twenty-four hours before I filed the report. But they didn't seem that concerned. The detective closed the case after a month. He thought she just ran away. I was at the station every day, trying to convince anyone to look for her. I checked everywhere I could. And then I went to Saints and Sinners, walking through the place looking for her." I laugh sadly. "Something wasn't right, so I asked if they had any openings. I knew how to dance from Cassie."

"She worked there first?" he asks.

"Yeah, she got a job there first. She told me to stay far away from the place. She was like a big sister to me, so I listened."

"Is that where she was the night she went missing?"

"Yes." There's a tear running down my cheek when I whisper the answer. I hadn't realized how much I was holding in. Looking for her was the only thing that kept me going. I hadn't talked to anyone about what it was like to not have her in my life. My dad had other things going on, Detective Ellison didn't listen, and Cassie wasn't here. I had no one left to talk to me.

But John is leaning on the railing, watching my face as I process the emotions.

"Keep going." John covers my hand with his, the warmth permeating my skin.

"That was three months ago." I shrug. "I heard some whispers that one of the girls who doesn't work there anymore was sleeping with Marcus. It would… make sense?"

"You think she was with Marcus?"

"I don't know. Cassie was sleeping with someone before she went missing, but she never told me who. We were supposed to get drinks the next night, but… she didn't come home. So it could have been Marcus."

John's face doesn't change much as I tell him my story. He's comforting in his own way, though. His hand squeezes mine. "Where do you think she is?"

I tug my bottom lip between my teeth. This is the part I don't want to tell John. I've seen what he can do. Madi says he doesn't feel, and if that's true, then how can I possibly believe he cares about me? How can I trust him with my secrets if he doesn't care about me?

"You can tell me," he whispers, his palm coming up to meet my cheek. It rests in the warmth of his hand, and I want to trust him.

"There are girls at the club sometimes." I look up, scared to meet John's eyes. They don't look angry, intrigued maybe. "They don't speak English, and they're covered in bruises… I think…"

"They're trafficked?" He doesn't look surprised.

"I think so," I choke out the word, my chest tight. "Did you know?" The thought of him knowing about these girls and doing nothing makes my stomach swarm angrily.

"I suspected." John shakes his head. "It makes sense."

John's statement catches me off guard.

"Marcus wanted to get into selling girls before, but my uncle told him no," John admits. "It would make sense that he would make a deal with LaFontaine. He's got good connections with the cops here."

"That makes no sense." I admit. I think John is ten steps ahead of me or in a completely different book. What does LaFontaine have to do with Cassie?

"If the cops covered up Junior's murder for him, he can sell his girls."

"So he killed your uncle… just so he could *sell* girls?"

John pulls me into his chest, wrapping his arms around me. "It's not a kind world we live in, kitten."

"John." I pull back, looking up into his dark eyes. "Where's Cassie, then?"

TWENTY-FIVE

John

I solved the mystery of Zoe.

Proneness to boredom, that's one of the traits of a psychopath. Another check mark on the list that defines me. But even knowing her secret, I'm still interested in her. I still want to take her home and fuck her madly.

Or maybe that's because she knows who I am, what I am, and she hasn't run off yet. Hasn't abandoned me.

I don't have an answer for her about where her friend is. Something about the look in her eyes makes me want to figure it out, though. I hadn't guessed that our puzzles would be so tightly intertwined. Her connection to the club and Marcus, Marcus to LaFontaine, and LaFontaine to Sam. I need to unwind the ropes that twist this all together and let it come crashing down.

But first, I need to fix Zoe's problem. I need to figure out what happened to Cassie.

Marcus is at the club when I arrive, sitting in the VIP room with a drink in his hand. Zoe promised to actually listen to me today and go to the private room I booked, which eases my nerves. I don't want anyone looking at her, and I don't want her to be around when I have this conversation with my cousin.

"I haven't seen you in a while, Johnny." Marcus puffs on a cigar as I slide into the seat across from him. The red tie he's wearing hangs limply from his neck, like he's loosened it up. His suit jacket is folded haphazardly over the back of his booth, and his eyes watch the dainty stripper as she sways in front of him. Her eyes are glassy, and she's stumbling on her heels, probably on something.

"Could say the same about you." I unbutton my jacket and lean forward, pressing my elbows to my knees as I watch my cousin. It's only been a day since I killed LaFontaine, so I don't expect him to be suspicious of me yet, but he will be soon. Once he puts together that I was the last one to see him.

I want to say killing the congressman was a mistake, but it felt too good to call it that. It's been too long between kills. My fingers were itching for it and watching the life leave LaFontaine's eyes was all too satisfying. Relieving.

Death is a rush.

"What's she on?" I nod up at the petite blonde who doesn't even hear me. Her body's moving, but her eyes have closed; she looks completely out of it. Marcus looks up at her and rolls his eyes.

"She's a lightweight," he tells me. "Hey!" he shouts at her, and when she doesn't respond, he reaches out with his foot to kick her. She stumbles, her eyes opening from her stupor as she trips over her own feet. When she hits the table and spills Marcus's drink, I can see the anger rise in his eyes.

"Stupid fucking bitch!" he screams, standing from the booth. His arms reach out, pushing the girl again as she struggles to get her bearings. "What the fuck is wrong with you, huh?"

The girl doesn't answer, just pushes herself up into a standing position and mumbles an apology. "Get outta here."

Marcus points to the door, and she goes, her heels scrapping as she drags her feet out of the room. I'm not sure if she'll even make it back to the dressing room. Her body looks sluggish under her, like it's not fully connected to her brain. Or her brain isn't working.

I don't interfere, though, just sit back further in my seat and take a long sip of my gin. Once she's gone, it's just me and Marcus in the VIP room.

"It's hard to find a good girl," I mutter.

"Yeah," he scoffs. "How's yours? Is she good in bed?" I cringe internally at Marcus's question. I want to slap the smug look off his face, but I don't. If I expect him to open up, I need him to trust me, so instead, I spread my lips into a wide grin.

"Yeah, she's good."

He nods his head, laughing. "I had one girl here who gave the best head. She was so fucking desperate, it was too easy to get her on her knees." He smiles. I think half the fun for Marcus is putting girls in these situations, where they rely on him to fuel their addictions. He wants to be the only man in their life, the only one who can quench their thirst. That way, they'll do whatever he wants.

And *I'm* the psychopath.

I lean forward, pretending to be interested in his little story. "She still here?"

"Why, you wanna taste?" He chuckles, taking another puff of his cigar.

"Maybe, if she's that good."

"Nah, *cugino*." He waves a hand. "She's long gone."

"What happened?"

"Ahh, same old. She wanted more, thought we were in love or some shit." He seems irritated as he taps the ash from his cigar. "She's gone now."

"Dead?" I ask.

"Yep."

I don't know if this is Cassie or not. I can't be sure. But it would fit, I think. Cassie went missing three months ago, according to Zoe, so it could make sense for Marcus to have killed her about then.

"What'd you do with the body?" I ask, leaning back in my seat and taking another sip of my drink. I'm mirroring his actions, looking as relaxed as he is in an attempt to comfort him. Just two old friends talking about dead women.

His eyebrow lifts, and he looks at me. "Need some new ideas," I add with a smug smile. This makes Marcus laugh.

"Listen to this." He leans forward, and that's when I know I have him hooked. The thing about men like him is they like to brag about their accomplishments.

I lean forward too, continuing to mirror him as he begins to tell me his story.

"The bitch tripped and fell, banged her head off the side of my desk. A lot of fucking blood." He looks annoyed by that fact, as if having to clean up her blood was her fault. I'm not convinced she *tripped*; I'm sure he really pushed her, but I don't interrupt his story.

"So I called Joey to come wrap her up," he continues. "And we have this guy, Martin Bailey, who owes me a shit ton of money. So I tell him I'll forgive all his debts if he gives me his shitty Toyota Camry." Marcus laughs loudly at this part. "I mean, the guy jumped on it. So Joey puts the girl in the trunk of the Camry, and we tell Martin all he has to do is park the car in long-term parking at the airport, and we'll have a guy pick him up. Idiot didn't even know he had a body in his trunk."

"Jesus." I mimic Marcus's laugh as I lean back into my seat. "That's genius. Anyone find her?"

"Nah, not yet anyway." Marcus puffs on his cigar.

Good, I think to myself, that means I can still get Zoe some closure.

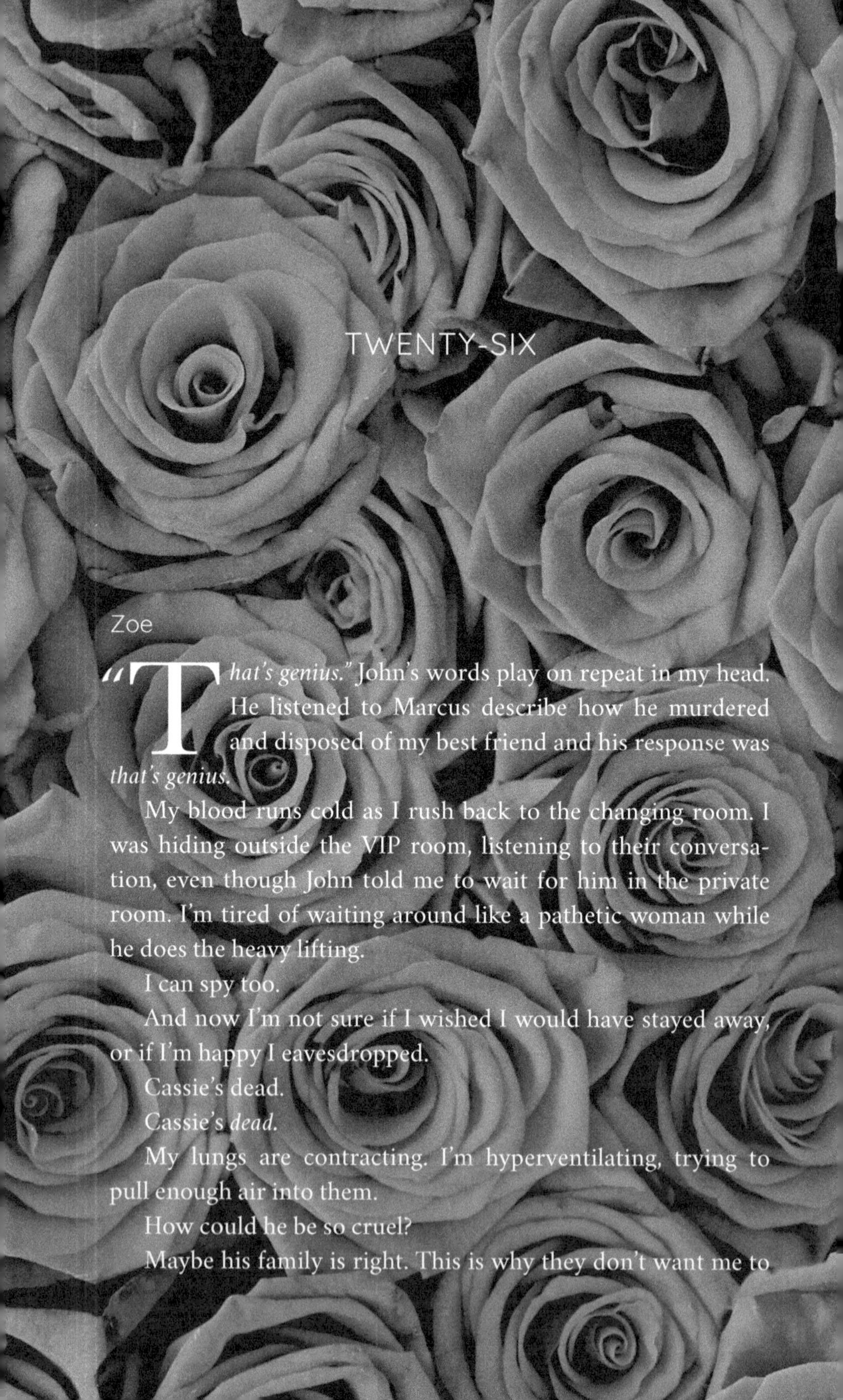

TWENTY-SIX

Zoe

"*T*hat's genius." John's words play on repeat in my head. He listened to Marcus describe how he murdered and disposed of my best friend and his response was *that's genius.*

My blood runs cold as I rush back to the changing room. I was hiding outside the VIP room, listening to their conversation, even though John told me to wait for him in the private room. I'm tired of waiting around like a pathetic woman while he does the heavy lifting.

I can spy too.

And now I'm not sure if I wished I would have stayed away, or if I'm happy I eavesdropped.

Cassie's dead.

Cassie's *dead.*

My lungs are contracting. I'm hyperventilating, trying to pull enough air into them.

How could he be so cruel?

Maybe his family is right. This is why they don't want me to be with him. He's a psychopath. Cold and emotionless. Who am I to think that he would change because of me? That he'd be capable of feeling anything.

I'm a dumb girl. Naïve and fucking stupid.

I barely reach my locker before I collapse onto the floor, my breathing labored as I try to pull myself together.

It doesn't even matter anymore, though. Who do I have left to live for now? Cassie's gone. Marcus all but admitted it. Trembling, I sink into myself, my chest pulsing as the sobs escape my lips. My eyes are running, wet tears dripping from my chin. I wipe at my face, smearing my makeup and staining the backs of my hands. My entire body aches, and I wrap my arms around myself, hugging them against me.

I've never felt as alone as I do at this moment.

I have no one left.

Are my fingertips laced with poison? Why does everyone I love die?

I think I might be dying as my heart races behind my ribcage. My fingers clutch against the lacy fabric there, trying to calm my heart by touch alone. It doesn't work, not as my lungs gasp for air. I'm hyperventilating, everything feeling insurmountable.

They say panic is a response triggered to keep you safe, a protection mechanism. But I don't feel protected right now. I feel like I've been sliced open, my insides on display.

Look here everyone! The broken girl who thought she could trust a man!

Cassie became bitter after every breakup. Shouting about the monstrosity of men. She was in a vicious loop. Hate them. Love them. Hate them. Love them. A predictable cycle.

I always loved her in the hate them cycle; it left more time for me, more time for us. When she was with a man, she became consumed, as if he was the succubus and she was the sailor unwittingly falling for him even when all he wanted was sex.

I promised myself I wouldn't be like that, yet here I am, crying on a changing room floor over a man I met a month ago.

I'm better than this.

Pulling myself off the ground feels impossible; my limbs are weighted down, heavy as lead. It takes time for me to sit up, to let the waves of grief pass.

When I meet my reflection in the mirror, smeared mascara coats my cheeks like war paint. I can't help the laugh that bubbles from my chest. *Fitting*, I think, *like I'm going into battle.*

I need to re-strategize, get my head back in the game.

Cassie's body is at the airport, so now I just need to get someone to find her. Maybe Ellison? I wipe at my face again. Will he listen if I tell him where she is? But then again, John said the police might be working for Marcus, doing his bidding. That's how they framed his cousin.

My stomach rolls. I can't trust John. Can't trust Marcus. And I can't trust the police.

Who the fuck is left?

I want to cry again, collapse into myself and give up. But I can't. Not yet. Not until Cassie's body is recovered, and I'm able to properly bury her. Then I'll sink under my covers and never come back out.

I pull myself off the tiled floor, running my hands over my bare legs and attempting to put myself back together.

"Are you okay?" It's a garbled voice that asks the question, muffled and slurred, like she's not all there. I turn to find Daisy slumped against the wall opposite of me. Her dirty blonde hair falls limply, sticking to her sweaty forehead. Her legs are sprawled out in front of her and her head rolls from side to side as if she can't hold it up on her own.

"Are you okay?" I ask back to her.

Red lips pop open, and her hand lifts as if she's about to say something, and then confusion draws on her face, pulling at her eyes. "I don't know," she says.

She's high.

That's clear.

"Daisy." I move closer to her. She looks pathetic in this state, too high to function or even to remember what she's doing. She can't possibly dance like this.

I'm not sure what I should do. Get Donnie? Who knows how he'll react to her being unable to work.

When I get closer, I can still see the faint yellow and blue marks on her skin, an arrangement of bruises changing colors. Knots twist in my stomach. Marcus is relentless with his abuse, yet she keeps going back to him. Is it the drugs?

"I don't feel good," she mumbles, and right as she does, vomit spills from her lips. She convulses as I rush over to her. Her skin is pale and clammy. My heart begins to race again as I look at her.

"What did you take?" I ask, but her response is mumbled, incoherent. "Daisy!" I yell. "What did you take?"

Her head lulls to the side, and her eyes droop closed. "Daisy!" I yell again as I shake her body, but she doesn't respond.

"Help!" I shout as I run out into the hallway. "Help!" Guests turn and look at me, most of them confused.

"Why are you screaming?" It's Robby who comes to me first, backing me up in the staff hallway and out of the main floor.

"Daisy, I think she's overdosing."

Robby shakes his head but goes into the dressing room anyway. It's John who I see next, even though Marcus is ahead of him. "Shut the fuck up," Marcus growls at me.

"I think she's overdosing!" I feel panicky as the words leave my lips. Marcus pushes me against the wall as he passes, his dark eyes glaring daggers at me.

John puts a hand on my shoulder, and the skin burns under his touch. Even in my panic, I remember he's a liar. A psychopath. I can't trust him. "Don't touch me!" I push his hand from me.

I need to leave, get the hell out of this club. But Daisy?

I decide I don't care, instead pushing past John and running toward the back door. I don't care that I'm still dressed to go on stage, my five-inch heels clicking against the tile. Don't care that my ass is hanging out from the booty shorts I'm wearing or that the skin of my stomach is completely exposed.

I just run. Outside. Down the block. I keep going until my lungs burn and my skin's on fire. Then I collapse against the nearest wall and let the tears flow.

TWENTY-SEVEN

John

The blonde is seizing when I enter the dressing room. Zoe ran from me, and I think I should chase after her, but this truce with Marcus is fragile, and I can't let him think I value a stripper over him. Even if Zoe is much more than that.

I text Roman instead, telling him Zoe ran out of the club and to go find her, and then I slip my phone in the pocket of my suit jacket.

"Jesus," Marcus mutters. He doesn't look too pleased by the girl overdosing in front of him. He scrubs a hand down his face and turns around to me. "Wanna job?" he questions.

The girl isn't even dead yet, but I know exactly where this is going. I nod my head.

"Get rid of her," he tells me, and then he marches out of the room.

"I need you to keep the other girls out of here," I tell Robby, who is on his knees, holding her head as she seizes. He does a double take, and I can practically see the words on his lips. We should take her somewhere, do something. But we won't.

Zoe will be upset. Her morals are too strong, too high. She'd want to help the girl. But helping her does nothing for us. It would only piss off Marcus and add an extra layer of complexity to our situation.

Getting rid of her, on the other hand, helps us. The trust it will build with Marcus is more valuable.

So I sit with her until the shaking subsides and her pulse drifts off and I know she's no longer in the land of the living. Then I find a dress bag hanging on one of the racks, and I slip her body into it. In one of the maintenance closets, I find a roll of duct tape and I use that to wrap the bag tightly around her.

Death doesn't bother me much, it's a part of my job. But something is nagging at me, something I'm not used to. Zoe's face when she ran from me. This is going to hurt her, knowing that I watched someone die and then disposed of their body.

Will she still love me once she sees how big of a monster I truly am?

I'm wishing I had the Escape now as I try to shove the girl's body into the small trunk of my Porsche.

I take her to my guy, Luther. He rubs sleep from his eyes as he leaves the shack he lives in on the edge of the swamp. He has a small motorboat, and he helps me carry her body into it. I slip a few thousand into his hands and get back in my car, leaving him with the girl's body.

She'll get to meet LaFontaine out in the swamp, their bodies resting with the alligators who will carry them back to their homes for a meal later.

Zoe will find my method of disposal horrible, I think, and I wonder if I should even tell her. I push the thought to the back of my mind. I can deal with that later, because right now I have other priorities.

"No missing person's report?" I had asked Marcus earlier while he gloated about getting rid of his last girl's body.

"Nah." He smiled. *"These girls don't get reported. Someone would need to care for them for that to happen."* His laughter hit a nerve in my chest. That may be true for the rest of the girls in this place, but not Zoe.

I care about her.

She might be the only person I've ever cared about, other than Junior and Sam. I failed to protect them, but I won't fail Zoe.

I need to get her out of this situation, out of the club.

I need her to be safe.

I leave an anonymous tip for Detective Ellison and then watch from across the street as the cop cars roll into the airport parking lot. It takes a few minutes for the dogs to track down the scent of the rotting corpse, and once they find something, more cop cars come their way.

The parking lot gets roped off with caution tape as they wait for the coroner to come collect the body. I try to tell myself that this is good, that this will solve Zoe's search, but deep down, I know this will only make her pain worse.

She wanted her friend to be alive, but she's not.

She's dead. Rotting away for months while Zoe dug through the club, searching for any clues. This is going to gut her. I scrub a hand over my face and pull my car away from the airport.

I need to go check on her.

TWENTY-EIGHT

Zoe

The first time I had a panic attack was the night my mom died.

"Why are you crying?" The small, lanky blonde girl plopped down on the cot next to me. The arena was packed, families loaded in to fill every inch of the space. My father was somewhere, trying to convince someone to go look for my mom. It was in that moment, when I was alone and no longer felt the crushing weight of having to be the strong one on my shoulders, that the floodgates opened. The tears flowed from my eyes, and my chest rose and fell quickly as I hyperventilated.

The girl next to me was older, and at the time I didn't know by how much. She wasn't crying like many of the people who gathered in the Superdome, but she was alone. Just like me.

I hiccupped my next sob and turned to face her with my tear-streaked cheeks. *"I don't know where my mom is,"* I told her.

"Me either." She shrugged her shoulders like this was the most normal thing in the world and squeezed her raggedy teddy bear to her chest. From the moment I met her, Cassie had a way

of making me feel like things were going to be okay. Or maybe it was that I finally had someone to share my pain with.

Dad never recovered after mom's death. He spent that night crying on the cot we shared, his body shaking violently while I rubbed circles on his back with my small hand. He was never the caretaker, that was always my mother, but now it was different. Gone were the days of the fun dad, who took me out for ice cream and sang Disney songs at full volume in the van. This version of my father was heartbroken, and I learned early on that broken hearts don't heal.

There were days when he would get up, when he would try, but even on his best days, he was never the same.

Part of me, a desperate part, wants to go to him now. I want to be held and rocked while my world falls apart around me. But he's not the father he used to be. I know that. He won't hold me and whisper affirmations while I cry my way through this.

I got good at managing my panic attack after that first one.

"Try breathing, that always helps me," Cassie had suggested. And then she sucked in a deep breath through her nose, dramatically tilting her head back with the action. I mirrored her and when she blew the breath out of her open mouth, I did too.

That was the first instance of me following after Cassie.

"Zoe?"

My eyes shoot open at the sound of my name and everything around me rushes back in. It feels like sensory overload. The sounds of the Quarter, the smell of fried food and powdered sugar mixed with alcohol. My stomach revolts, and before I know it, I'm on my hands and knees, throwing up my dinner.

"It's okay." It's Roman who rubs my back. And when I'm done, he helps me stand up and leads me to the car.

"Don't take me to John's house," I mutter from the passenger seat, leaning my head back against the smooth leather.

Roman sighs, his fingers tapping against the wheel. "Zo-"

"I don't care what he asked you to do, Roman." I face him

now. He's become sort of a friend over the time I've spent with John. Driving me around and spending time with me when John is out. I'm pleading with him now, banking on the little bit of friendship we have. "Please don't take me there. I want to go home."

"Did something happen? Did he do something?" he asks the question, but even if John did do something, I don't believe Roman would stand up for me. He's a soldier in this world, a pawn for John to push around his chessboard.

"It doesn't matter." I turn my cheek so I can watch the streets as he begins to drive.

"Okay."

I'm surprised when he listens and takes me back to my apartment.

The place feels strange, like a foreign memory I'm seeing again for the first time. I've barely been back here since John took me to his place. How stupid could I be? I let the man sweep me off my feet, pull me into his life of luxury. And I went willingly, leaving everything else behind.

But he never cared about me.

Jesus, I'm stupid. I sigh, running my hands down my face as I fall back on the thrifted sofa. Self-loathing runs rampant through my body, and all I want to do right now is collapse on this couch and let all the memories float away.

And then I remember I still have a joint left.

I rummage through my desk drawer, pulling the joint from the old pencil case I store it in. I don't even have enough energy to take it outside, so instead, I slide down to the floor and light it up, inhaling the smoke as if it's my last dying breath.

When the knock sounds on my door four hours later, I'm not surprised. I'm also not surprised when he lets himself in after I don't answer. I don't move from my spot, huddled against the wall between my bed and desk as I hear his loafers tap against the hardwood.

John appears in my doorway, dressed in another one of his designer suits hugging his features perfectly. His dark hair is held back with gel, and the sharp lines of his face are high-lighted by the moonlight that filters through my open window.

"Hi," he says the word softly.

"Hi," I say back.

I don't know where this relationship stands, but I do know that I don't want it anymore. I don't want to be with a man who can be so casual about death. My stomach churns when I think about finding him outside the gala with Congressman LaFontaine's body at his feet. How naïve was I to think that he only killed when he had a good reason to?

Yet, he was so chummy talking about death and disposing of bodies with Marcus tonight.

"You're gonna have to tell me what I did, kitten." His lips curl up into his signature charming smile, but that's not going to work on me tonight.

When I don't answer, he crosses the threshold into my bedroom. His shoes that probably cost more than my rent take soft steps across the floor until he's standing in front of me. It's not right how handsome his face is, with his sharp jaw ticking as he looks down at me.

"Kitten," he purrs as he squats down until he's level with me.

"I heard you," I say, and John's eyebrow lifts, waiting for me to continue. "Marcus was telling you about how he killed Cassie, and you were nodding along with him, telling him how awesome it was!" I don't even realize I'm yelling at him. He just sits there and takes it, waiting for me to finish.

"I had to make him think I was interested, kitten, or he wouldn't have told me."

He sounds too logical, and my anger doesn't care for his reasoning. Maybe he's right, but my chest is burning, the hope-lessness and rage mixing together and radiating through me with such intensity, I'm unable to control it. I don't care about his reasons; all I know is my best friend is dead.

If she would have never walked into that strip club, she might be alive. But the Costello family devours everyone around them. Maybe James is right; maybe I should get away from John before he takes me down with him. Before I follow in Cassie's footsteps for the final time.

"I think you should leave," I mutter.

"I'm not going to do that."

"Leave!" I shout the word this time, rising from my corner and pressing my hands against his chest. He doesn't move, though, he's like a brick wall in front of me. I punch him next, my fists beating against his chest, to no avail. He doesn't falter, his face remaining a sheet of stone as he waits for my meltdown to subside.

I collapse at his feet, my breath coming out in heavy pants as the tears spill from my eyes.

I hate him.

I hate that Cassie is gone. That my father is dying. And that John Vitale made me fall in love with him.

"I don't want anything to do with you," I hiss.

"That's not true, kitten. You're just hurt right now."

"No!" I shout. "I don't love you, John!" The words leave my lips tasting like a bitter poison. "Get the fuck out of my apartment!"

"Zoe." His hands grab each of my shoulders, holding me in place and forcing me to look at him. "That's fine. You can hate me, you can claim you don't love me. I get it. But right now, I need you to listen to me."

I swallow back my tears and stare at the man in front of me. His face is concerned, wrinkling at his forehead while he talks to me.

"I need you to leave the city."

"Fuck you!"

"Zoe!" he scolds me, shaking my shoulders a bit to get me to listen. I press my lips into a thin line and stare at him. Nothing he says will make me leave.

"I'll give you money, a million dollars, you can take your dad. Go anywhere you want, just get out of here." His dark eyes are pleading with me, showing more emotion than I've ever seen from him.

"Why?"

"I have a few things I need to wrap up, and I would feel better if I knew you were safe." I don't know if I believe him, or if I should believe him.

"I'm not leaving, John."

"Please, Zoe. Please, just let me put you in a safe house or something."

I shake my head. "I don't want anything from you."

His head drops, and finally he lets me go, and I slump back against the wall, watching him as he scrubs a hand over his face. "You don't mean that," he says, and when his eyes find me again, they have more emotion than I've ever seen from him. They're glassy, waiting for me to take back my words.

Maybe he does love me.

Or maybe this is just another form of manipulation.

Maybe he truly is a psychopath.

TWENTY-NINE

John

The first time I killed a man, I was fifteen. By this point, my uncle was well aware the day was coming. He knew I was going to be a killer, and despite his awareness and lessons, he had yet to send me out to kill a man.

"It's different, killing a man with your bare hands versus ordering his death. You can send a soldier out to slit his throat, but when you feel his blood on your own hands, feel his body go limp beneath yours - that's a feeling that you don't get sitting behind a desk." He was trying to tell me you can't take it back, that the blood you spill will haunt your dreams. But his warning went the opposite way with me. It made me want it more.

And finally, one day, when the anger bubbled over, I killed a boy for cutting in front of me in line. Waited for him after school, led him into an alley, and sliced his throat. Junior was right; the feeling of his blood on my hands was like nothing else. I was still bleeding him out when someone found us, stumbling into the alleyway and looking at the mess of blood and guts with pure shock lacing his features.

I'll never forget that look, the face someone makes when they find out who you truly are. What kind of evil lurks beneath your skin.

I killed that man too.

A week has done nothing to erase Zoe from my mind. Her face is still glued to the walls of my mind, a fresh wallpaper that won't fade no matter how much I throw at it. She wasn't scared when she saw me with the congressman's body at my feet. She should have run, gotten as far away from me as she could, but she didn't. Instead, my kitten walked right up to me and let me fuck her in the bathroom.

I never believed in true love, but maybe I'm an idiot for letting Zoe walk away. I scrub a hand over my jaw and flag the bartender down for another drink. Maybe I'm spending too much time at my cousin's club. I used to drink from the comfort of my own home, sealed away in my library with nothing but alcohol and books. Now, I can't stay away.

I'm not even sure if Zoe will come back here now that she knows she won't find her friend. I want her to listen to me, to get the fuck away from New Orleans and the Costello *famiglia*, but she won't do that either.

"You did good, Johnny." Marcus has a wide grin spread across his cheeks as he claps a hand on my shoulder.

Disgust rolls through my stomach, but I plaster my normal uncaring face on and give my cousin a small nod before bringing my glass of gin to my lips.

The smile on his mouth is still present as he leans in closer, closing the space between us. "You want more work like that?"

One of my brows ticks up. "Yeah, I do," I tell him, trying not to come off too eager. I don't need work, don't need money from Marcus. I killed for Junior simply for the thrill of it. I'll kill for Marcus to get close to him. Just one little confession is the only thing keeping me from killing my cousin.

"I'll call you when I have something for you." This time, his smile reaches his eyes, crinkling the corners. He's too happy. I haven't seen him like that since we were kids. Marcus used to howl with laughter whenever he did something menacing, like leaving bugs in the girl's shoes, or holding his pet snake too close to their faces.

My gut churns with discomfort; something isn't right here.

"Oh, and by the way, Davis LaFontaine is missing." His eyebrow ticks up when he says the statement, like it's less of a fact and more of a question. I mimic a surprised look.

"Do you know what happened?"

"Nah," he's still staring at me, assessing me. "He never came over after the gala. Weird, huh?"

"Yeah, weird."

When Marcus leaves me, I chug the rest of the gin, letting the alcohol burn my throat before I set the glass back down on the bar top and go in search of my kitten.

It's been a week. I've given her space. But I want her back now. Maybe we're a fucked up pair. A psycho and a liar. A rich man and a poor girl. Maybe we shouldn't be together, but I don't give a fuck right now. Not with the liquor burning through my system and my need for her growing stronger with every step.

I want her back.

I'd do anything to have her.

I don't find her at any of the stages. "Hey." I find Robby next to one of the doors. "Where's Kat?" My fingers itch at my sides when I say her name.

"Should be out soon. She was late." He rolls his eyes in annoyance. I ignore his answer and turn away, finding a seat at the bar where I watch the hall from the staff area. My kitten finally comes out five minutes later, her skin glowing under the purple lights. She has on the thigh high black boots again with a simple black set that has far too many straps. There's a choker wrapped around her throat, and immediately, I feel angry that it's not my collar she's wearing.

She steps up onto one of the stages, finding a chrome pole and spinning around it. I watch her body as she dances, the way she moves and sways her hips. She's sexy, easily every man's fantasy, and rage boils in my chest.

I don't want her up there, showing every man in this club what's mine. By the time she steps off the stage, I'm angry, heat simmering within me. And then one of the guys finds her, whispering in her ear. She tilts her head back and laughs, and then I watch as she leads him to a private room.

Something inside me snaps, the anger bubbling over. My feet move to the private room without my brain's participation. I swing the door open, finding the man sitting on the velvet booth and Zoe hovering above him.

She smiles when she sees me, the corner of her lip ticking up into a smirk.

"Get out," I demand. The guy looks between me and Zoe, confusion lacing his features. "Get out," I tell him again. This time, he listens, adjusting his boner as he shuffles out of the room. I kick the door closed behind him, coming face-to-face with my kitten.

I don't want to scream at her, don't want to scare her, but I wish she would listen. Why is she here? Why won't she leave this club, leave this city - do anything but stay here where Marcus could get to her.

"So demanding," she tsks. "Are you jealous, John? Maybe you do have feelings after all."

I let my feet take me to her, until we're inches apart, breathing in the same air. "What's this?" I ask, my finger slipping under the elastic choker.

Her steel gaze drifts down to where my finger meets her throat, and then slowly lifts back up to meet my eyes before she answers. "You don't own me, John." I watch her painted red lips as the words leave them, wanting nothing more than to fuse mine to them. My fingers weave through her hair, finding the back of her neck.

"You want me to let you go, kitten?" It pains me to ask the question. Everything in me wants to bend her over the nearest surface and remind her who owns her.

But I can't do that. Can't force her to stay with me through sex. She needs to figure this out on her own. She needs a choice.

"Yes." The word leaving her lips feels like a dagger to my chest. I release my grip on her, smoothing my hands on my pant legs as I step away.

"Okay," I tell her, my fingertips grazing the handle of the door, willing myself to leave. "But here's the thing…" I let myself look at her one last time, not knowing if she'll forgive me. Not knowing if I'll be able to see her again. "You can hate me all you want, Zoe. You can believe my parents when they tell you that there's something off inside me, something not quite right. And maybe there is, maybe I'm not normal. But I know that what I feel for you is unlike anything I've ever experienced. The world was cold and numb before you. The only thing I've ever cared about is killing people and making money. But I care about you, more than anything else in the world. More than money, more than blood. I won't force you to love me, to stay with me. You're a grown woman, you can make your own choices. But please, for the love of God, don't stay here. Leave this club, leave this town. Go somewhere, anywhere. You're the best thing I've ever had, and you're far too good for a place like this."

I give her one last look, ignoring the way her glassy eyes find me. "Goodbye, Zoe."

THIRTY

Zoe

There's a hollow feeling in my chest when I walk through the familiar door of my father's house.

"Zoe? That you?" he calls from his recliner in the living room.

"No, dad, it's an intruder."

"Ah," he groans as I hoist the overstuffed plastic bags onto the counter. "Don't joke like that with your old man."

I take my time unloading the groceries. He's still living in squalor, still unwilling to let anyone take care of him.

Overwhelming dread hits me, tunneling my vision and weighing down my bones. I try to hold on to the counter, but my weight is too much, forcing me to sink to my knees as the tears start to flow. Everything hits me so quickly. It's too much. Cassie, John, my dad. I can't save everyone, can't take care of everyone.

The word *failure* repeats in my brain, chanting at me like a middle school bully.

Worthless.

Stupid.

Can't get anything right.

My breath comes in shallow strokes, feeling like fire burning through my chest. I can't breathe, can't suck in enough air to get the oxygen to my brain. My heart is hammering against my chest, convincing me that this might be a heart attack. Maybe I'm dying. Maybe that's a good thing, maybe I shouldn't be able to go on anymore.

"Zoe." I can hear my dad's voice, but it's muffled, like he's above the surface, and I'm miles beneath the water. "Zoe," he says my name again, and this time, I feel his hands on me, his grip tightening as he shakes me. "It's okay,"

"It's not okay," I manage to spit out. "Nothing is okay."

He sinks down to the floor next to me, his arms wrapping around my body as he pulls me against him. I can't remember the last time my dad hugged me like this. Normally, it's side hugs or me leaning down to give him a half hug while he sits in his chair. But this is real. His arms squeeze me, and my head finds his shoulder. The moment it lands, the tears burst through in thick waves, leaving me sobbing and shaking against him.

"Shh," he tells me, his palm finding my back and rubbing slow circles. "It's okay, I have you."

I melt into his embrace and let the emotions flow from me. Everything that's been pent up inside me escapes, leaving me as nothing but a sack of bones.

When I finally calm down, my breathing evening out, I can see the worry that's settled in my father's eyes as he pushes the hair off my face.

"I'm so sorry, kid," he breathes.

"Dad, it's not-"

"No, let me say this, Zo." He scrubs a hand over his stubbled jaw. "I messed up as a dad. I should have been there for you. I've been thinking about it a lot lately. After your mother died... something in me died too. It sounds stupid, but..." he trails off, wiping under his nose as he tries to prevent the tears from fall-ing. "I loved her so much, she was my best friend. And I should have been there for you instead of chasing ghosts, but I just… it isn't an excuse, but I just *missed* her."

"It's okay." A year ago, I might have screamed and yelled at him. Accused him of not loving me, or choosing a ghost over me. But I get it now. It's hard to let go when you love someone. You build a life with them, a relationship, and suddenly they're gone.

My chest aches again with the realization.

Cassie's gone.

But John's not.

It's hard being with him, knowing what he does, who he *is*.

But it's harder being without him, feeling the loneliness creep in, the longing for him. I don't want to be dependent on him. I want to be half of a partnership, not a girl he's saving. But I want to be with him, I think, and the rest can fall into place as we figure it out.

"I get it," I tell my father through glassy eyes. "You loved her. I'm not mad at you." He hugs me then, his own eyes glossy as we embrace.

"I love you, Zoe," he whispers.

"I love you too, Dad."

"Now," he pauses to pat a wrinkled hand on my leg and leans back against the cabinet. "Tell your old man what's going on."

"I think I messed up,"

"I don't believe that." He waves a hand dismissively. "Every-thing is fixable, Zo."

"I told him to stay out of my life, Dad. I screamed it at him."

"Did you mean it?" His eyes are serious when they question me. I've never spoken to my father about men before; it was a subject we just pretended didn't exist. He gave me a poor excuse of the birds and bees speech at fourteen and we never spoke of it again.

"In the moment. But I was hurt."

"Do you love him?"

Do I love John?

I love the feeling of being with him. The way he calms my soul just by being near me. I've felt happier with John than I have most of my life. It's been two weeks since I told him to go away, and I've longed for the tiny sliver of paradise we created together. Not to mention the way he owns my body and soul.

"I think so," I whisper.

"Then you should tell him. You deserve love, Zoe. You deserve happiness, and you should go after it."

A stray tear leaks from my eye. "Thank you," I whisper.

"But once you two make up, bring this man over here. I need to make sure he's good enough for my daughter."

I can't help the laugh that escapes me. I can't imagine what that would look like, John in his thousand-dollar suit in this tiny house.

When I get home to my apartment later, I want nothing more than to sink into my bed and sleep for a million hours. I lock the door behind me and flip on the light, exposing a shadowed figure leaning against my far wall.

"Why, hello, Zoe."

THIRTY-ONE

John

"I have a job for you," Marcus says as soon as I answer the phone. He's had more jobs for me lately, since I ended things with Zoe and got rid of the blonde stripper's body for him.

He likes my disposal method better, less chance of being found than his airport scheme. No chance of being found after the gators digest them.

"Sure." I run a hand through my dark hair. The strands are too long, and I need a haircut. I feel unkempt, but that's how everything has felt for the last few months. Like my entire world has shifted off its axis. Nothing feels right anymore. I was fine before. Before Zoe, before Sam's imprisonment, before Junior's death. Everything was clean and orderly. Everything had a place in my life.

I want to go back there, but nothing can be like it was anymore.

"What is it?" I ask. Killing for Marcus is different than killing for Junior. My uncle was methodical; I watched first, killed later. Marcus doesn't watch, he doesn't listen to reason. Once he wants me to kill someone, there's no backing out, there's no changing his mind. Even if I would find something to exonerate the person, a reason why they may not be an enemy. Even something that makes them useful… it doesn't matter. They're still dead.

"I have a girl locked in a crate down at the dock. She needs to go."

I nod my head. "Consider it done."

Junior would have never sent me to kill a girl, but Marcus isn't Junior.

He starts to turn away from me, but then he stops, his body turning and his knuckles knocking on the bar top. "Oh, and John?"

"Yeah?" I down the rest of my gin as I wait for him to finish.

"Get a nice suit. My sister's getting married." His words hit me like a bucket of ice water, coating my body with an icy chill. He steps closer to me, invading my personal space until our faces are level. I can see the darkness in his eyes as he speaks his next words. "I expect her not to run out of the church." When he pulls back, his lips twist into an unsavory grin. "Saturday."

He steps away from me, but it doesn't ease the bubbling sickness in the pit of my stomach. No one had tried to prevent Lily's arranged marriage and it ended up in her taking her own life to save herself. I couldn't blame my older cousin; I wouldn't want to share a bed with Davis LaFontaine either. And then Lana was given to him in her sister's place. Sam and I couldn't shut that down as easily as we wanted to, so we got her out instead.

The idea of a third cousin, the baby of the family, being married off like cattle to serve some asinine business purpose makes my blood boil.

My grandfather had always preached *family above all*, and even after his death, when our beloved family ignited a war, I wanted to take that notion to heart. But now, after all this, I don't believe for a second that my cousin is a good man, or that he deserves to be spared.

I know it's pot calling the kettle black and all that, that I'm not a good man either. But I like to believe I wouldn't marry off my sister if I had one. Marcus is already gone before I can even ask him who the groom is. With Davis dead, I can at least sleep in peace knowing he won't be marrying Madi, but it doesn't tell me who is. Or what kind of deal Marcus is getting by giving away his only sister.

I swallow thickly as I head out to my car. I'll do the job, and then I'll go home and sit back in my chair while I dream about getting Sam released from prison and how to save my cousin.

The dock where Marcus sends me is only about a thirty-minute drive, fifteen in my Porsche going over the speed limit. There's a large white crate sitting there, and I see one of Marcus's men guarding it. I'm not sure why one of them couldn't have killed the girl if they were already there.

My skills are probably better used to hunt, kill, and dispose, but I won't tell Marcus his jobs are beneath me. Not when they quench the thirst that runs through my blood.

I give the man at the container a nod as I approach. Smells of the bayou greet my nose with a hasty takeover, infiltrating my senses with the lazy mossy scent. The doors to the container open right up, no lock in sight, but the girl inside has her hands tied behind her back. The outside light fills the dark container, and her legs scramble beneath her to scoot away from the edge, away from me.

A flip of dark hair comes over her shoulder, and steel-gray eyes shoot up to meet mine.

Shit.

We both stare at each other for a long, hard moment.

I must be an idiot for not expecting to see Zoe, my sweet kitten, tied mercilessly at my feet. She, on the other hand, looks scared of me, and I think she finally might be the smart one between the two of us. My heart floods with something I've never felt before. Grief? Sorrow? I don't know what to call the emotion that nags at my chest, threatening to bring me down to my knees.

My gut instinct is to untie her, wrap her in my arms, and take her back to my home. But I know there's at least one guard out there, waiting for me to be dragging a dead body out of this container.

I run a hand over my face, trying to think of the best way to get us both out of this situation. Why haven't I just killed Marcus yet? Why have I been so hesitant, waiting for the final proof that he's the one who set up Sam and killed my uncle in order to do the thing that needs to be done? That's what put me in this situation, put Zoe tied up at my feet.

I could sit here and think of *if onlys* all day, but that won't save Zoe.

This must be a test, and I'm about to fail it. But suddenly, I'm okay with failing Marcus's test.

Sorry, Junior, I think, but I'm not getting proof on this one.

"Zo?" I whisper, crouching down until I'm face-to-face with her. A stray tear leaks from her eye, and the duct tape over her lips prevents her from talking. "I'm going to take this off. Are you going to scream?"

She shakes her head no. "Brace yourself." I rip the tape from her lips, and she hisses a painful sound. I untie her wrists next, watching as she rubs the raw flesh.

"What are you doing here?" she asks, her voice a soft, near silent whisper.

That's a great question.

Zoe

The deception has a bitter taste. Slimy and sour as it trails through my insides. *Is this the end? Is this where my desire to save everyone around me finally takes me down?* My back is pressed against the rusty metal of the container Marcus shoved me into. The Louisiana sun beats down on it, heating the metal and searing my skin by proxy.

I wonder if someone will kill me before I die of heatstroke or starve to death.

Anxiety swarms my stomach, not unlike the butterflies that had settled there only months ago. But this time, it's not out of excitement or the anticipation of having John alone. No, this time, it's fear that rages its war inside me.

I don't know what will happen next.

I should have walked away, let it all go, but I was petty with anger. Grief had struck and with no one left, I'd suddenly become careless.

And then the door swung open, the bright light infiltrating my tiny metal box. For a moment, I wondered if this was *the light*, the one people talk about seeing before the end. But then John's face broke through the blurry haze, his features tilting into a deep scowl as his dark eyes met mine.

Part of me wanted to leap up and hug him, but the logical part of my brain withdrew, scurrying backwards until my back was pressed tightly against the burning hot metal.

John scrubs a hand through his thick black hair, messing up the perfectly gelled strands. He tells me to brace myself as he rips the dirtied duct tape from my lips. It hurts like a bitch, but I do my best not to scream.

"I'm sorry," he breathes.

"Why? You didn't kidnap me…"

"You're in this mess because of me." He looks anxious; it's the first time I've ever seen John not be in control of the situation.

He scratches at the back of his head, turning between the exit and me and the floor.

"Are you here to save me…?" I trail off my question. I want to add *or kill me,* but fear prevents the words from leaving my lips. What would I do if he said yes?

Dark eyes stare at me for a long moment. "I'm supposed to," he finally answers the silent question I haven't asked. "But I'm not going to."

He moves toward me, bending down so he can cut through the tape that binds my wrists and ankles with his pocketknife. Heat swirls in my gut, my heart hammering in my chest. He's supposed to kill me… but he's not. "Why?" I ask.

"Zoe, this isn't the right time."

"Just tell me. Why aren't you going to kill me, John?"

"You know why," he huffs.

"You're not broken," I whisper once he cuts through the last of the tape. His dark eyes rise from the task to meet mine again. My newly freed fingertips reach out to graze his face. There's a day or two of stubble where he's normally freshly shaved, but as soon as my hand makes contact, his eyes drift shut, and he leans into my touch. "You might believe you can't feel, but I don't. If you were really the psycho you say you are, then you'd kill me. But you're not going to do that, are you?"

"No," he whispers. "I love you, Zoe. I've never loved anyone before. I don't know how to…"

"We'll figure it out. Together."

He leans down, his lips pressing against mine. "Together," he repeats.

THIRTY-TWO

John

"We need to get out of here," I tell Zoe.

"What are you going to do?"

I scrub a hand over my jaw; she's not going to like what I have to say. "I'm going to kill the guard, and then you're going to get in my car, and I'm going to get you out of here. Once you're safe, I'll take care of Marcus."

"No." She stands now, her face twisting in pain when she straightens her sore muscles. "You're not leaving me to do this all yourself. I can help."

"I can't risk you getting hurt."

"We're a team." Her statement catches me off guard. I've never been a team player, never worked well with anyone before. Even Sam, my only friend, wouldn't tell you I play nice with others. I want Zoe out of here, want her tucked away safely somewhere where Marcus can't get to her.

But I like the idea of her working with me. Of us being a team.

"Fine," I tell her. "I'll kill the guard, and then we'll find Marcus."

"And then what?"

"We kill him."

I take a deep breath, steadying myself before I take Zoe's hand and lead her to the end of the container. There's a single guard I can see, and he's facing away from the container. I tug my gun from the back of my waistband, checking to make sure it's loaded and ready before I take my next step.

I have the device aimed at the guard, pointing toward the center of his head when I take my first step out of the container.

"Put the gun down, *cugino,*" Marcus's voice interrupts me.

My heart stills in my chest as he steps around the container, out from my blind spot. He shakes his head, running a hand through his dark hair. Behind me, Zoe squeezes my hand as she presses herself against my back.

I lift my arms, slowly lowering to set the gun down at my feet.

"Kick it to me," Marcus demands, and I do, nudging the gun with my black-booted foot and sending it across the pavement to my cousin.

"You failed," he announces. "I should have known better. I really wanted to trust you, John." He shakes his head with a laugh. "I was hoping that you'd choose correctly, but you didn't."

"You can trust me," I say the lie with confidence, hoping it will stop whatever villain speech he's going for.

"I told you to kill her." He waves the gun he's holding in Zoe's direction.

"You did." I nod my head. "I'll kill anyone you ask me to, *cugino,* just not her."

A roaring laugh leaves Marcus. He's amused by my request. "This was a test, John. A test that you failed."

"Maybe, but you'd be killing family. Your cousin. A made

man. I might have failed your test, but you'd be breaking our code. Defying your oath."

Marcus scoffs. "You think I care about that?"

"I think you vowed to care."

A mischievous grin rises on his features. "Oh, Johnny, you won't even be the first family member I killed."

Lead settles in my stomach, making it convulse. Something in my gut had always told me it was my least favorite cousin that killed my uncle. But hearing the admittance makes it too real.

"That's right," he confirms. "I killed your precious Uncle Junior."

"Just tell me why?" I ask. "Give me that, and then you can kill us both." I can feel Zoe still behind me at my words.

"Fine." Marcus smiles. "Because Junior was a selfish asshole. He wanted to make our businesses *clean.*"

He says the word *clean* like it's filthy. Junior did want to make the business clean; he wanted funds that weren't tainted with our dirty businesses. He wanted us to be respectable businessmen, the same thing my grandfather wanted.

"And you wanted?" I prompt.

"Do you know how much money I'm making with these girls? Using them in the club, and then selling them off as the offers come in." His grin widens. "It's more money than you could possibly imagine. And Junior was going to shut that down."

"So you killed him for money?"

"Yeah. You should have seen his face, Johnny. He never saw it coming."

"Yeah, I guess you won't either."

Zoe acts faster than I expect her to. She pulls the second gun from my waistband, flips off the safety, and shoots over my shoulder. The kickback shakes her, and since she's unprepared, she stumbles backward. She misses her target, only nicking

Marcus's shoulder, but it's enough for me to grab the gun out of her hand and take a second shot.

I don't miss, and the bullet lodges itself directly into Marcus's forehead, leaving a tiny trail of blood from the wound.

My mind flashes back to Junior, to that day in his living room while he was bleeding out on the floor, staining the white carpet.

Protect Sam.

I'm trying, *zio*.

THIRTY-THREE

Zoe

There's blood. More blood than I could ever possibly imagine. It leaks from Marcus's body, spilling around him and covering the pavement with a dark red. I don't even realize that my hands are still out in front of me, an imaginary gun gripping between my fingers, until John takes them into his own hands.

My eyes dart up to meet his. "I've never killed anyone," I blurt out. The words sound stupid coming from my lips. Of course, I've never killed anyone. John's lip ticks up at the corner.

"You didn't kill him, Zo, I did." He pulls me into him, wrapping his thick arms around my body. His grip calms me, stops the tremors that were wracking my body.

I didn't kill Marcus, but I did shoot him. That's bad enough on its own.

"Whatever bullshit narrative you're telling yourself, stop it right now," he tells me, his lips coming down and pressing into mine before I can say anything back. He kisses me softly, a gentle exploration of my mouth. He lulls me into him, erasing the current circumstances from my mind. I start to melt into his touch, and when I do, John wraps an arm under my legs and scoops me up. He carries me to his Porsche, sitting me in the passenger seat and fastening the seat belt. I feel like a child, but I don't complain or stop him. He strips his suit jacket from his shoulders and rolls up the sleeves of his dress shirt before he walks back over to the two bodies. I watch as he hoists them over his shoulder one at a time and stuffs them into the trunk - a feat I can't even imagine is possible in this small ass car, but he manages.

When he's done, he drives me home, not speaking of the body of his cousin that's in the trunk of his car.

I forget how to speak as John takes care of me, lifting me from the car and carrying me into his townhome and straight upstairs to the master bath. He sets me on the toilet as he fills the tub with warm water, testing the temperature with his hand. Then he strips me down until I'm naked before him and leads me over to the freestanding tub.

It feels heavenly as the warm water touches my skin, cleaning the dirt and grime from my body. John grabs a wash-cloth, wetting it with the water and using it to clean the dirt and blood from my skin. He does my hair next, soaping it up with the shampoo I'd left here and working his fingers into my scalp. I begin to relax, the tenseness melting away from my bones.

"Thank you," I murmur.

"You don't have to thank me, Zoe." He turns my face gently with the tips of his fingers until we're looking at each other, his dark eyes boring into my lighter ones. "I'm sorry, kitten. I'm sorry I got you into this mess, but I promise I will spend every day for the rest of my life making it up to you."

"It's okay," I whisper. "You didn't get me into anything. I walked in willingly."

"I should have stopped you." He looks like he's in pain as he says the words.

"Maybe." I shrug. "But I'm glad you didn't, because then you wouldn't have had to spend the rest of your life making it up to me."

He smiles ever so softly. "What did I do to deserve you, Zoe Carson?"

After he rinses the remaining conditioner from my hair, he pulls me from the tub and wraps me in a big fluffy towel before he carries me back into the bedroom and lays me down on the king sized bed. "You, my kitten, are absolutely fucking perfect. Do you know that?"

I can't help the grin that rises to my face and the blush that shows on my cheeks as John leans forward, placing his hands at the end of the bed as he hovers over me.

"Yes," I breathe. "But you can tell me again."

The corner of his mouth ticks up into a grin. He's stunning like that. Somewhere along the way of bringing me home and cleaning me up, he lost his shirt and dress pants, instead displaying a bare chest and pair of low-slung sweats.

I tug my bottom lip between my teeth.

His eyes darken at the action, and he moves forward, crawling until his body is directly over mine. "You know how that makes me act." His finger comes to my mouth, releasing my lip.

"I've missed you," I whisper, my words hanging in the air, the emotional sentiment heavy. I never should have walked away from John, not when being under him feels righter than anything I've ever experienced.

"I've missed you too, kitten." He presses a long and soft kiss to my lips. When he pulls away, he lifts himself so he's kneeling with his legs straddling me. My body is burning in anticipation, longing for him to move faster. For his clothes to come off, for him to touch me.

His hand reaches into the pocket of his sweatpants, and when he pulls it back out, the black collar is dangling from his fingertips and the rose gold charm glints in the moonlight.

"I'm not letting you go again, baby. You're mine." Dark eyes look down on me, waiting for a response. "Tell me," he demands.

The fire in my body ignites, his possessiveness making me overheat in response.

"I'm yours," I whisper, watching as a wide grin spreads across his face.

With deft fingers, he unties the robe, pulling my arms free of the material and letting it fall beneath me. Soft lips pepper me with kisses as he moves down my body ever so slowly. Every inch of me is vibrating with need, begging him to touch my most sensitive parts.

"So fucking beautiful," he murmurs against my thigh, the vibration of the words buzzing on my skin. "You tell me what you want, sweet girl." He kisses me again, slightly closer to where I want him. "Tonight is all about you." Kiss. "Taking care of you." Kiss.

"I want..."

"Tell me," he demands when I pause.

"I want you to taste me. I want you to make me come with your mouth,"

"Wicked girl," he murmurs, his breath ghosting over my slit.

Heat rises on my flesh, coating me in a crimson blush as he dives between my thighs, licking me like I'm the most delicious treat. I feel beautiful and cherished beneath him as he devours me, sucking on my clit as I writhe.

"So fucking stunning," he murmurs to my pussy. "So fucking *delicious.*"

I suck in a breath as he goes back to my clit, overwhelming the bundle of nerves with his tongue and mouth. And when I fall over the edge again, John is there to catch me, whispering sweet words of encouragement while everything around me explodes into pure bliss.

The high of my orgasm begins to melt away, and the room comes back into focus right as John pulls the sweatpants down his legs. He crawls back onto the bed and straddles me again, leaving his thick cock right in front of my eyes.

"Tell me what you want." His voice is demanding, forcing me to make the decisions tonight.

"You," I murmur. "I want you *inside me*."

A grin flashes on his face and he palms his cock, wasting no time as he moves between my legs. He slides himself between my folds, coating his tip in my wetness before he pushes inside.

"Fuck," I hiss, my hands shooting forward to grab onto his shoulders.

"You look so pretty when you take my cock, kitten." He pulls back and drives into me again, making me moan out from the action. "Such a cute little slut."

I can't help but to smile at his praise. Something about his words, the dirtiness of them, ignites me, making me come alive.

My hands explore his body, tracing every inch of his chest and forearms, reaching up to the column of his throat and over the lines of his face. I want to memorize every detail, every inch of him. Burn it into my mind so I never forget what it feels like to be his in every way.

"Stunning," he whispers. "Where do you want me to come?"

"On me." I smile. "I want to be covered in your cum."

"Fuck," he hisses out a breath. "My beautiful little cum slut." He lifts himself up, just enough so he can reach a hand down to my clit, rubbing his finger over it in quick circles. "I want you to come, baby, thinking about how pretty you're going to look when I shoot my load all over you."

I don't need much more encouragement to make me come undone all over again. Stars shoot behind my eyelids and my body tenses as euphoria takes over. I scream out, calling John's name as he whispers praises. And when I come back down to earth, he's pulling out of me, his own release falling onto my stomach in thick ropes.

He collapses beside me, both of us panting and covered in sweat, but it feels right. Everything settles around us, and for once, I feel like I can breathe again.

Like everything is the way it should be.

THIRTY-FOUR

John

I slide a large stack of money across the mahogany desk to Detective Ellison, watching as his eyes dance between the stack and my face.

"I'm assuming you're the one who framed my cousin."

Ellison leans back in his chair, not touching the money and focusing his gaze on me. "I don't know what you're talking about," he deadpans.

"Well, I suggest you figure it out real soon." I give him a sly grin. "Marcus is no longer with us. So if you want to continue making payments on your Beemer, you should take my money." I nod at the stack of hundred dollar bills. "Misplace whatever bogus evidence you have on Sam Costello, and make sure his charges get dropped."

Ellison taps his fingers against his thigh as he replays my message in his head. I can see the wheels turning, trying to figure out who he should give his loyalty to. He leans forward, his eyes finding the stack of cash for a brief moment. "Or what?" he asks.

"I'm sure you know I can be *very* persuasive." What I don't add is how I plan on being *persuasive* if he doesn't take the money. Shaking down a detective isn't the best idea, but there are other ways to make Ellison miserable.

He ponders my statement for a brief moment before he snatches the cash off the desk and tucks it inside the pocket of his suit jacket. "Consider it done."

I LEAVE the police station in exchange for the cemetery. Zoe's already there when I arrive, with her father's hand on her arm as they walk slowly through the large iron gate. There's a priest waiting for us in the section of the Costello tombs, his black garb covering his skin with only the smallest bit of white on his neck. He watches the three of us as he clutches his bible to his chest. Ultimately, whether he wanted to or not, he took my money and agreed to this funeral. Just like the Lafayette cemetery took my money for the tomb, even though these are reserved for the Costello bloodline only.

But I could see the grief still clinging to Zoe. She needed peace, a place to lay her best friend to rest. And even if she wasn't blood, Cassie was her family and Zoe is mine. So it seemed right to give her this space.

"You must be John." Her father extends his hand to shake mine. "I've heard a lot about you."

I slip my most charming grin into place as I shake the man's hand. "All good, I hope."

"Eh, well she did cry."

I think he's trying to tease me, but my eyes flash to Zoe's anyway.

"Dad." She pokes his ribs with her elbow. "It wasn't his fault."

"I sure hope not," he retorts. "But you should know, if you ever do anything to hurt my daughter-"

A well-timed cough from the priest cuts him off.

"Trust me, I will never hurt her." Zoe looks at me with bright eyes, but her father still has a skeptical look on his face.

"Sure," he says, unconvinced.

"Shall we." I gesture to the priest who opens his bible.

The words drone on as he reads, going right through my brain without stopping to process, but it doesn't matter because Zoe stands behind me, clutching a tissue to her face. I wish I could erase her pain, but the best I can do is stand in it with her. Give her a place to rest it while she mourns her friend.

And later, once the funeral is over and we take her dad home, I hold her in my arms and make sure she knows how loved she is.

That I'm here with her.

And that she'll never be alone again.

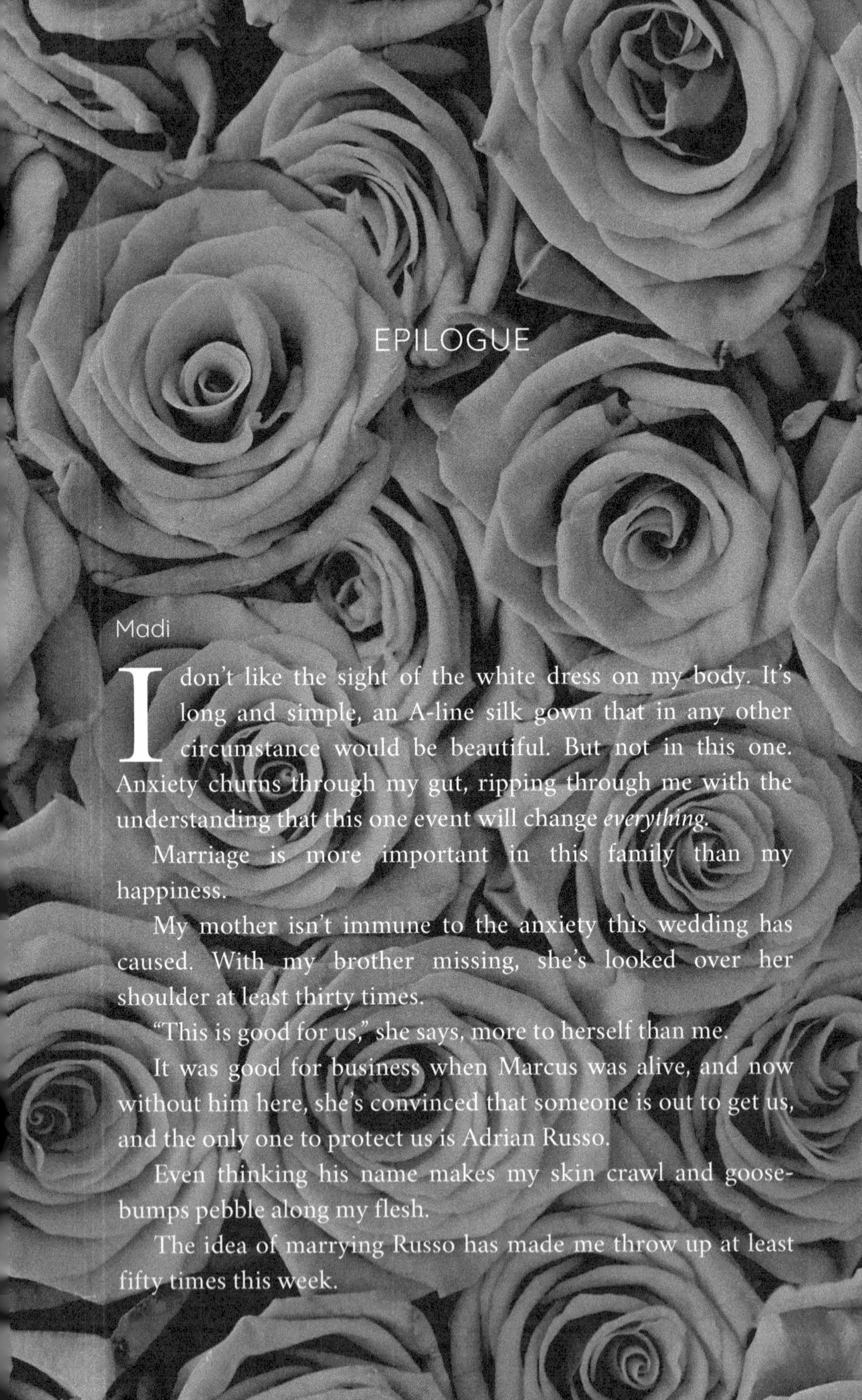

EPILOGUE

Madi

I don't like the sight of the white dress on my body. It's long and simple, an A-line silk gown that in any other circumstance would be beautiful. But not in this one. Anxiety churns through my gut, ripping through me with the understanding that this one event will change *everything*.

Marriage is more important in this family than my happiness.

My mother isn't immune to the anxiety this wedding has caused. With my brother missing, she's looked over her shoulder at least thirty times.

"This is good for us," she says, more to herself than me.

It was good for business when Marcus was alive, and now without him here, she's convinced that someone is out to get us, and the only one to protect us is Adrian Russo.

Even thinking his name makes my skin crawl and goose-bumps pebble along my flesh.

The idea of marrying Russo has made me throw up at least fifty times this week.

Like my mother, I've also been looking over my shoulder, but unlike her, I'm waiting for John to come and save me. Have a getaway car parked outside like he did for Lana. But even I don't think my cousins can pull that off twice.

"Come on." My mother ushers me with a wave of her hand. I've been staring at my reflection for far too long, mesmerizing the girl I am before I become *his*.

The churning sensation in my stomach is still there as she escorts me out into the entrance of the church. There're not many people here, just a speckling of guests that takes up a small fraction of the pews.

My mother glances between me and one of the enforcers meant to make sure I don't run away before she walks down the aisle to the front of the church. From here, I can see the altar where the priests stand, and next to him the tall, lean body with a sharp jawline and a head of dark hair.

Dressed in a black tux with a white silk shirt and a teal bow tie that matches the color my hair used to be before Ma drug me to a salon and dyed it back to its old chocolate brown color. From his spot at the front of the church, he watches me before giving me a wink.

And when the processional music begins to play, I'm ushered forward.

Whether I like it or not, today I'm marrying Adrian Russo.

***

WANT MORE MAFIA ROMANCE? Check out Gio's story in the Delgado Trilogy.

ACKNOWLEDGMENTS

Thal - This is the fifth book you've supported me through. I wish there was a better word than support... you texted me through breakdowns, plot changes, and insecurities. Reassured me when I the words weren't coming. And read every version of this book. I think I say it every time I finish a book, but I'll say it again: I could not do this without you. Thank you for being my bestie!

Anna, Laura, and Julia - y'all are the best. Thank you for supporting me on this venture, for reading all my words, and for putting up with my general craziness. I love you!

Val @ Book n Moods - Thank you for making pure magical covers out of the nothing I give you. I don't know how you do it, but I won't question it. You rock!

Kenzie @ Nice Girl Naught Edits - Thank you for working with my craziness, for editing a book that had no ending, and for all the love on this manuscript. I appreciate you so much!

Savannah @ Peachy Keens - Thank you for keeping me organized and supporting the hell out of this release.

Jake - This might have been the worst I've ever been while writing a book. My insecurities were crazy with this one. Thank you for listening to me explain the plot easily 100 times and for feigning interest each time. You're my MVP.

To my street team, Natalia's Famiglia - Thank you for promoting the hell out of this release, and for supporting all of my work. You gals are the best!

And finally my readers - THANK YOU! I couldn't do this without your continued support.

ABOUT THE AUTHOR

Natalia Lourose writes angsty romance about broken people figuring out life and finding love along the way. Television and far too much smut as a teenager left her obsessed with dark-haired bad boys who are moody and wear leather jackets. Tucked away in her office with a dog at her feet, two cats on her keyboard, and husband doing something she is always writing something, or trying to.

She loves interacting with fans and fellow book lovers on social media, here's where you can find her:

instagram.com/natalialourose
tiktok.com/@natalialourose